Mordecai Richler, as prolific as he is gifted, is the author of eight novels including the recent, much acclaimed, *Joshua Then and Now* (also available in Granada Paperbacks), writer of many screenplays (among them the film version of his own *The Apprenticeship of Duddy Kravitz*), and observer of curious societies from the Klondike to Hollywood – in articles that have appeared in leading British and American periodicals. He lives in Montreal, where he was born and brought up and to which he returned a few years ago after two decades in London, with his wife and their two daughters and three sons.

By the same author

Novels
The Acrobats
Son of a Smaller Hero
The Apprenticeship of Duddy Kravitz
The Incomparable Atuk
Cocksure
St. Urbain's Horseman
Joshua Then and Now

Stories
The Street

Essays
Notes of an Endangered Species

Mordecai Richler

A Choice of Enemies

A PANTHER BOOK

GRANADA

London Toronto Sydney New York

Published by Granada Publishing Limited in 1960
Reprinted 1982

ISBN 0 586 05540 1

First published in Great Britain by
Andre Deutsch Limited 1957
Copyright © Mordecai Richler 1957

Granada Publishing Limited
Frogmore, St Albans, Herts AL2 2NF
and
36 Golden Square, London W1R 4AH
866 United Nations Plaza, New York, NY 10017, USA
117 York Street, Sydney, NSW 2000, Australia
100 Skyway Avenue, Rexdale, Ontario, M9W 3A6, Canada
61 Beach Road, Auckland, New Zealand

Printed and bound in Great Britain
by Cox and Wyman Ltd, Reading
Set in Plantin

For
Joyce Weiner

Part One

I

Ernst was still in the Eastern Zone, about ninety kilometres from Berlin, when the truck emerged so inexplicably out of nowhere that it seemed to have been created by the rain itself. Ernst waved. The truck stopped. He jumped in beside the driver.

'Where are you going?'

'Berlin,' Ernst said, slamming the door.

'Have you a travel permit?'

Ernst pointed to the FDJ badge on his jacket lapel.

Heinz indicated his own badge, 'Friends of the Soviet Union', and said, 'If you don't mind, I would like to see your permit anyway.'

'Don't be stupid.' Ernst wiped his dripping head with his sleeve. 'All members of the Central Cultural Group of the FDJ must be at the Lustgarten by four this afternoon. I'm late as it is, so please hurry.'

The truck swished ahead into the rain again.

'As you can see,' Heinz said, 'I don't pick up people without checking. After that mess provoked by fascist agents in Berlin I decided to follow all regulations to the letter. Heinz, I said to myself, Heinz Baumann, you cannot be too careful.'

'Admirable of you.'

'Heinz, I said to myself, these woods are crawling with bastards trying to sneak into the West. You cannot be too careful, Heinz.'

'Thank God for the road blocks,' Ernst said.

Heinz had a red pockmarked face. He seemed to Ernst to be the simple sum of all the thick, docile women, beer and sausages he had consumed. Ernst glanced surreptitiously over his shoulder. The truck was carrying paint. But there was a box covered by a tarpaulin hidden behind Heinz's seat.

9

'We want to be one nation bound by brotherhood,' Heinz said.

'Exactly.'

'If the West rearms all the old boys will come back again.'

'Exactly.'

'It's good to see our youngsters in such a hurry to get to political meetings. In the West boys your age are bikini-ists.'

Ernst didn't reply.

'Germany should sit at one table.'

No answer again. Ernst had fallen asleep.

Heinz tugged at his cap and cursed the windshield wipers and, more impersonally, his luck. He began to hum an old Afrika Korps marching song. The rain gradually softened into a drizzle and the truck began to pick up speed. Looking the pale skinny boy over again Heinz decided that in the old days he had cut a finer figure. Not that he had anything against the present regime. A man could earn a living anyway. Better the S E D than the old crowd.

'Where are we?' Ernst asked.

'Did you have a good sleep?'

'Yes,' he said. 'Where are we?'

'Take it easy.' Heinz glanced at Ernst's boots. 'We don't reach the check point for another ten minutes.'

'I'll get off here, if you don't mind, and catch a train into the city.'

'How did you get the mud on your boots?'

Ernst froze. He felt inside his jacket cautiously. He wore a knife strapped inside.

'Let's see your papers.'

'Don't be a fool. If you turn me in at the check point I'll say you were helping me.'

'Who said I was going to turn you in?'

'I'm telling you just once more. I'm in a hurry.'

'Everybody's in a hurry these days.'

'All right,' Ernst said, 'I insist you take me to the check point. But don't think I didn't notice the eggs and butter in the back. Profiteering will interest the *vopos*, I'm sure.'

The truck coughed to a stop and Ernst opened the door and leaped out.

'I wasn't going to turn you in,' Heinz shouted. 'I was only teasing.'

Ernst ran, he stumbled, he broke for the woods again.

'You should have trusted me,' Heinz shouted after him. 'I could have . . . helped . . .'

But Ernst was gone.

II

The visitor from Toronto, a short, squat, bearded man with an unused boyish face – his name was Thomas Hale – smothered the door knob in a hairy wad of fist and, his smile muddy with assurance, said to his host once more:

'You ought to come home—'

It was four a.m. and his host, Norman Price, was awfully tired.

' – Europe's had it, Norman. England's not a battlefield any more, but a playground for sentimental, visiting Canadians like myself. Nothing more is going to happen here, except that Churchill will die. But in Canada—'

Norman glanced at his watch. 'I wish we could talk some more,' he said, 'but your taxi is waiting downstairs.'

'It's a pity. A waste. You ought to come home and teach.'

Hale, Norman thought, is what the obituary writers mean when they call somebody 'a fighting cock', but Norman was fond of him all the same. Hale was a magazine editor. A fierce champion of periphery causes, he had, for instance, taken an outspoken stand against capital punishment. Yet, even if Hale hastily rejected anything that might impose on his slippered ease, he was also unfailingly decent. You couldn't dislike him simply because he was cautious.

'Your taxi is—'

'Well,' Thomas Hale said warmly, 'see you next year, I hope.'

Norman raised his glass 'To next year in Toronto,' he said.

Hale gone at last, Norman returned to his smoke-filled living room and slumped back in his chair. Norman was thin, a little taller than average, with a long narrow face. His black curly hair, already grey around the temples, was beginning to recede. His steel-rimmed glasses made him look rather solemn. Norman, in fact, was extremely self-conscious about what people told him was his remote expression, his severe face, and so, hoping to please, he smiled often. His smile was shy, hesitant, and gentle. But a smile on his face, like a sun in the London sky, was so incongruous that it startled rather than pleased. 'A spectre is haunting Swiss Cottage,' Winkleman had once said. 'It is the spectre of Norm's *Goyishe* conscience.' Norman was thirty-eight; he was thickening around the waist.

Whenever Norman thought of his country he did not, as Americans were supposed to do, recall with a whack of joy the wildest rivers and fastest trains, fields of corn, skyscrapers, and the rest of it. There were all these things in his country. There were magical names in abundance. A town called Trois-Rivieres; a mountain pass named Kicking Horse; Saskatchewan – a province. But there was no equivalent of the American dream to boost or knock. The Canadian dream, if there was such a puff, was how do I get out?

I got out early, Norman thought.

Norman had been eighteen when he had come to study at Cambridge. He had been back to Canada many times since, for periods of from one month to a year, but after he had resigned his job at an American university four years ago he had come back to London again.

Norman thought he was doing very well. That's why he was so annoyed with Hale. For looking over his hard-come-by Kensington Church Street flat with Hale's Canadian eye he was aware for the first time of the chipped bureau, the frayed sofa, and the absence of a frigidaire, television set, and deep-freeze. What only this morning had seemed very cosy indeed now struck Norman as seedy. He cursed Hale. This morning he had been proud to think that here he was an academician, a disgraced professor, doing reasonably well as a writer of thrillers and the occasional film script. But Hale wasn't impressed. I'm decadent, he thinks. Me, Norman thought, decadent. Jesus.

Feeling better, he went out for a walk.

Norman, unlike the other *émigrés*, had taken London to his heart. It didn't yield itself to strangers with nearly so much ease as Paris, but in the end the city's beneficence, its quality of being used, feasible, sane, took you prisoner. New York was more spectacular, but London, perhaps because you were not the saint or irresistible lover you longed to be, was the more reassuringly human. Greatness and power and youth had passed: the city, like you, was relieved.

Norman remembered a more febrile London. The London of blackouts and dancing the raids through at the Dorchester and the boys you flew with going down one after another. Whenever he recalled his crash he remembered that he had tried to shield his face from the flames even before his groin, as though he would rather have suffered impotency than a disfigurement he couldn't conceal from society. There was something else. He had not prayed.

When he had suffered his first failure of memory, about two months after his crash, he had put himself in the hands of the psychiatrists. A month later he had been discharged. But there had been other lapses. One had lasted nine days. They said his amnesia was not organic; it was functional, of the fugue type, and inexplicable. So some time ago Norman had resolved to keep his life free of disturbances.

Walking home again in the widening light Norman wished once more that he could be a better, more intelligent man. It would be fun, he thought, to have been one of those brilliant sensitive Englishmen who, at the age of fifteen, is seduced by an exotic lady novelist in his uncle's villa at Florence or Dubrovnik. Brilliant, sensitive Americans, he knew, were heartier types. Their first woman came at fourteen, either in a field of corn under a symbolically bloody sun or, if the weather didn't permit, in the barn where he and she took refuge, with the symbolic storm raging out-side.

Norman turned up Church Street. There he saw a pretty girl with a furled umbrella waiting at the bus stop. She had nice legs. The sun was stronger in the sky now, it was spring, and all at once he yearned for toast and coffee. What I need is a wife, he thought. Maybe I'll meet a nice girl at Sonny Winkleman's on Saturday night.

He picked up his mail downstairs and took the steps to his flat two at a time. There was a copy of the *Intelligence Digest* – a magazine he needed for an article he was prepar-ing for Hale – and a telegram from Charlie Lawson.

'ARRIVING SOUTHAMPTON TWELVE TUESDAY. MEET US WATERLOO.'

Tuesday, Norman thought. This *is* Tuesday.

'CAN YOU SUBLET APARTMENT AS HINTED. SALUD. LOVE AND KISSES. CHARLIE AND JOEY.'

No, Norman thought, I certainly can't. He did not intend to leave London that summer. But pouring himself another cup of coffee he read Charlie's telegram again. They're two, he thought, and I'm one. They don't know London. No, he thought, I'm not letting them have the flat. That's final.

He turned to the rest of his mail. His agent in New York had sent him a copy of the letter from Bill Jacobson of Star Books. They liked his latest thriller, but they wanted it expanded to a minimum of sixty thousand words. There was also a copy of the Montreal *Star*, a friend at home always sent him the Saturday edition, and a few bills. Nor-man returned to Charlie's telegram. They're two, he thought, and I'm one. Then, remembering all the good times they had shared, he decided that the least he could do was to let them have the flat until they found something more permanent at a reasonable rent. He phoned Karp.

'Karp? Norman speaking. Listen, I'd like to ask you a favour. Have you any empty rooms in your place?'

Karp's house was in Hampstead. He said that he had two empty rooms.

14

'I'm going to sub-let my flat for a while. Can you rent me one?'

'Remember,' Karp said, 'last week I arrived early for dinner? I had to wait an hour for you in your flat. There was nothing to amuse me, so I went through your drawers. I found some letters from a girl called Joey.' Karp paused. 'Do many women crawl to you like that, Norman?'

No, Norman thought. Unfortunately no.

'Can you rent me a room or not, Karp? It won't be for long.'

'*I* am to be your landlord. Imagine that.'

Norman had first met Karp in the hospital. Karp had been an orderly.

'You'll be able to read my mail more often that way.'

'You mustn't take offence,' Karp said. 'After all, who read your letters to you in the hospital? Not to mention bathing and hair-cutting and—'

'Then I can count on a room?'

Karp said he could count on a room.

Norman poured himself more coffee. He had been saving his letter from Nicky for the last. Now he opened it eagerly. After their mother had died Norman's younger brother Nicky had gone to Boston to join her family; he had even adopted their name – Singleton, and that's how he came to be in the American Army.

'DEAR UN-COMRADE TROTSKY:

Here in Munich, up to my neck in krauts and beer and brass I often think of you among the more civilised Britishers.

The only thing I don't miss are those crazy Church Street church bells breaking my head on Sunday mornings.

How are you, are you married yet, and please send me more Evelyn Waugh penguins.

re Evelyn: A buddy here, one Malcolm Greenbaum, spotted *A Handful of Dust* on my pillow and said, quote, I hear she writes very good. But Malcolm is real people.

15

Honestly, Norman, when I think of my buddies here – Malcolm and Frank in particular – I am really grateful for the army. I would never have met any of these cats at Harvard or in Uncle Tom's law cabin after (not that I'm going into the law firm any more).'

Norman remembered Nicky as he had last seen him in London. Tall, boyishly awkward in his uniform, with their father's brooding blue eyes and tender smile, and with a lot of Dr Max Price's brilliance too. Nicky inherited the gift, he thought, not me.

'Please don't send me any more *New Statesman's*, books like that one by Ring Lardner, Jr, or back issues of *Pravda*. This is the American army not Abe Lincoln's Brigade. Do you want me to end up in the stockade? Besides, I don't dig that red or pink or plain off-colour preaching. I don't care if the next president is Ike or Harpo Marx, as long as you haven't forgotten that you promised to take me on a trip once I'm discharged.'

Norman had promised to take Nicky to Spain for a few months. They were going to rent a villa together. Norman could hardly wait.

'Oh yes. I'm going to make 21 in four days, man. No time for more now.

Auf wiederShane,
ALGER HISS
P.S. Don't forget the Waugh, old thing.'

He had sent Nicky a hundred dollars for his birthday. That was a lot of money, it made him feel guilty, but recalling Nicky's stay with him again he was glad that he had done it. They had sat up into the early hours every night talking about their more eccentric relatives and only on the last day of his leave had they realised with a sudden panic that Nicky had yet to see a play or the sights.

Norman read Nicky's letter twice more. He had time to write him a brief note before he went off to meet Charlie and

Joey, but it wouldn't do to write I love you, everything you say makes me feel good. A letter to Nicky had to be a funny letter. Norman sat down by his typewriter. He was in a very good mood.

III

A damp copy of *Reveille* clung to the concrete at Norman's feet. He glanced again at the picture of the bathing beauty that had been smudged and ripped by footprints and then looked up just as the boat train rounded the bend. A brief shock of sunlight suddenly illuminated the cracked, soot-soiled glass overhead, but then the clouds closed again and a thin rain began to fall on the black concrete platform of Waterloo Station. Two West Indians with flashing ties passed a Woodbine between them. Norman felt elated, but he was apprehensive too. He wasn't sure whether Joey had ever told Charlie the truth.

Norman saw them first.

Charlie was bent over a little boy who appeared to be lost. One look was enough, one look at Charlie and you could tell that the child wasn't, couldn't be, his. He was too rigidly attentive for a father. And once you saw him stand upright and smile and then pat the boy's head and smile even fuller you knew him for a childless man who kept pockets full of candies and never forgot to bring a toy when he visited. Charlies was a small rotund man, bald except for the thick unruly horseshoe of hair that ran from ear to ear. His face, the face of a middle-aged cherub, had a remarkably gentle quality. He returned the little boy to his parents and then looked about him, confused, as though he was expecting to be accused of a misdemeanour.

Joey was talking to a young girl. They made an odd contrast. For Joey, slim, fair-haired, and thirty-five, with a brown bony face and enormous brown eyes, was a fully-realised woman. She was smartly dressed. The young girl, who had wild streaky blonde hair and a white creamy face, was dishevelled from her journey. Joey, had she been as plump as the young girl, would never have risked slacks. But it was the young girl who caught Norman's eye. She seemed so refreshingly American.

'Norman!' Charlie rushed up to him. 'Norman!'

Joey hugged Norman; she held him close.

Norman noticed that the girl who Joey had been talking to earlier was smiling at him faintly and he returned the smile. The girl looked down at her shoes.

'I couldn't sleep all night, Norman,' Charlie began. 'I was so excited. Ask Joey.' He squeezed Norman's arm. 'I've got so much to tell you.'

Joey, after a perfunctory backward glance at the girl, took Norman's other arm.

Sally waved half-heartedly. Then forgotten on the platform, she watched the three of them walk off arm-in-arm. Sally had a grievance. Over the years, what with all her father's stories about him, she had fabricated a romantic picture of Norman Price. He was to incorporate the most alluring characteristics of Hemingway and Fitzgerald heroes into one tall expatriate. In the flesh, however, he looked just like another socialist schoolmaster. Norman and Joey went into the tea room while Charlie looked after the baggage.

'It's wonderful to see you again, Joey.'

'And Charlie?'

'And Charlie. Of course, and Charlie.'

The uplifted brown face she turned to him, the hardened brown face, hadn't altered.

'You're staring, Norman.'

'I was wondering what would have happened,' he blurted out, 'if I had agreed to go to Mexico with you.'

Joey laughed her bony laugh.

'Do you despise me?' he asked.

'Don't flatter yourself, Norman.'

Norman reached out impetuously and stroked her cheek. 'Are you happy,' he asked, 'happy with Charlie?'

'I've made my peace.'

'Oh. Oh, I see.'

'He's the kindest man I've ever known. Underneath it all, that's what he is.'

'You sound like you're recommending an hotel.'

'Let's change the subject. Are *you* happy?'

Looking at him, waiting for his reply, she remembered sadly that there had used to be things you couldn't do or write or say because Norman, Norman Price, Asst Prof. Norman Price, would call them dishonest. Today he wrote thrillers. And all at once she wanted to sting him, but, warming to his slow tender smile, she realised that would embarrass him for her sake rather than hurt him. Writing thrillers would be a game to Norman. He had no creative pretensions. He was still the tallest of the group.

'Do you still think I'm pretty, Norman?'

'A smasher, you are. Scouts honour.'

As he leaned over to kiss her on the mouth he felt Charlie's hand on his shoulder. 'You can look,' Charlie said, 'but you can't touch.'

Norman grinned.

'I've been standing over there—' Charlie pointed towards the door ' – and spying on you for the last minute. You looked so cosy, the two of you, that just for a second I hated you both. Hell, am I ever going to miss my analyst.'

In the taxi, Charlie slipped into a long denunciation of American foreign policy. He had the manner of someone who had forgotten some little task or errand but couldn't, try as hard as he would, remember exactly what it was, so while he talked to you he seemed to be thinking of, or seeking out, other issues. Charlie began to curse those who had informed.

'Not so fast,' Norman said. 'This choice was a difficult one. Fifteen hundred a week is a lot to give up for honour, for people and ideas you no longer believe in . . .'

'What Norman is trying to say, Charlie, is that you weren't earning anywhere near that on the coast.'

Charlie applied his hand to his forehead like a poultice. 'I'd have done it,' he said. 'You did it.'

'I was only earning a hundred odd dollars a week at the university, Charlie. Besides I was bored with my job.'

'Let's talk about something else,' Joey said.

'Well, here we are.' Charlie squeezed Norman's knee and smiled. 'Joey and I. Still together after fifteen years; always smiling, always right. Canada's Sunshine Kids.'

They all laughed.

'How long since we've seen you, Norman? Five years.'

'Six,' Joey said quickly.

Norman told them about Nicky. He also told them that they could have his flat for a while.

'What a town,' Charlie said. 'Oh, I'm going to love it. Really I am. I feel lucky.' He grinned. 'Wait till you read my new play. It's sensational. Sally loved it.'

'Sally?'

Joey told him who Sally was. She explained that they had met her on the ship. Charlie said that he had asked her to come to Sonny Winkleman's party on Saturday night.

'That's nice.' Norman took a letter out of his pocket. 'Do you mind if I ask the driver to stop at the next mail box? I mustn't forget this letter to Nicky.'

'Can't it wait?'

'No,' Norman said, 'it can't. My brother Nicky is the most. It's his birthday tomorrow.'

IV

As the sun suddenly broke through a heavy wad of clouds over the grey barracks of the McGraw Kaserne, Malcolm Greenbaum, a hefty boy with a big open face, hitched up his trousers with his elbows. Malcolm suffered from boils. His thick knotted neck was bandaged. 'Remember,' he said plumply, 'if we're going into town we must conduct ourselves like matoor representatives of the *U*-nited States abroad.'

A responsive grin spread like butter over Frank Lord's

freckled face. But Nicky frowned. He didn't appreciate it when Malcolm remarked on his own reserve. He didn't want the others to think him 'different'.

The three boys raced across the street and leaped aboard the army bus. Inside, Milly Demarest, a pretty blonde crafts director, sat by the window. 'Hello, boys,' she said, flicking her greeting at them like cigarette ashes, 'going into town?'

'You guessed it.'

As the bus pulled out of the Kaserne gates Frank said: 'It's Nicky's birthday.'

Frank Lord was six foot three, maybe more, with hair red as fire. He never cursed. They said his father was a Baptist preacher. Frank could play a banjo. They said that, too. They also said that his brother had been hanged, but nobody knew for sure. Unless Nicky, maybe. For Frank didn't talk much, except to say that he was going to study pharmacy when he got out of the army. That was for sure.

'Oh,' said Milly, 'how old?'

'Sixteen.'

'You act it,' Milly said.

'*Touché*', Malcolm said.

Big American cars, a casual proof of the conqueror's affluence, were parked without care on either side of the Grunwalderstrasse. Looking out of the window, Nicky noticed the usual set of army wives, in pincurls and blue jeans, drinking beer morosely in the *gasthaus* garden. They struck him as a curiously touching group.

'Nicky's brother sent him a hundred dollars for his birthday,' Frank said.

Nicky was skinny and tall and awkward with his fair hair clipped short and his eyes blue and brooding.

'Nicky's brother is a square,' Malcolm said. 'He can't forgive cats our age for not having been killed in Spain and all.'

'Is your brother a commie?' Milly asked.

Nicky looked pained. 'He's a paraphrase writer,' he said.

'A what?'

'Tell her, Mr Bones.'

'A paraphrase writer,' Malcolm said, 'is a guy who can read a story in *Collier's*, rewrite it, and then sell it to the *Saturday Evening Post* for more loot. Right?'

'Young man,' Nicky said, 'you have just won a bar with a built-in Cadillac and your choice of three of the Philippine Islands. Would you like to try for sixty-four dollars?'

'For heaven sakes,' Milly said, 'can't you answer a question?'

'My brother,' Nicky said, 'was an English lit. prof. until it was discovered that he was an agent of the Kremlin. A fact uncovered by close examination of his income tax returns. So he was fired. And just about then a publisher got after him for his confessions. But he refused. On that day in fact Norman Price made that now historic statement: "I'd rather be left than vice-president".' Nicky pulled frantically at his cigarette. 'So what happened next?' laughed the pretty young crafts director. 'He was deported to Canada,' snarled the young soldier with the wrinkle in his eye. 'And from there he came to Europe where he is now otherwise employed as a witch-hunt hunter. More specifically, honey-child, my brother is compiling a list of anti-communist front organisations for Hollywood-hacks-in-exile, Inc. The afore-mentioned hundred bucks is hush money. Moscow gold. I'm the Munich fingerman.'

'A hundred dollars is a lot of money,' Milly said. 'Does Peggy know yet?'

'Peggy bugs him,' Malcolm said.

'Well, maybe Peggy is getting just a bit tired of Nicky picking up stray Germans here and there. Maybe Peggy' – she turned to Nicky – 'is beginning to find you just a bit too moody . . .'

'Come on,' Nicky said as the bus came to a stop, 'let's see what's doing at the American Way.'

Soldiers slumped in easy chairs, in the immense lounge of the American Way Club and a jukebox hillbilly hollered:

'Wahoo, somebody ughed on you
And I know all about your secret, I'm afrai-ai-aid.'

The three boys stopped before a cardboard figure of a hillbilly who advertised a barn dance. Pappy Burns' Tune Twisters, the poster promised, would play on Friday night. Another poster, this one on the wall above the information desk, read:

DACHAU

Bus Leaves Every Saturday at 1400

VISIT THE CASTLE

AND THE CREMATORY

The boys walked through the lounge into the snack bar.

'What's happened to Nicky?'

Malcolm looked round. 'He's probably upstairs playing ping-pong.'

They looked, but he wasn't there. They found him drinking beer with a German in a bar around the corner.

'Meet Ernst,' Nicky said.

Ernst had a lean, quiet face. His hard blue eyes were mindful. Vigilant. Had he been dressed differently he could have passed for a man who considered himself better than his job, but obviously he had none. Yet he did not seem cunning or squalid. That (the possibilities of a true friendship) is what had attracted Nicky to him at first. For Nicky, more than the others, was conscious of the hatred evoked by his uniform. He yearned to be recognised as something more personal than just another occupation soldier.

Ernst wore a G.I. combat jacket that had been dyed blue and under it a strikingly clean white shirt opened at the collar. His baggy, cuffless black trousers had originated with some other army, probably the Russian, but his tan loafers were distinctly unmilitary.

'Ernst's from East Germany,' Nicky said. 'He's on his way to Paris.'

'Who's holding him back?' Malcolm asked.

'No money.' Ernst spoke softly, his accent was thick, but his American, just like his Russian and his French and his English, was incongruously colloquial. He spoke the language of soldiers. 'And no papers.'

23

'That's crazy, you wanting to get out of Germany,' Malcolm said, his thick neck reddening. 'Real crazy.'

'Cut it,' Nicky said.

But Malcolm edged closer to Ernst. 'My name's Greenbaum,' he said. 'G-R-E-E-N-B-A-U-M.'

'All right,' Nicky said, 'he was a kid when all that happened.'

'A kid sure.' Malcolm turned to Ernst again. 'Were you in the war?'

'Yeah. During the last weeks.'

Malcolm grinned triumphantly and afraid.

'And I'll bet you come from a leading family of anti-Nazis . . .'

Ernst averted his eyes. 'I would like to be your friend,' he said. 'I have nothing against—'

'Nothing against the Jews, huh? That's very white of you.'

'I am not an anti-semite,' Ernst said.

'Shake with him,' Frank said to Malcolm. 'Come on.'

'Over my dead body.'

'I was with the communist youth,' Ernst tried again. 'They have lots of Jews.'

'If there's anything I hate worse than an anti-semite,' Malcolm said, 'it's a commie.'

Frank walked away in disgust, put a coin into the juke-box, and asked a heavily made-up girl, who had been sitting with three men, to dance with him. Malcolm ordered a round of drinks and then pulled Nicky into a corner. 'I don't dig the kraut,' he said. 'I thought we were going to have us a ball, just the three of us, and then maybe later some *schatzies*.' A boil had burst on the back of his neck and Malcolm fingered the yellowing bandage tenderly. His quick black eyes pleaded for assurances. 'Be a pal,' he said, slapping Nicky on the back. 'Let's ditch him here and go to Peg's party.'

'Nobody's stopping you from going to Peggy's party.'

'It's your birthday but. The party's for you.'

'Drink your beer, man. And try to be friendly.'

The bar, cheap but not quite a dive, smelled of cooking fat. The tinsel decorations over the mirror were covered with dust. There were many salesmen and office workers and small business men about. Men with uniformly spic faces. There were a few more girls, but no other soldiers. Frank held his girl tight and she giggled and pushed his hand away from her breast – and all the men heard and watched.

One of the men, a big one with cold little eyes, came up to Ernst and pressed his arm. Ernst tightened and slipped his hand into his jacket. Malcolm watched.

'Get them out of here,' the big man said. 'The girl is with us.'

Ernst recognised the type, and he would gladly have started a fight but remembering that he had no papers, remembering the dreary Nissen huts and the drearier lectures on democracy in the refugee camp at Sandbostel – what he would have to return to if he were caught by the police – he decided that a fight would be foolish.

'All right,' Ernst said, 'but let them finish their drinks first.'

So the four boys left. Frank and Malcolm walked ahead.

'The kraut's packing a shiv,' Malcolm said.

'Do you think there's going to be trouble?'

'Not if we warn Nicky.'

'You can't tell Nicky anything. Don't you know that yet?'

The four boys picked their way between bars and churches and brothels in the constricted grey streets of the old town and finally emerged into the broader twilight of the up-and-coming streets at the Marienplatz. For several years now men had been working day and night rebuilding what had been almost totally destroyed by allied bombings. Week by week Munich was being restored and pushed higher. A scaffolding came down here, another shot up there. This changing of the face of the city day by day lent a certain excitement to the streets, but, as far as Nicky was concerned, it was difficult to believe in the boom. Everywhere there were busy bosses and busy workers, but the new shops of the Theatinerstrasse had the ephemeral quality of a carnival big top and one could never be sure that the circus would not be dismantled and pulled out of town during the night. Men of a certain age were scarce. The cafés were too thick with unaccompanied women. You could believe in nothing these days. Nicky sensed that, Ernst knew it. And as they crossed the Stachusplatz Ernst said, 'In 1919 the Reds held this square against a whole regiment with only two machine guns and four men.'

'Are you a communist?' Nicky asked.

'I used to be. I was an official in the FDJ, but now—' Ernst hesitated; he would have liked to have said something sardonic about East and West—'now I have no politics.'

'Neither have I.' Nicky waited until Frank and Malcolm had turned the corner and then pulled a pile of papers out of his pocket. 'Here,' he said, separating three twenty dollar bills from the other papers. 'I know you're broke. Pay me back when you have it.'

Ernst took the money, but he was puzzled.

'Come on.' Nicky felt hurt because Ernst had not thanked him for the money and yet he disliked people who were effusively grateful. 'Let's catch up with the others.'

Malcolm and Frank were waiting around the corner. 'Let's go to Peg's party,' Malcolm asked for the tenth time.

'Look, man,' Nicky said, 'if we go to Peggy's party she's going to want to know why I didn't see her yesterday and the yesterday before yesterday. She bugs me, man. I want a swinging gal and she ain't it.'

Frank suggested that they go somewhere where they could dance.

'That's my boy,' Nicky said.

The *jazzkeller* had served as an air-raid shelter during the war. As the four boys descended the musty concrete steps a thick-lipped blues, washed up with the yellow smoke and laughter, slapped against the stones. They picked their way through a dark winding passage, tripping over abandoned beer bottles, before they finally made it into the crowded anteroom.

'Maybe,' Malcolm said, confronting Ernst heatedly, 'you'd like to buy a round for a change?'

'This happens to be my round,' Nicky said. But Nicky was ashamed. He watched sadly as Malcolm, conscious of his spilling belly again, hitched up his trousers sullenly. Nicky punched him affectionately on the shoulder. 'We'll go to Peg's party from here.'

'If you don't mind my tagging along,' Malcolm said.

Nicky pushed his way through the mob and back again with four bottles of beer. Then, with the others following after he squeezed his way under a low door into the immense cellar. The arched ceiling was visible only where cigarette clouds parted grudgingly here and there. To Nicky's right, long wooden tables faded away into the endless gloom. Bodiless heads and hands gripping beer bottles appeared through punctures in the eye-stinging haze. The din, whenever the music let up, was deafening. A girl was shoved against Nicky – they embraced. Then she was consumed again by the mob and his beer bottle was gone with her. Another girl swiftly took her place against him as though a body alone, like an open wound, was something to be quickly bandaged. Above them, the band played badly in a blaze of five hundred watt bulbs, and all at once Nicky and the girl were flung free into a clear space. Malcolm was there, watching, rubbing his damp yellowing bandage.

'Where's Frank?' Nicky asked.

'Gone to the can with—' Malcolm pointed at Frank and Ernst approaching. 'Here they are.'

Frank's flaming hair was damp with sweat.

'He's been sick,' Ernst said. 'I think we should go.'

Outside, Malcolm caught up with Nicky. 'Frank's lost his wallet,' he said.

Nicky wiped his head with his arm.

'Frank's lost his wallet,' Malcolm said, 'and you and I both know who swiped it.'

'Don't be crazy. One of the whores must have lifted it.'

'Yeah, some chance.'

'He didn't steal Frank's wallet. *He didn't*. Why can't you

be nice to him? He didn't shoot your *zeyda* or – Ernst's probably had it tougher than either you or I can imagine. Give him a break, huh?'

'Will you lemme search him?'

'Go to hell, Malcolm.'

'I'll bet you my next month's pay against one lousy buck that Ernst's got his wallet.'

Ernst and Frank were coming.

'You touch him, you just put your little finger on him, and I'll break your neck.'

'Scared he did it, huh?'

'Why should I give a damn?'

'You tell me, man, I'm listening. *He packs a shiv.*'

'Who?'

'The man in the goddamned moon, that's who. Wow! Can I have the next dance, momma?'

'You remember what I said,' Nicky said as the two boys drew nearer.

'Some buddy you turned out to be. Jesus H. Christ.'

Nicky broke away and took Frank by the arm. 'Feeling better?'

Frank, tall and awkward, grinned weakly. And Nicky wondered whether Frank's brother, the one who they'd hanged, had been so tall, so gentle. He hoped not.

'I'm fine,' Frank said. 'Honest I am.'

'We're going to Peg's party now. You'll be able to lie down there.' Nicky hailed a taxi. 'You two go ahead. We'll follow.'

'You're trying to get rid of us,' Malcolm said.

Nicky pushed the two of them into a taxi and turned to Ernst with a shy, hesitant smile. 'Thanks for taking care of Frank,' he said.

Ernst reached into his pocket. 'Here.' It was Frank's wallet. 'I saw one of the girls take if off him. Here.'

Nicky slipped the wallet into his pocket. 'Let's get a taxi,' he said, his voice unnaturally hoarse.

'You think I stole his wallet?'

Nicky felt as though he was going to be physically sick.

28

'It doesn't make any difference.'

'Yeah,' Ernst said. 'It does.'

They got into a taxi.

'If you say you didn't steal it then I believe you,' Nicky said.

'Malcolm's a Jew,' Ernst began. 'That's why—'

'Why you filthy—'

'Listen, my father spent most of the war in —'

'Yeah. I know. In Belsen. Everybody's father—'

'But mine did.'

Nicky wished they'd both go away. Malcolm and Ernst. He wished they'd take their sickness elsewhere.

'If I had stolen Frank's wallet I would have kept it.'

'You might have heard Malcolm suggest searching you. You were close enough.'

'You would never have allowed him to.'

'Why?'

'Because you were sure I had stolen it.'

'Look, let's just forget it ever happened. You didn't take it and I apologise, O.K.?'

The brownstone house on Runtgenstrasse was a Special Services, B.O.Q. A house rule forbade male guests from going upstairs where the bedrooms were, but nothing had been said about the three basement rooms, which were unoccupied. There was a patio and a garden around by the back of the house. Peggy's bedroom, overlooking the garden, had a window that could be reached from the patio roof.

Peggy seized Nicky and spun him around.

'Happy birthday, keed!'

The party was well under way. But because it was still early the homely had not yet settled for one another. The handsome and the beautiful, assured, conscious of their obligations, favoured even the most ungainly with promising little attentions. The dancing at this stage was still fairly inhibited. Jimmy Marko sat at the piano.

'Oh, my girl's got Wrigley, Wrigley eyes.'

And upstairs, upstairs where men were forbidden, teddybears lolled on double beds. And, in the case of Peggy's bed, all the ladies' wraps and handbags were piled.

Nicky avoided Peggy. He knew that she probably had things to say to him, that she had most certainly bought him an expensive gift, and he did not feel up to either prospect. He noticed that Ernst was eating sandwich after sandwich, indifferent to the whole crowd. Nicky was confused; he felt blue. Why had Ernst lied to him? Why, now that they were together at the party, didn't he make some show of friendship? I'll go, Nicky thought defiantly. I'll finish this drink and I'll cut out. But when Malcolm approached, smiling a boyishly triumphant smile, Nicky grinned back at him gratefully. This he knew; Malcolm he understood. Malcolm wore the lipstick smudges on his chin like a medal of honour.

'Hey, those college chicks,' Malcolm said.

Nicky handed Malcolm Frank's wallet.

'One of the girls in the jazz cellar took it off him. Ernst got it back from her.'

'You kidding?'

'Look, I was with him. We went back together. He pointed out the girl and we got it off her see?'

Malcolm knew that Nicky was lying. He looked hurt. Cheated.

'What in the hell's the matter with you?' Nicky yelled.

'Nothing.'

But Nicky understood that Ernst, even if he never saw him again, had already cost him one of his best friends. More confused than before, his sense of frustration and his temper both rising sharply, he went into the kitchen and refilled his glass.

'Can't you morons do anything but neck?'

A tall West Point man and his girl broke apart.

'You looking for a fight?' the West Point man asked.

I am, Nicky thought. I sure am.

And just about then in the parlour, the first of the beautiful, Milly Demarest, made her move. She took a likely young man by the hand and slipped down to the basement. The party pitch heightened. Pimpled boys, girls with little breasts, cast their frightened eyes about searchingly. Couples danced out on to the patio and then retreated into the garden. A soldier complained that his eyes hurt and out went the lights. Giggles, a few mock shrieks of protest, then the rustling of skirts. Those who had been left out fired frantic jokes into the dark.

Nicky drifted over to the piano and began to play *Lady Be Good*. Peggy smiled at him adoringly. A brown, long-legged girl, Peggy, at twenty-seven, still had the impulsive manner of a girl ten years younger, but she had already swept through most of the European capitals collecting travel posters and beer labels and theatre programmes with which she hoped, one day, to paper the walls of a dream. A dream, an apartment, which included the famous Nicky Singleton knocking out his latest hit tunes on the parlour piano between television appearances.

'Everybody says you play something divine, Nicky,' she said.

Nicky stopped playing. He got up.

'What's wrong? Have I said something?'

'No.'

'I was talking to your German friend,' she said. 'I like him.'

'Well, I don't. I wish I hadn't brought him here.'

'Do you want my car, Nicky? You can borrow it tomorrow, if you like.'

Nicky realised that her gesture was no less crude, no less desperate, than his having offered Ernst sixty dollars. God, he thought, searching the room for Ernst, God. He took Peggy into his arms and kissed her on the forehead. 'Thanks for the party,' he said. 'You're very sweet.' And then before she could spoil things with an unfortunate remark he moved away.

Jimmy Marko sang:

'You're whispering why you'll never leave me,
Whispering why you'll never grieve me . . .'

31

Having eaten his fill, Ernst collapsed into an armchair and lit a cigar that had been given to him by a visiting professor from UCLA. These wild, amazingly affluent Americans both delighted and horrified him – look at the size of those cigarette butts – but what was to be done about Nicky? Ernst had indeed taken Frank's wallet in the toilet of the *jazzkeller*, but he had never meant to keep it. Because Nicky had been kind to him, Ernst had wanted to make a gesture in return. He had hoped that by giving Frank's wallet to Nicky, and saying that he had discovered it on one of the girls, he would ingratiate himself with him. But his scheme had backfired. Ernst sucked drowsily at his cigar. A thin pretty girl loomed up before him. She had obviously had too much to drink. 'Aren't you Terry Lewis?' she asked thickly.

'No, I am not.'

'My name's Nancy.' She swayed slightly. 'Would you like to dance with me?'

Ernst got up slowly, unsure of himself.

'You don't *have* to,' Nancy said.

As they danced round and round in the dark, bumping against other couples, Ernst took fright. Nancy rubbed against him; he felt her lips on his neck. If he didn't respond she would be insulted. But if Malcolm, or another unfriendly soldier, caught him with her, he might start a fight. A fight, and the police, would mean Sandbostel again. Maybe worse. Another consideration was that he didn't want to embarrass Nicky. Nicky was his friend.

'You're the strong, silent type,' Nancy said. 'I can tell.'

'Come into the garden with me.'

'Want to show me your etchings? Mm?'

'Come,' he said.

Nancy led Ernst out into the hall and to the foot of the stairs. 'Look,' she whispered, 'you can't come up with me. It's not allowed, you know, and Captain Hodge might see.' She squeezed Ernst's hand. 'I'll go first. You count to ten and then follow. But for God's sake don't let anyone see you, and *no* noise. I'll meet you at the top of the stairs.'

Before Ernst could protest, she was gone. Not that he was against her little scheme. It would be nice to have a girl, he thought.

Ernst counted to twenty-five, looked around twice, and then started softly up the stairs.

He didn't see Malcolm, however, Malcolm, who had nobody to dance with himself, watched Ernst sneak up the stairs and then hurried off in search of Peggy.

Ernst couldn't find Nancy anywhere.

'Here,' she whispered.

She was in the bedroom where all the coats and hats were piled. Ernst took her in his arms and kissed her expertly. Her cheeks were very hot, but her breasts, as he had feared, were small. Suddenly Nancy broke free of him. 'I'm going to be sick,' she said, and she ran off, holding her hand to her mouth.

Ernst heard the toilet door slam. He sat down on the bed and lit a cigarette.

Malcolm and Peggy found each other at last.

'Malcolm,' Peggy said, 'have you seen that German boy around?'

'You mean the one who swiped Frank's wallet?'

'The one who what?'

'You heard me.'

'Oh, Nicky'll drive me nuts yet. He's always picking up people and things and five minutes later, he can't stand them.'

'Nicky told you that?'

'He told me himself that he couldn't stand the German boy.'

'Look, I just saw the little bastard sneak upstairs. I'm sure he's after the coats and stuff. You go phone the M.P.s Peg, and meanwhile I'll keep my eyes open for him. Hurry.'

Nicky passed from room to room, but he couldn't find Ernst, so he refilled his glass and went down to the basement. He found Milly sitting there, alone.

Frank, who had passed out on the sofa, was snoring loudly.

33

'I'm clobbered,' Milly giggled and drank from Nicky's glass. 'Happy birthday,' she said as Nicky took her in his arms. 'Happy – Oh, no, Nicky, I've got the curse.'

When Nicky came upstairs again Peggy was waiting for him.

'Wipe the lipstick off your mouth,' she said. 'You could do that. At least that.'

And then Peggy ran off.

Turning away Nicky caught sight of a girl sprawled out on an easy chair with her legs dangling over one arm and her head resting on the other. Her partner had just left her, maybe to get another drink, and so she was alone in the dark. The girl brushed back her brown hair with a white little hand and then absently did up one or two buttons of her blouse. Next she lit a cigarette very slowly and without concern, as though time and headlines and coarse boys could never strike at her. There were beads of sweat on her forehead, a little golden slipper dangled from one foot. Bright eyes, a pretty polished face, a tiny waist. Nicky was afraid to stir lest he distract her attention. The absolutely unselfconscious poise with which she smoothed down her skirt made him almost unbearably happy. Then, as the girl smiled a full satiated smile, Nicky hoped that she would fall asleep and that her soldier, whoever he was, would not return and make more demands or talk obscene about her in the barracks the next morning. The pretty girl rubbed her lips where they had been bruised a little. Nicky, watching, suddenly wished that this stuffy room could be transformed into a wood and that all the girls, full of sun and pain and laughter, could go dancing round the trees. The soldier returned. 'Hell,' he said to the pretty girl, 'Peggy's locked herself in the can. She's crying her goddam heart out.'

Nicky heard the police sirens in the distance. He turned away and began to improvise at the piano. That's when Malcolm showed up, obviously drunken.

'You were never my friend,' Malcolm said. 'You with all your big words and big talk and big books. You yeah you. A college kid. Money? Stinking with money. You were pre-

34

tending to talk like us and feel like us when all the time you were laughing at us behind our backs. Well, I'll tell you something you Nazi-loving son-of-a—'

'Rain, rain, go away, come again another day.'

'And I'll tell you something else. Don't think—'

'Lady-bug, lady-bug, fly away home, your house is on fire, your children all alone.'

'And I'll tell you—'

'Go away Malcolm. Breeze.'

'Your little friend is upstairs going through the coats and purses.'

Nicky stopped playing. The police sirens sounded closer.

'Peggy sent for the M.P.s,' Malcolm said.

'She sent for what? Oh you fools!'

And Nicky, seized by a sudden and uncontrollable anger, anger against Ernst's betrayal, anger against Malcolm and the pretty girl's soldier, anger against all things unbeautiful, pushed past Malcolm and, smashing a beer bottle against the wall and gripping the stub tightly in his fist, started up the stairs.

Jimmy Marko took Nicky's place at the piano and sang:

> *'Ain't misbehavin'*
> *Doodle-de-dum,*
> *Ain't misbehavin'*
> *Dada-da-dum.'*

When the West Point man and his girl heard the thud above them, they broke apart briefly thoughtful. But as no other sound followed immediately they embraced again.

Malcolm had stepped outside to wait for the M.P.s, so he heard nothing.

Harvey Jones, a slight corporal with rimless glasses who suffered from acne, cornered the professor. Harvey, was a preacher. 'Yes,' he said, 'this is my last week here. Next Tuesday I'm being sent back to the land of the Big P.X.'s. But I want you to know that it's been a real joy to work here and that when I go stateside I'll continue to work as a vital witness for Jesus.'

35

'I'm glad you feel that way, son, but if you don't mind—'

Peggy heard the next thud and froze where she stood, trying, trying desperately, to hear something more above the din of the party.

'Two years ago, when the letter came from my draft board, I was mighty sorrowful. The first question I asked myself that day was why, *why* has the Lord allowed me to be inducted? Wasn't I spreading Christian fellowship at home? Was I being punished? Then, Sir, when the Lord sent me overseas again I asked myself why? Why has the Lord sent me overseas? The answer is as clear as crystal to me now. The Lord sent me overseas to spread His Word and, believe me, friend, it has been a real joy for me to do that very thing. The Lord—'

'Excuse me, son, but—' a confidential nudge ' – I think I'd better go and test the plumbing. All—'

'The Lord has led me to some wonderful victories here in Germany.'

'All this beer, you know—' and a sunny smile ' – I'll be right with you.'

A soldier smoking on the patio ducked as glass came splashing down on the grass. A girl screamed. Two couples emerged from under the trees. 'There's a man,' a girl began breathlessly, 'he—'

'Some guy – he was all bloody – just jumped out of the window and took off into—' the soldier pointed '—That way . . .'

Two soldiers started after the man who had jumped out of Peggy's window. After Ernst.

Inside, everybody was swiftly conscious that something had happened. Couples broke apart. The boys adjusted their ties and the girls fiddled with their hair. A fat girl began to whimper softly. Then, mercifully, the M.P.s burst into the room.

Peggy stared at the ceiling with tears in her eyes and prayed to God, please God, please he's not hurt.

The lights were switched on at last. Upstairs, a girl screamed.

Malcolm started up the stairs. Two M.P.s followed, then four more. They had guns, but they were too late. Ernst was gone.

'I know his name,' Malcolm screamed. 'It's Ernst. Ernst Haupt. You've got to find the bastard. You've got to find the dirty bastard and kill him.'

Nicky had lost a lot of blood in his fight with Ernst. But they rushed him off to hospital just in case something could still be done.

V

The following evening, in London, Norman went to Sonny Winkleman's party. Sonny lived in a big red brick house in Hampstead. The Americans who gathered there on Saturday nights were mostly blacklisted writers, directors, and producers from Hollywood and New York. Winkleman, who had been a successful producer in Hollywood, was a stout, middle-aged man with a head of shaggy red hair, a wart the size of a dime on his neck, and a somnolent manner. The manner was a ruse. For those heavy colourless eyes which seemed to see nothing were lit fiercely from behind and saw everything. Winkleman was always on the alert. He was a fortunate man. He had money and he had settled his accounts with the Home Office with a surprising *élan*.

The lesser producers, the acolytes, had a much harder time. Budd Graves, for instance, did not even have a passport. When the actors managed to get work permits they did well. So did the directors, although they often had to work without credits. The most gifted of the writers, Bob Landis, had had to struggle at first, but although he too wrote without film credits, he was once again earning big money.

Everybody came to the party at Sonny Winkleman's. Even Karp, who had helped Sonny find a house, was there. Sally, a stranger to the group was also there.

'Nobody gives a damn about the murders in Kenya,' Bob Landis said, 'but when a shipload of horses bound for the slaughter houses of Holland suffer ill-treatment at sea the *Manchester Guardian* makes it front page stuff for days. British hearts have been touched.'

Somebody made a crack in Yiddish and Charlie, although he didn't understand it, laughed happily. Charlie was a Roman Catholic but he was short and fat and better still his name was Lawson, possibly derived from Leibovitch, so many people believed him to be O.K. Charlie seldom corrected this sometimes helpful misunderstanding.

And tonight, Charlie was happy. For the *emigrés*, Winkleman in particular, had considered Charlie bargain basement, a Monogram hack, in Hollywood; he had never really been accepted. That, of course, was before some of the brightest radical stars had paid for and printed their public confessions of error. That was when wit and achievement had still been the criteria of acceptance, while here in London all that was asked was that you had acquitted yourself honourably before the committee.

Sally, provocatively pretty in a green taffeta dress, perched on the arm of Norman's chair. He was excruciatingly conscious of her breasts, but her creamy smile was without guile. 'What's a "property"?' she asked. 'Everybody seems to be talking about "properties".'

'A "property" is a script.' Norman eased away from her thigh a little. 'This is a market place for scripts.'

'My father made me promise to look you up, Norman.'

Sally MacPherson's father was a high school principal. Norman had known him in Montreal.

'Your father is a very gentle man.'

'Gentle men,' Sally said, 'don't shake the world.'

Her throat was very white. She smelled sweet, freshly washed. Norman laughed indulgently. At her age he had felt just about the same. Sally told him that she was going to teach school in London. She was twenty-four. She told him that too.

'I have a brother a little younger than you,' Norman said. 'Nicky was twenty-one yesterday.'

Sally was slightly drunk. Norman attracted her. For the pursuit of whatever quality it was that made some men smoke pipes, and others grow beards, seemed inherent in Norman. He had no need for appendages.

'This crowd,' she said, 'reminds me of my father in a way. He won't buy South African sherry these days, but before he never kept sherry in the house at all.' She caressed his neck with her fingers. 'Do they all belong to the Party?' she asked with a scythe-like sweep of her glass.

'Which party?' Norman asked.

Sally giggled.

Norman kissed her on the forehead and then went to replenish their drinks. He felt very good.

Charlie, in his corner, was stuck in a puddle of theatrical people. There was a producer who had no backers but a sensational script and a director who had no script but an option on a sensational theatre and a starlet whose husband was potentially a sensational backer and a sensational British gossip columnist who was under the pay of all except Charlie. So it was on Charlie that he focused his dulcifying gaze. 'Glad to have you with us, Mr Lawson, I'm rather keen on Americans myself.'

'You ought to be,' Charlie said. 'Seeing how you've let this island become an American colony.'

Joey smiled apologetically, 'He's joking,' she said.

'I'm making anti-American propaganda,' Charlie said.

Karp, who had been contemplating the group like a meal, suddenly broke into the circle. 'Ah, Mr Jeremy,' he said to the director, 'I don't think I've ever had the chance to tell you how much I enjoyed your last picture.'

Karp had a peculiar physique. His face was round, but his limbs were so thin that his belly, sudden as it was huge, sprung forth as a surprise. Karp had a hurt flatulent face with protuberant eyes. With his pink little hands, like apples with fingers, he massaged the top of his cane.

Boris Jeremy shrunk from Karp's small smile. 'I have no pretensions about *Murder Monday Next*,' he said. 'It was a piece of shit.'

Bob Landis clapped Jeremy on the back and grinned widely. 'Don't overestimate your own work,' he said.

Winkleman floated drowsily but watchful between his guests like a whale among smaller fish. He trapped Norman when he was on his way to the bar again.

'Charlie mailed me some scripts from New York, Norm. He's waiting for me to speak to him.'

Norman looked to where Sally perched on the arm of his chair. He smiled at her. I wonder, he thought drunkenly, whether she's wearing black underwear.

'Technically, they're fine,' Winkleman said. 'What are you smiling at?'

'Nothing,' Norman said. Blue, he thought. Blue would be nice.

'But they don't spark me.'

Somebody was talking to Sally. Karp it was.

'That's tough luck for Charlie,' Norman said.

'One of them is a comedy with a strong story line. It's set in New York. The dialogue is strictly from hunger. But if I buy it, Norm, will you – Hey, am I annoying you?'

'No.'

'Does this talk of money depress you?'

Norman laughed.

'If I buy it, will you work on it, Norm?'

Norman often thought that Winkleman and the others made deals and entered into publicised secret partnerships only to keep in practice, like generals disputing imaginary deads in a battle exercise. Sometimes, however, an imaginary battle yielded a real casualty. Only the odd deal materialised, but making one undoubtedly helped to keep the *emigrés* sane.

'Charlie's very touchy; he wouldn't like that.'

'I'm asking you a question. Tell me to buy it and I'll buy it.'

40

'On one condition, Sonny. Pay him a good advance right now and he's not to know that I had a thing to do with it. If the picture's ever produced I want him to get the credit.'

'It's a deal,' Winkleman said. 'When can you start work?'

'Tomorrow.'

Winkleman grinned sleepily. 'You ought to get married,' he said. 'You don't deserve to stay single any longer.'

'You're a filthy old man.'

'I should hope so.'

'Charlie, try to understand,' Joey said, 'all I'm saying is please don't count on anything.'

'Sure, sure. But listen. I could *feel* that Winkleman just loved my script. Of course he couldn't make me an offer right here. But he as much as told me that he wanted an option. He said my story sparks him – don't forget that he was one of the biggest on the coast – he said that he may have to call in a hack to touch it up here and there, but . . .'

'About Norman Price I have a different feeling,' Budd Graves said. 'What do Sonny and Bella see in him anyway? He's so cold he could freeze you with a look.'

Bob grinned affectionately. Though they were infrequent, he enjoyed his afternoon visits with Norman immensely. It gave Bob pleasure – as his own life came to be more and more dominated by the weekly Nielson ratings – to stop and think of Norman writing calmly at his desk, sitting there each afternoon in a jacket with leather patches or in an old sweater, his walls bulging with well thumbed Oxford editions of the poets, copies of *Les Temps Modernes* the pages of which had been cut, and coffee stains and cigarette burns everywhere. In another age, he thought, Norman would have been a monk.

'That's a lot of woman Norman's got there,' Bob said.

'You don't like Norman,' Karp said to Graves, 'because he has dignity.'

Graves, who knew that Karp was a concentration camp survivor, did not want to argue with him, so he ignored him

41

instead. 'No, Bob, there's something funny about Price. I think the war and all that time in the hospital loosened a few screws here and there. I mean if a guy suffers from attacks of amnesia and . . .'

'He no longer suffers from amnesia,' Karp said.

'I wonder who she is,' Bob, grinning like a satiated panda, turned to Karp. '*A Yiddish maidel?*'

'I do not speak Yiddish,' Karp said emphatically. He glared, leaning belligerently on his cane. 'One should not take it for granted that just because I – Ach!' Karp turned and walked away from them.

'Him,' Sally said. 'That man over there. The corpulent one.'

Norman, reaching over Sally's lap, put his drink down on the end-table. 'Oh, Karp,' he said. 'Well, if you're renting a room from him we'll be neighbours. I'm moving into his house tomorrow.'

'Why, that's wonderful!' Sally leaned back and stretched her legs. 'Why does Charlie's wife hate him?'

That seemed to annoy Norman.

'God,' Sally said, 'he gave me his play to read on ship. He's a lousy writer, isn't he?'

This time, when Norman reached for his drink again, he let his arm rest on her lap. He told her angrily that she had not earned the right to judge Charlie. Charlie was always a participant. His hands were dirty. He had never been one to be afraid of looking like a fool in the eyes of the world and that, Norman said, was saying plenty in times like these.

'Oh, no. Not coming from you. Look at them—' she indicated a huddle of long acquisitive faces with a wave of her arm. 'They use Spain like a hormone conditioning cream.'

'And your father?'

'You know better than that. My father isn't a socialist because everything else about him is too ugly to face. He's a high school principal. He earns ninety-two fifty a week. God, if he ever met up with these people he'd have to stop admiring them. He'd have to give up sending badly needed ten dollar bills to "fighting funds" and writing angry letters to the editor that never get printed anyway.'

'I count on these *phonies* for a living.' He laughed. 'My kid brother also talks faster than I can keep up with.'

Winkleman joined Karp in the hall. 'Going so soon?' he asked.

'Mr Sonny Winkleman,' Karp said, 'I find your friends obscene.'

Norman and Sally came out to get their coats too. Bella Winkleman was with them. She was a dark, graceful woman with black hair.

'This way, Sally,' Bella said. 'The second door to your right.'

Karp took Norman aside. 'Sally will be good for you,' he said.

Karp's face wrinkled, his eyes squeezed shut. This smile of his always horrified Norman for he was afraid that once the face unsqueezed again the eyes would have been consumed by the flesh. He waited anxiously and at last the eyes reappeared as provocative as ever.

'I'll see that you get the room next to hers,' Karp said.

Norman stiffened. He watched sadly as Karp, the sway of his back slightly feminine, retreated down the hall; his steps short and quick and angry, like bites.

'Horrible creature,' Bella said.

'Oh, no,' Norman said. 'Don't say that.'

They looked at each other, surprised. Then Bella smiled. Winkleman had left them to return to his guests.

'Sonny is thirteen years older than me,' Bella said, 'and we've been happily married for more than twenty years.'

'Thanks,' Norman said sheepishly, 'but, really, I just met the girl today.'

'Bring her around with you anytime you like.'

'Thanks, Bella, but—'

'And I'll make sure that Bob Landis keeps his distance.'

'Really, Bella, I just met the girl.'

43

Charlie and Joey came into the hall. They were leaving too.

'Hey,' Charlie said, 'we'll see you later, huh? He winked.

VI

Sally's room was on the fifth floor of an hotel near Piccadilly Circus. Norman watched as she bent over a suitcase, looking for the whisky bottle.

'I got it on board ship,' she said. 'It's tax-free.'

Norman poured himself a drink and sat down in the armchair near the window. Sally curled up on the bed.

'Mr Karp told me that if not for you he would still be a hospital orderly. He's very grateful to you, you know.'

Norman didn't want to talk at all. He just wanted to stare.

'Before the war Karp was a GP in a small Polish town. He – he's one of the unlucky few who survived the camps.'

'How do you mean unlucky?'

'The price of survival came high in Karp's case.' Norman twisted his glass round and round self-consciously. 'But let's not talk about him.'

'Why are you smiling?'

'Am I smiling?'

'You've been smiling without stop ever since we left Mr Winkleman's house.'

Norman put down his drink and started towards her. 'No,' she said, 'please don't. There's something so sordid about hotel rooms.' He sat down again. 'You've been looking at me like I was a meal ever since we got here,' she added. But then she rose to fill his glass and Norman circled her waist with his arm. He did that almost absently, giving her a chance to withdraw without embarrassment. She looked at him severely.

'Your friends are so sharp and cruel and witty,' she said. 'I don't want them to make something dirty of us.'

44

'My friends,' he said thickly, 'have nothing to do with us.'

'Don't you see that I could do this just as well at home. Go to bed with a man, I mean. This is Europe. I want things to happen to me here that could never happen to me at home.'

Norman noticed with pleasure that her hair was not blonde in the dry refulgent way a movie bad girl's hair is blonde. Sally's hair was thick, healthy, and streaked with brown. Her calm, sensitive face, however, was not yet fully formed. Absent were the hard lines that made Joey so attractive.

Sally, made uneasy by Norman's stare, shifted her position on the bed. 'Were you a pilot?' she asked.

He wished people wouldn't ask that question with such amazement. Maybe it was because he wore glasses. No, he thought, there's more to it than that. They expect that I would have been something behind the lines. An interpreter, perhaps.

'I was a fighter pilot. I didn't wear glasses then.'

Sally noticed for the first time that there was something odd about the lower lid of his left eye. It was a Tiersch graft, Norman explained. A layer of skin as thin as cigarette paper taken from the inside of his left arm. Luckily, however, his face had only been slightly scarred. Luckily, he said, his crash had come after they had given up the use of tannic acid for burns. Then he told her in a constrained voice of Hornstein.

'He was a dark, intense man,' he said, 'with all the unfortunate characteristics the anti-semite attributes to his people. Whether it was a room full of girls, a pub, or even if it was only the mess, Hornstein always played it the same, like a Hollywood air ace. He was always the guy on the spot when a Canadian correspondent wanted a story.

'Hornstein wasn't a bad pilot – that much you had to give him. He had three 109s and two probables to his credit. But he was a fixer. He wangled the longest leaves and the best girls. If it was liquor, a week-end pass, a phone number, or

45

money you wanted you went to Hornstein and hated him for it. I avoided him like the plague. But Hornstein tried everything – he wanted to be accepted at any cost. One evening in the mess he read us a Bnai Brith pamphlet which proved that in proportion to the population of Canada, there were more Jews than Gentiles in the armed forces. None of us gave a damn one way or another, really, but one by one we got up and left him alone at the table with his pamphlet.'

'I know the kind of man you mean,' Sally said.

'The next day – at the time, you know, the Germans were putting everything into knocking out our advance fighter bases – we ran into a formation of about twenty 109s at 20,000 feet. They had the height – the sun – everything. We were occupied with the twelve Dornier 215s below us. Hornstein was flying close to me. Before we peeled off to join the battle he winked and made a thumbs-up sign to me. That made my stomach turn.' Norman poured himself another drink. 'The battle was brief, fierce, and explosive. Hornstein was hit. I watched as at a height of about two thousand feet he prepared to bail out of his blazing machine. Hornstein was over a thickly-populated area. I saw him climb in again and crash his machine into the Thames.

'That takes courage, madness, or a Jew terrified of doing the wrong thing. At that moment I hated Hornstein more than I've ever hated anyone in my life.

'I would have bailed out, you see. There's no doubt about it.'

'Come on,' Sally said, 'how do you know what you would have done?'

'Because I had visualised just such a thing happening to me.'

'How can you tell for sure?'

'I had figured out that in rounder terms my life was worth more than any deaths or damage my crashed Spitfire might have caused. After all, I was a trained fighter pilot. So on top of everything else I hated Hornstein for being braver than I was.'

Norman paused, much as though he had given Sally something – a pill, perhaps – and he didn't want to continue until it had had time to dissolve.

'After I saw him crash like that I went temporarily out of my mind. I still had some ammunition left so I didn't return to the aerodrome with the others. I moved up into the sun and saw four 109s heading for home. I must have chased them half way to France before bullets suddenly started appearing on my port wing. Two 109s had been flying even closer to the sun than me. I pulled up and away desperately, but black smoke was already pouring out of the engine. The fire spread inside – that's how I crashed.'

Having told her about Hornstein, a grief he had not shared with anyone else, he felt, and she seemed to understand, that they were now free to make demands on each other. She was already in his debt.

'I think I'd better be going.'

Sally came close to Norman and kissed him on the mouth. But the kiss was affectionate; no more. Norman seemed resentful. And Sally, a little perplexed, said:

'Will you call me early tomorrow morning?'

'Sure.'

'Really, though. You're not just saying that?'

'I'll call you early. I promise.'

Sally stood by the window with her cheek and hands pressed against the cold pane and watched Norman get into a taxi. There were all those stars – she hated them for 'twinkling' just the way they did in cheap novels – and below the endless noises of the night.

At home, in Montreal, right now her father would be seated at his desk steeply and severe, *The Lusiads* opened at one elbow and an exercise book at the other. Mother in the parlour with knitting and Mozart and below the 3a streetcars and next door Mr O'Meara calling, 'Hurry, Ros, hurry. Ed Sullivan's just beginning . . .' and in the park the boys in blazers calling hi, *bee*-utiful and smoked meats and Frankie Laine at Ma Heller's and boning for Psych 103 and

47

Sheldon saying, 'If you *insist* on going to London I guess that's it . . .'

But she missed them. Already she missed them.

Sally lay down in the dark with a cigarette. I'll never get to sleep tonight, she thought.

VII

'If you want a script that's nifty,' Charlie sang, 'I'll write it in a jiffy, Lawson but does nuttin' for ya 'olesale.'

'Not so loud,' Joey called out from the bedroom.

Sure, Charlie thought. Not so loud. The Chairlady of the Bitcher's Club will now say a few words. Charlie stuck out his tongue. 'You made lots of women in '22,' he sang *sotto voce*, 'you let other hacks make more gold than you, why doncha do right, and make me a movie to-ooo?'

Charlie was going to get work. He had made a good impression. Invitations to dinners and parties from Winkleman, Landis, Jeremy, and Graves would soon come down on him like rain. They would please Joey so much. And once he was rich Charlie would be handsome with his money, not like some other guys he knew.

Money, Charlie thought. Charlie required lots of money. Money to support his in-laws, the Wallaces, and money to pay Selma's tuition at drama school. Joey's sister Selma was cute but a weirdie, too. There was still that nose operation of hers to be paid gff. And what if the Wallaces took it into their sinus soaked heads that they needed Arizona again next winter? (Perish the thought, Charles.)

'Maybe it's because I'm a Torontonian,' Charlie sang, 'that I love London so.' He raised his voice. 'London's going to be lucky-ducky. We've finally made it. I've got that certain feeling.'

Charlie could hardly wait for Norman to get back. Meanwhile, shifting through the top drawer of his desk he came upon a thick airmail letter addressed to Norman Price, Esq.

'As long as you can earn a living,' Joey said, entering the room, 'I'll be pleased. Remember what you said when you first came to New York?'

'New York was different.'

'Maybe, but all the same – What have you got there?'

'A letter from you to guess whom?'

'If I were you,' Joey said, 'I wouldn't read it.'

'I was looking for a pencil. I can wait until he leaves before I go through his personal papers.'

Joey took the letter into the kitchen, lit it, and then let the ashes fall into the sink.

'Why did you do that?' Charlie asked.

'Charlie, do you remember that Norman used to come round every night for weeks and then didn't show up for months? You know why, don't you?'

Charlie didn't answer.

'Don't you?'

'Sure, Joey, sure. I mean I know you could have . . .'

'You should have seen the wild letters he wrote me, Charlie. But I wrote him no. Absolutely no. That was the letter I just burnt.'

'I love you,' Charlie said. 'I trust you completely.' He hugged her. 'You know what I'm going to be?' he asked, lifting her off the floor. 'An Irish Sean O'Casey.'

Joey laughed. She kissed him.

The door opened. 'Hello,' Norman said cheerfully. 'Still up?'

Joey broke away from Charlie.

'Ah,' Charlie said, 'The satyr of Church Street returns. He's abandoned his *soubrette* at last.'

Norman grinned.

'We didn't expect you back until morning,' Joey said. 'Wait, I'll get you a drink.'

'Thanks,' Norman said.

'Feel free.' Charlie filled his glass again. 'We want you to treat this place like your own home.'

'Do you think you'll like it here?' Norman asked.

'We'll adore it,' Joey said.

'Wait till I tell you about Rinky-Dinky Winkleman. A few days in London and I've as good as got a film contract in the bag. Not bad, huh?'

'Please, darling. He hasn't even taken an option yet.'

'Am I or am I not seeing him first thing tomorrow morning?'

'Charlie's right. Sonny likes his script a lot. He told me so himself.'

'I'll believe it when I see the cheque. Not before.'

'Thank you, Madame Defarge.' Charlie turned to Norman. 'You didn't have to go to her hotel, old chap. You could have brought Sally here. We're very liberal-minded.'

Norman slept on the sofa in his little study, and there, he remembered Sally's freshly washed smell. He recalled her wild blonde hair – the creamy smile – and all at once he felt foolish. He had made an unsuccessful pass at the sweetheart of the Sigma Something. No more. That kind of stuff was O.K. for Nicky, but not for a man of his age.

I shouldn't have told her about Hornstein, he thought, just before he fell asleep.

VIII

But the next morning at nine-thirty, Norman, feeling uncomfortably like a college boy again, was waiting for Sally in her hotel lobby. They ate breakfast together.

Sally was small, no more than five feet four, and she was cursed with a plump figure and the most useless big feet. Her blessings – Sally considered them few – were her streaky blonde hair and slender ankles. But what attracted Norman most were her warm, quizzical blue eyes, and the absence of hardness about her. They were extremely polite with each other. Norman intimidated Sally. His long narrow face was solemn; his manner was exacting. She felt that she was being examined like a potential sexual belligerent, and this she found disquieting.

After breakfast they walked through Soho, down Charing Cross Road, and to the Strand. They ate an enormous lunch at Simpson's. Then, because Sally was momentarily panicked by the strangeness of it all – the streets of little black cars and sexless black men and old blackened buildings – they hurried back to Leicester Square and went to see an American film. Inside, Sally pretended she was in Montreal again. Norman fell asleep half-way through the film and that, oddly enough, made her like him very much better.

From there they went to the Arts Theatre Club bar for drinks and, her assurances regained, Sally was very cheerful indeed. They exchanged old and tested anecdotes that were, all the same, fresh to each other, and whenever Sally laughed – and she laughed spontaneously and often – her head fell against his shoulder. They were so happy together that they did not realise they were being loud and conspicuous. As the crowd in the bar thickened they reached that point of intimacy where a nod of the head for a foolish face discovered, a nudge for a pompous snatch of conversation overheard, was enough to send them off into further fits of laughter. At dinner Norman squeezed her knee under the table and Sally leaned over and kissed him once.

Later, in the Theatre, East Stratford, they joined the Winklemans and Charlie and Joey to see a new play by a left-wing theatre group. Norman began to sober up. A fuzzy-haired Jewess with a wide red mouth sat beside him. Her boy friend, a skinny boy with a little sandpaper face, chewed his nails endlessly. The play, a political comedy, was spiked with puerile jokes about Eden, Rhee, Dulles, and the rest of them, but the audience responded with laughter wild and febrile. Tense, thick faces. Partisans. A kinky West Indian with a flash of pink tongue. A hunchback in a corduroy cap with a smile like a clenched fist. Young girls in rumpled clothes hand in hand with boys who required beards just as older, sunnier men needed desks before them. The virtuous failures; the good people. A middle-aged woman made in Bethnal Green of headlines and mashed brussels sprouts and unuseful memories. They laughed, they applauded, and their laughter was so sad, so savage, that Norman was immensely relieved when it was time to leave the theatre.

Sally held on to his arm, just like she was his girl, and that made him feel better. They were joined by the Winklemans and Charlie and Joey, and together they piled into Winkleman's car and drove to his house in Hampstead. Winkleman was in one of his more expansive moods. He told them how he had settled his accounts with the Home Office.

Norman, who had heard the story many times before, joined Sally in the laughter that followed all the same, but he was not aware, as the others certainly were, that he was also holding her hand. He and Sally didn't realise that the Winklemans and Charlie had been nudging each other whenever they looked in their direction. Joey alone remained aloof.

Finally, it was time to go. Before Norman could protest Joey announced that she had called a taxi and that they could easily drop Sally off on their way home.

The Winklemans went upstairs to bed.

'I'm so glad for Norman,' Bella said. 'I think she's a very sweet girl.'

'I hope it works out for Nòrm, too. That guy's so lonely it's a crime.'

Charlie was too excited to sleep. 'They're like a couple of kids together,' he said to Joey.

'Norman's going to get hurt.'

'How come?'

'She's far too young for him.'

'Me,' Charlie said, 'I like them under fifteen. Sixteen tops. Yum, yum.'

The next morning, at nine-thirty, Norman presented himself at Sally's hotel again. This time she was waiting for him. They kissed eagerly, and after breakfast Norman helped to move her things into Karp's house. The cooking facilities in Sally's bed-sitter looked fine and there was even a telephone extension on the table, but the gas heater seemed inadequate. The kitchenette part of the room closed like a cupboard. The walls, originally a bright yellow, were by this time a depressing brown. Bright yellow squares, where the last tenant's pictures had used to hang, glared angrily at you. There was an abandoned Penguin on the mantelpiece. *Ballet* by Arnold Haskell. The kind of room, Norman imagined, where once or twice a year there had been bottle parties. Warm punch out of sticky glasses. A red-stained slice of lemon adhering to the bottom of your glass all night. A bearded boy with a guitar, perhaps.

Sally was enthralled. She told him excitedly of her plans to make the room more 'homey'. Norman was briefly conscious of the years that separated them. For her a rented room was an adventure. He remembered it as a place where you were alone. Terribly alone.

Karp told Norman that his room would not be ready until Monday and then Norman went off to have lunch with Charlie.

'I'm surprised you've got time for me these days,' Charlie said.

'What do you mean?'

'Hey,' Charlie said. 'Hey there.'

Norman grinned foolishly. 'Do you like Sally?' he asked.

'What are you trying to promote – a triangle?' Charlie laughed. 'She's crazy about you.'

'I wish I thought so.'

'Are you kidding?'

'No.'

'Hell, that girl can't keep her eyes off you. You're like a couple of honeymooners together. An iceberg of a guy like you. I'm shocked. Personally, I think you're a couple of dirty pigs.'

Norman laughed self-consciously and then quickly changed the subject. Charlie was disturbed. He complained to Norman that Winkleman was stalling. He had not yet been paid his advance on the script. So that afternoon Norman phoned Winkleman, told him to give Charlie some money, and promised to begin work on the script on Monday.

'That's a nice girl you've got there,' Winkleman said.

Norman and Sally became inseparable. On Wednesday he borrowed Bob Landis's car and took her to Cambridge. They rented a canoe, ate a picnic lunch beside the Cam, and on the midnight drive back to London she slept with her head on his shoulder. The next afternoon they visited Hampton Court together. They managed to avoid the Winklemans and Charlie and Joey until Saturday night, when Norman had promised to bring Sally home for dinner. In all that short febrile time, though everyone had put them down for lovers, they had not been to bed together. Norman, after the first night's failure, had shied away from trying to make love to her again. He lived in perpetual fear of rejection. With the fear, though, he also had his dream. He and Sally were married, they had three children, and they were uniquely happy. They did not hang impressionist prints on their walls. Sally, like him, enjoyed making love in the mornings. But when the kids came that was seldom possible. The kids woke them early each morning, jumping up and down on their not-Swedish Modern double bed.

After they had dinner with Charlie and Joey on Saturday night, Sally invited him into her room for a drink, even though it was quite late.

Sally sat on the floor, her legs tucked under her wide green skirt and her blouse sufficiently open at the neck so that he could see where her breasts began. Norman told her about the time he spent with his father in Spain and Sally spoke about her parents. Their conversation was forced. Norman was always so annoyingly a man of no frivolity that she was constantly afraid of making a fool of herself with him. When Sally wasn't getting up to twist a dripping faucet tight or to pull the curtains or replace a book, she seemed just a little petulant.

'Well,' she said at last, 'here we are.'

'Here we are.' Norman cleared his throat. 'Bob says we

can have his car again tomorrow. We can drive down to Brighton, if you like.'

Sally gathered that Norman was particularly proud of his community of friends. There was, to be sure, an instinctive generosity about the way they lent each other money, their cars, and even – as in Norman's case – a flat. There was plenty to be said for a group of men who, though they were naturally competitors and professionally jealous of each other's success, still did their utmost to share out the available work. But what astonished her was the ways in which the 'enlightened' left was similar to the less intelligent groups it despised. The loyalties, the generosity, like those of the Rotary, lost in purity by being confined to the group strictly. You didn't wear a badge with your first name on it, you weren't asked the name of your 'home town', but your contributions were 'concrete', your faith 'progressive', and your enemies 'reactionary'. *Joe Hill* ousted *Down By the Old Mill Stream*, but, though the sentiment was loftier, it was still uncritical, still stickily there. It seemed to Sally that Norman and his friends were not, as they supposed, non-conformists, but conformists to another rule.

'All right,' she said. 'If you like.'

This time when she rose to fill his glass again, and Norman circled her waist with his arm, she did not withdraw or look at him severely. Instead she came closer to him.

'Oh, please,' she said. 'Hurry. I want you to.'

He raised a hand to her breast. Sally shut her eyes, murmured something inaudible, and fitted her body closer to his. As they sank down on the bed together he began to undo the buttons of her blouse. Sally leaped up, her slip coming off with a black swish, and, in a moment she stood naked before him.

'You're beautiful,' he said.

Then, as they fell into another embrace, the phone began to ring. That startled them. Norman sat up, he began to sweat. The phone rang again and again. Sally, trying to pull him down to her, said huskily, 'Let it ring. Who cares?'

It was Joey. He knew it. Anger knotted inside him.

'It's probably not for me.' Sally offered him her mouth again, but as he took her in his arms the phone rang and rang. A buzzer sounded. Obviously the phone call was for her.

'All right,' she said sharply. 'I'll get it.'

But just as she reached the phone the ringing stopped. Standing there in the nude on a cold floor, a dead receiver in her hand, she was consumed by a searing rage, but she did not weep.

'I can't understand,' Norman said, 'at this hour . . . who . . .?'

Norman slipped into his trousers. Sally poured her slip over her head, wriggling to help it down, and then sank wearily back on the bed. She rose quickly again and poured him another drink.

'I suddenly feel like the heroine of a smutty story. You know, the school teacher visiting Europe and . . .'

'I'm sorry.'

'You needn't be sorry.'

Norman got up and replaced the receiver on the hook.

'Say something,' she said. 'Please.'

'I could tell you how I feel about you, but I'm afraid—'

'—of Joey?'

'Why should I—'

'I was only joking,' she said.

'It was a bad joke.'

'All right. It was a bad joke. I'm sorry. But there's no need for you to be angry.'

'I'm not angry.'

He took her in his arms once more. They kissed; he fondled her breast. But it was no use. It was too late. They broke apart.

'Oh,' she said. 'I feel like I'm being scratched all over inside. I feel terrible.'

Norman frowned helplessly. His excitement, his longing for her, had been so urgent, that he had reached a climax while they had embraced. Now, all excitement temporarily spent, he felt tense. Though he ached with love for her, he was afraid that if he was called on right now he would prove inadequate, so Sally's presence embarrassed and angered him, and with himself he was absolutely disgusted. Norman reached for his jacket.

'Don't go,' she said. 'Stay and have another drink.'

'No. I must go. That was probably Joey on the phone.'

'So what. Do you think I care if she knows you spent the night here?'

This was an invitation. He realised that. But he didn't sit down again; he slipped into his jacket.

'I've hurt you,' she said.

'No.'

She came close to him. 'I like you so much, Norman Price,' and rested her head against his shoulder. 'Are you very angry with me?'

'No,' he said. 'No, my darling,' and was gone.

'Darling.' Sally was alarmed. Coming from Norman 'darling' was far too solemn. He had never called her 'darling' before.

IX

Charlie and Joey were ready for bed when Norman arrived.

'Ah,' Charlie said, 'here he is.'

Norman turned angrily on Joey. 'Did you phone Sally about half an hour ago?'

'Yes,' she said coldly. 'Why didn't you answer?'

'It looks to me that you phoned at *one* in the morning simply to see if I was with her.'

'A telegram came for you. I thought it might be important.'

'I told her that it could wait until you got back.'

'A telegram?'

'It must have come this afternoon,' Charlie said. 'I went out for a coffee, and found it in the mail box Here, maybe you won something on a quiz show . . .'

But Norman turned very pale.

'Anything wrong?' Joey asked.

'What is it, Norman?'

'It's from my Aunt Dorothy in Boston . . .'

'What?'

'Nicky's dead.'

'Who?'

'His brother.'

'There are no details,' Norman said. 'Nothing.'

'Oh Norman, I *am* sorry,' Joey said.

Norman retreated into his cramped little study and shut the door after him. He sat down on the tattered sofa and read the telegram over and over again. Removing his glasses, he wiped his eyes and lay down on the sofa and rested there until a soft knocking at the door startled him.

'Can I get you anything?' Joey asked.

'No.'

'A drink might help,' Charlie suggested meekly.

'No. No thanks.'

'Are you sure?'

'Please go away.'

Before he turned out the lights, Norman wrote out his name and address on a piece of paper and fastened the paper to his arm with an elastic band. Eventually he got up and undressed, but he didn't sleep.

Dawn came. Buses began to lumber down Church Street.

Tall, he thought. Nicky had been tall with our father's eyes and smile and with a lot of Dr Max Price's brilliance too. Nicky had inherited the gift, not me.

Norman got up at last around ten and joined Charlie and Joey in the kitchen.

'Did you sleep?' Joey asked.

'Yes.'

'I guess there's nothing I can say, is there?'

'I'm O.K., Charlie.'

Joey served him coffee. 'You were very fond of him, weren't you?'

'I'd rather not talk about it.'

But he was grateful to both of them just for being there. They were old friends. He wasn't required to show a stiff upper lip or a drooping one, either. Being himself was good enough for Charlie and Joey.

The bells of St Mary Abbot's began to chime.

'Sally phoned,' Charlie said cheerfully. 'She seems to think you're angry with her or something . . .'

'Look, Charlie, there is something you can do for me. Would you call Air France and see if you can get me on the next plane to Paris?'

Charlie looked imploringly at Joey.

'Go ahead,' Joey said. 'It'll do Norman good to get away.'

Charlie went into the living room to phone.

'What happened?' Joey asked. 'Is it the girl?'

'Her name is Sally,' Norman said sharply. Then, as he told her something of Sally, he realised for the first time that he was grateful that Joey had phoned last night. He had been afraid to make love to Sally.

'So you're going to use your brother's death as an excuse for running away.'

Norman did not want to discuss Sally any more. Not this morning. 'Jesus,' he said, 'I'm not serious about her. I—'

'Are you sure?'

'Of course I'm sure. I wanted to go to bed with her, that's all.'

'You're sure you're not running—'

'I'm not running away.'

The bells of St Mary Abbot's started up again.

'What am I to tell her if she phones again?'

'Tell her anything you want.'

'O.K.,' Charlie said. 'You leave in two hours. Is that too soon?'

'No. Thanks a lot, Charlie.'

'How long will you be gone?' Joey asked.

'A couple of months at least.'

'Look,' Charlie said, 'I'm flat broke right now but—'

'I don't need any money, Charlie.'

' – but I'm going to see Winkleman in half an hour, he

phoned earlier, and I'm getting a pretty big advance on my script to begin with, so—'

Norman's face clouded. 'Don't tell him I'm going away.'

'Why?' Joey asked quickly.

'No special reason,' Norman said. 'I'll write him.'

It's no use, Norman thought. Charlie won't get a second payment until I get back. I hope he isn't counting too heavily on the money.

The bells of St Mary Abbot's began to chime again.

'I'm going out for a walk,' Norman said. 'See you soon.'

Joey poured Charlie another cup of coffee.

'Poor guy,' Charlie said at last.

'He's a coward,' Joey said.

'A coward? It's not easy, you know. He was crazy about his brother.'

'Norman has never faced a crisis in his life. He's always run away.'

'You know,' Charlie said. 'You know everything.'

X

A mist from the Seine. Ernst yawned. All his bones ached. The bum who was curled up next to him on the cobble-stones began to cough wetly again. Ernst was afraid that he was dying. He ran off into the night to the nearest café and returned with a small bottle of cognac. The bum accepted his drink gratefully, but just as Ernst was falling asleep a few moments later, his coughing worsened. Ernst took the bum in his arms and pressed more cognac on him until he passed out or fell asleep; Ernst couldn't tell for sure. By then it was nearly 5 a.m. The bums began to stir as one by one they were nudged by the sun. An old man rose and stretched. Another, still stiff with sleep, heaved his pack over his back and urinated under the bridge. Ernst rose and hopped first on one leg and then on the other. As soon as he felt warm enough he started up the concrete steps to the street.

This was Ernst's tenth day in Paris and he was still without prospects. He had a letter from his mother. She was in Hamburg. She needed money. His father had sent him a postcard from Berlin. He needed money.

Ernst's father was a grey, shrunken man with weak moist eyes and an annoying habit of bowing his head when he spoke with strangers. He had not always been like that. When Hitler had come to power Karl Haupt had not joined the Nazis, but neither had he worked against them. Always a little inclined towards anti-semitism, never very fond of the British, he had, nevertheless, found Hitler offensive. As he was in the legal business his attitude was very costly to his family. You could not practice law unless you were a party member. During the war Karl Haupt, who was in and out of the punitive camps, did odd jobs for lawyers. His friends pleaded with him to be sensible.

Karl, did not the Jews overrun most of the professions before Hitler?

Exactly.

Karl, isn't it our sacred duty to defend the fatherland from the Jewish bolsheviks?

Exactly.

So Karl, why make it hard for yourself and your family? Join the party.

No, Karl would say, your party is rotten, and into prison he would go.

After the war Karl Haupt enjoyed a brief time of money for the first time in his life. The Americans made him a judge at minor denazification trials in a provincial town. As all his old advisers came up before him they got sentences of from six months to two years. Then, abruptly, the trials were over. A year, two years later, Karl Haupt was worse off than before. All the denazified were out of prison and back in the courts and, of course, they made sure that he got no work. So he took to the Soviet Zone, but there it was soon established that he had worked for the Americans and, what's more, he would not join their party either.

Ernst lit a butt he had saved from the night before.

At Les Halles the higher sun bit ravenously into exposed crates of melons and lettuces and peaches. Ernst wriggled through the sharp-smelling maze to where M. Krespe stood with his grimy little pad.

'I told you to be here at four.'

'I asked them to wake me at my hotel,' Ernst said, 'but they forgot.'

'That's a good one. At your hotel, eh?'

Ernst helped unload crates of oranges until nine a.m., until two cuts in his hands had reopened and his back was knotted with pain, and then he had to hang around the café for another half hour before M. Krespe paid him. The sun was wide in the sky, this was going to be another white hot day. Ernst went to the Gare St Lazare, had a cup of coffee at one of the wagons, and then went down to the toilets and rented a private cubicle and sat down and ate two oranges and a banana while he read a story by Kipling in a German translation. He dozed briefly. In his dreams he returned to the black market at the Potsdamerstrasse. Again the American soldier whom he had cheated the day before returned sobered and with two friends. Again he came to with his knife gone and his nylons gone and three teeth gone. The dream faded; Ernst woke in a sweat. He washed and shaved. But it was still too early. The boat-train wasn't due for another twenty-eight minutes. So Ernst sat down on a bench opposite track nine and counted his money. Seven hundred and twenty francs. Not enough to get him to Dieppe. Not a big enough stake for London.

He fell asleep. Once again he sat on the bed, waiting for Nancy to come back to him. Once again instead of the thin pretty girl there came the familiar shriek of M.P. sirens. Fortunately the window was directly above the patio roof. From there, a leap into the garden would be easy, and he would be gone. But as he turned to raise the window he had been suddenly yanked from behind. There was Nicky, a smashed beer bottle in his hand, and a crazed look on his face.

'You son-of-a-bitch. First you steal Frank's wallet, then you cost me one of my best friends, and now—'

'You don't understand.'

' – and now you come upstairs to steal.'

In another moment, Ernst had thought, the M.P.s will be here.

'Get away. I'm going through the window.'

Ernst had tried for the window once more and Nicky, the smashed beer bottle in his hand, had rushed him. Ernst had tried to take him by force, but then, in the distance, he had heard the whine of another police siren, so he had pulled out his knife. Nicky had lost all semblance of individuality for him, he had become simply another opponent. Ernst had worked swiftly and accurately. Then, acting from the memory of other encounters, he had removed Nicky's wristwatch, taken his papers, smashed the window with a chair, and jumped.

Ernst ran and ran and ran, until he had collapsed on the pavement in a little street in Schwabbing, the blood pounding through his head. His hand had been bloody. He had sat there – a panting, empty-eyed boy on the pavement – until he had risen at last and had been sick once, twice, in the gutter.

The following morning, and every morning since, he had rationalised his crime to himself, but once he was alone in the dark, the rationalisations had no longer served a useful purpose. Each night Nicky came and was knifed and murdered again.

Ernst jerked awake. A scream died, unheard, in his throat. Breathing heavily, he wiped his forehead with his arm.

After the boat train arrived Ernst waited at the head of the platform until the people began to come through with their luggage. There were many Americans, more than he had hoped for, and at last he spotted a man of roughly his own size. The Americans was struggling with three pieces of luggage; he seemed baffled. Ernst hastened to his side.

'Porter?'

'I don't think—'

But Ernst was already in charge. 'There are two more inside,' the American said lamely, pointing at the train.

'Wait for me here, I'll get you a taxi.'

Ernst picked up the heaviest of the three bags and boarded the train. Inside he picked up another bag and then raced ahead through four cars and descended to the platform again. By this time a camera was strapped to his side and he was wearing sun glasses. 'Porter', he called. 'Porter.'

A porter picked up his bags and Ernst followed him through the gates.

'*Vite*,' Ernst said. '*Je suis trés pressé*'.

Ernst gave the taxi driver the address of an hotel on the left bank. Inside the hotel he registered at D. H. Hollis, the name on his luggage tabs. He told the *patron* that he was in a hurry, he said that he had to get to the American Express before it closed and that he would return before evening to fill out the proper papers, then he followed a sluggish boy to a room on the third floor. As soon as the boy left, Ernst locked the door. Then, the shaking came. He tumbled on to the bed and brought his knees up to his chin and hugged himself tight. When the fear had passed again he took out his last cigarette and smoked it on the bed. He stepped out of the hotel again about an hour later. He wore a Brooks Brothers suit. Carrying a raincoat over his arm in spite of the cloudless skies, he took a bus to the Rue des Rosiers and entered a dark seedy café there. Albert bought the camera, a leica, for about a quarter of what it was worth.

Ernst walked to the café in the Opéra district, sat down on the terrace, and ordered a beer. This, he thought, is a good time for a spot of *Selbst-Kritik*. He had twelve thousand three hundred francs and some change. Ten thousand would go to his parents. The night mortician, he thought, will sell me identity papers for fifty thousand francs, but what then? My French is bad; I haven't got a trade. A tall middle-aged Texan drifted down the street clutching his pretty wife like an all-day sucker. Lanky Swedes with packs on their backs, boys of his own age, passed brown and confident before him. Ernst took the newspaper clipping out of his pocket again. As a special service to tourists this summer, the clipping said, the Brit-

ish and French governments have agreed to allow all-day
trippers to travel between Newhaven and Dieppe without
passports. But if I'm going to London, he thought, I'll need
more money.

XI

A week later, in London, Sally went to visit the Lawsons.

'Look who's here,' Charlie said, 'the teach. Isn't that
wonderful, darling?'

Joey was typing a script for Charlie at Norman's desk.
Perhaps it was the horn-rimmed glasses, maybe it was just
an off day, but she seemed depressed. Charlie, though, was
in excellent spirits. Wearing a patched cardigan, corduroys
and slippers, he was perched high on a ladder, running gaily
coloured streamers from wall to wall.

'Welcome to the Young Pioneers, Kensington Division,'
he said. 'Mandrake Lawson's show begins at four.'

Charlie was giving a party for the *emigré* children. An
amateur magician, he was going to perform for them as
well. Sally discovered that Joey was worried because Charlie's deal to do a picture for Winkleman had hit a snag. They
were broke, she gathered, and not very popular. But Charlie
was sure that the deal would work out. Sally let an hour go
by before she asked about Norman. Norman had been away
for two weeks and she had yet to hear from him.

'We haven't heard a word either,' Charlie said.

Joey told her about Nicky's death.

'Hold on a sec,' Charlies said, 'I'll go and see if there's
any mail.'

As soon as Charlie had gone Joey shed her glasses and
turned solemnly to Sally. 'Are you very fond of Norman?'
she asked.

'Why?'

'I'm not trying to snoop,' Joey said, 'believe me, but for
your own good you may as well know right now that Nor-

man is very erratic. He's also selfish, thoughtless, and irresponsible.'

'I don't see that this has anything to do with me,' Sally said coldly.

'Maybe not,' Joey said. 'But you're young and impressionable. I'm only telling you this because I don't want you to build up things in your mind when—'

'I'm fond of Norman,' Sally said, rising, 'but no more.'

Charlie returned, breathless. 'No mail.' He turned to Sally. 'Aren't you staying for the party?'

'I really must go.'

After Sally had gone Charlie noticed that Joey was in tears.

'What happened?'

'I'm not staying for your party, either,' Joey said, getting up. 'How can you do this to me?'

'Do what,' Charlie asked. 'Beat you?'

'A children's party,' she said. 'Haven't you any feeling?'

XII

The first weeks of summer in London were the loneliest Sally had ever experienced. Every day she raced eagerly forth to adventure: none came.

Bob Landis took her out twice. She was flattered, and she certainly would have gone to bed with him that night after the theatre if, no sooner than he had succeeded in removing her blouse, he hadn't said, 'You know that I've got a wife, baby, and that this is just for kicks,' which had given her the giggles.

At night Sally often cried herself to sleep. She visited the British Museum, she went to the theatre, she stood on Westminster Bridge and she swept through gallery after gallery until her feet ached. The West End except for the grand swing of Regent Street, was another disappointment. This seemed to be little more than a second-rate, inchoate

Broadway. America's hit tune of last year triumphant again in the record shops of Charing Cross Road. Broadway's hit musical of 1948 a hit again at the Hippodrome. Johnny Ray at the Palladium; Billy Graham at Harringay. At night the parade of depraved itchy faces, men in black rubber trench-coats and whores past the indecent age, was the most appalling she had ever seen.

So Sally, ordinarily the most inadequate of correspondents, wrote her father every night. She missed her family, her friends, her own comfortable bedroom and, most of all, her bath. Missing these conveniences made her feel even more wretched. For when friends of the family had returned after a summer in Europe only to complain about the filth and the inefficiency she had summarily dismissed them as 'middle-class', a word which until recently had epitomized everything she abhorred.

One evening Sally set out to fish for sexual experiences in the espresso bars of Hampstead. Her first bite came from an elderly roué who was unhooked like a catfish. The next few nibbles were hardly worth the bait. A non-objective painter with the necessarily rotten teeth, a Dane who translated Chinese poems from the English of Arthur Waley, and an assistant television producer who wore a black turtleneck sweater and corduroy trousers. Denis Patmore was the last boy's name, and he took her to a bottle party at a friend's studio the next evening.

'I just don't dig Freud on people,' a girl said, 'that's all.'

The floor was heaped with unwashed girls in blue jeans and sweaters. Bleached ones, black ones; plump and un-plundered ones. A long loony-eyes one with a fistful of teeth and another one with pillowy breasts. But the men, after you allowed for a few exceptions, were a much drier lot. They seemed afraid that they would be devoured like pret-zels after the next round of drinks. One of the exceptions was an obese art critic with stinging red eyes: 'Higgins is a clod. The silly fool can't get his roger up unless Inga wears handcuffs.' An emaciated man, who described himself as a writer of 'progressive space-fiction' sold Sally two tickets to a meeting of the Anglo-Rumanian Friendship Society. A Negro novelist wiped his wine-stained hands on her skirt. 'The world,' he said, 'is so completely,' before he staggered off.

That's when Sally was introduced to a tall, silent, dusty-haired boy. 'I am a student,' he said stiffly. 'My name is Ernst . . .'

'Are you a German?'

'Austrian.'

A few days later, nearly a month before Sally was to begin work, she ran into Ernst again. They met in the back room of Collet's bookshop on Haverstock Hill. Ernst was there first. When Sally entered he moved swiftly away from a shelf, then, recognising her, he smiled ambiguously.

'Do you read very much?'

She could have kicked herself for saying that.

'Adventure stories,' Ernst said guardedly, 'and books about medicine. I am very interested in medicine.'

'Is that what you're studying?' Sally asked.

'Studying . . . ?'

'You told me you were a student.'

'I am studying . . . law.'

They both recognised the lie at once. Then Sally recognised something else – there was a bulge under Ernst's jacket. 'Let's go,' she said, taking his arm. 'We'll have tea together.'

'I have no money.'

'Come,' she said impatiently, 'don't be an ass.'

Her heart pounded wildly as they passed the bookshop manager. But they made it safely outside.

'Halfers,' Sally said.

'What?'

'We split the books.'

Ernst frowned.

'You're not going to pretend,' Sally said, 'are you?'

'No.'

He brought out the books. A copy of *Kon Tiki* and a travel book on Africa and an English-German dictionary.

'I'll settle for the book on Africa, O.K.?' Sally's smile faded. 'You're not a student.'

'No,' Ernst said. 'I'm not a student.'

'I'm not a student either,' she said, as they turned down Belsize Avenue. 'I'm Moll Flanders; shop-lifter extraordinary.' She explained who Moll Flanders was. 'I'm being silly,' she said, 'forgive me.'

'Where are we going?'

'To my place,' she said, 'for tea and bickies.'

At last her meaning was clear to him. He wasn't shocked either. Usually they were older, less attractive.

'O.K.,' he said.

The room was in a chaotic state. Records and books were scattered all over the floor. The one hard-backed chair was smothered under a heap of clothes. But the clothes, Ernst noticed, were expensive. The leather suitcases piled slipshod over the wardrobe were of a superior quality.

'It's not much,' Sally said, 'but it's home.'

When she turned round again Ernst had already taken off his shoes. He was unbuttoning his shirt.

'What are you—'

Ernst took her into his arms and kissed her on the mouth. Struggling free, Sally slapped him hard across the face.

Ernst didn't move. 'Why did you bring me here?'

'Isn't it obvious?'

'Yes,' he said, 'I thought so.'

'You thought so! I thought you'd like a cup of tea.'

'Don't make me laugh.'

Sally stared at him. 'Are you serious?'

'What do you want?' Ernst asked.

'But I don't want anything.'

'You mean,' he said, 'that . . . *tea*?'

Sally held up the kettle and tapped it with her finger, but Ernst still seemed a little incredulous.

'I had thought—'

'—that I was some kind of sex maniac?'

'No, but—' He broke off with a cautious smile. 'Tea. I see. Tea.'

69

But he didn't see.

'I'm sorry that I slapped you,' she said.

Sally put on a record. Mozart's Prague symphony. 'Are you hungry?' she asked him. 'Can I make you something to eat?'

'If it ain't too much trouble.'

She made him an omelette. He ate six slices of bread with it. Meanwhile, Sally curled up watchfully on the bed with her legs tucked under her skirt. Mozart's Prague symphony began to play over again.

'Who are you?' she asked.

'My name is Ernst Haupt. I am a law student. I come from Innsbruck. I am here on a scholarship.'

'Come off it.'

Ernst rose. He was taller than she had thought. More formidable looking too. A lean, lethal man, with an unnervingly sensual manner. That late afternoon sun lit his hair fiercely. She wondered how old he was. At times he seemed a boy, but right now he looked thirty or more. Thirty or more, and frightening.

'Do you mind if I turn off the record player?'

When he bent over to turn off the player she noticed the running scar on the back of his neck. A knife scar.

'How old are you?' she asked.

'According to my father I would be twenty-two now.'

'According to your father?'

'The records were destroyed in a raid.' He looked at her searchingly, his expression severe. 'Are you afraid of me?'

'No,' she said too quickly, 'of course not.'

'I haven't had anything to eat since yesterday noon.'

'Haven't you any money?'

'Money . . .'

'Can't you work?'

'I'm here illegally. I'm from East Germany. I have no papers.'

'Where are you staying?'

'Here and there.'

'You haven't got a room. Is that what you mean?'

'I can take care of myself.'

70

'But what do you do?' Sally asked nervously.

'When I was fourteen they put me into the army.'

'I mean are you qualified for a job?'

Ernst smiled.

'*That's* not a job. I mean a proper job.'

'I can speak five languages.'

'That's something.'

'There are people who can speak eight. Ten. And most of them are without work.'

'What do you want to do then?'

'I want to go to America. I would like to be rich.'

'So,' Sally said, 'you're the same as everyone else.'

'Naturally.'

'*Natürlich.*'

'You speak German?'

'A little,' she said.

'I hate Germany. I hate Germans.'

'So do I,' Sally said.

Outside it was growing dark. Ernst walked over to the bureau and picked up a hairbrush. He came to her and sat down on the edge of the bed. Sally took a deep breath; she prepared to scream.

'It is so good when a girl brushes your hair,' he said.

'. . . what . . .?'

'Please,' he said.

Sally took the brush and began to stroke his hair.

'I'm warning you,' she said as lightly as she could, 'I don't like men who pamper themselves.'

'Would you like to do the back of my head now?'

He turned round. She began to do the back of his head.

'I am handsome,' he said.

'Bully for you.'

'I beg your pardon.'

'Skip it.'

'I'm very good with women.'

'Do you carry written testimonials around with you?'

'I will get a rich American one and she will take me to the United States.'

'I could write to my father. Maybe he can get you into Canada. Maybe he can even get you a job.'

Ernst was encouraged. 'I used to be a bigshot in the communist youth,' he said. 'I could write an exposé for the newspapers.'

'That wouldn't impress my father, I'm afraid. He's a bit of a Red himself.'

'A communist,' Ernst said. 'In Canada?'

'Not quite.'

'What do they know about communism in Canada?'

'A lot more than you'd think,' Sally said annoyed.

'Wait.' Ernst took off a sock and held a burning match to his foot. 'A whole winter without shoes. All our food went to Russia. That's communism.'

Sally watched as he lit another match to his exposed foot. She thought it vulgar of him to be so free about what he had suffered.

'Perhaps Germany didn't deserve better,' she said, 'after what they did in Russia.'

'Me? *I* did?'

Then, briefly speechless, they both realised that they were together on the bed. Sally reached out a little frightened and touched Ernst's face where she had slapped him. He smiled and kissed her on the throat, then behind the ear, and at last on the mouth. Oh, it was all so expertly done. Sally broke free.

'I wouldn't want you to think that I didn't invite you up here for tea after all.'

Ernst put his finger to his mouth and, with his other hand, pointed at the door.

'What is it?' Sally asked, alarmed.

Ernst tip-toed to the door. 'He's gone,' he said.

'What are you talking about?'

'There was somebody listening at the door.'

Karp, she thought. 'Don't be silly,' she said. His smile was so insufferably thick with superior knowledge that she'd be damned before she would agree with him. 'This isn't Germany,' she added.

'Perhaps I should go.'

'Why?'

'You're angry with me.'

'I'm angry with myself.'

Sally got up, turned on the hot water faucet with a fierce twist, and smacked two blouses into the sink. Ernst watched. He and Sally were almost the same age. He was sure that rain had ruined at least seven of her Sundays, that she had quarrelled with her brother over whose turn it was to wash the dishes, and that her mother had refused to allow her to stay out late one night and, as a result, Sally had sworn never to speak to her again. She came from an ordered past. She broke and made up with boy friends, and trusted strangers. He had read about such things in American books; they were probably true. Ernst got up and, too late to restrain himself, kissed Sally softly on the neck. He retreated quickly, before she could turn round to reprimand him.

'Throw me your shirt,' Sally said. 'It's filthy.'

He took off his shirt and passed it to her meekly.

'You want me to stay?'

'You'll sleep on the floor,' she said, 'but no funny stuff, understand?'

'You are very kind.'

'Have you any other things?'

'A little suitcase.'

'You can go and get it tomorrow morning. Tomorrow I'll speak to Karp about a room for you. We can go shopping for some clothes in the afternoon. I'll lend you the money.'

No sooner had she made her offer than Sally took fright. A whole night with him on the floor. He might be dangerous, she thought. 'I may be able to get you into Canada,' she said, 'but I'm not a rich one.'

'Don't make fun of me.'

Sally smiled. 'Would you like another omelette?' she asked.

'No.'

'Sure?'

'Yeah. But would you brush my hair again?'

'Nothing doing.'

'Tomorrow morning,' he said eagerly. 'I will wash and wax your floor for you. I will put your room in order.'

Tomorrow morning, she thought with sudden anger, out you go. I swear it. Enough, she thought, is enough.

Part Two

I

Karp was surprised to see Norman. He hadn't expected him back for at least another month.

'You look well,' Karp said. 'Are you glad to be back?'

'I can't tell you how glad.'

Karp spread himself out on the edge of the bed, holding his ham sandwich in his saucer and watching Norman shave. There were four back copies of the Saturday edition of the Montreal *Star* stacked on the bed; Karl forwarded the rest of Norman's mail.

'And the room,' Karp asked, 'it pleases you? I had it painted.'

Norman, who had just arrived that morning, grinned through his shaving lather. 'The room looks wonderful,' he said, 'and I feel wonderful.'

Karp ripped off a corner of his ham sandwich; he fell on his food like a conqueror. Norman, however, couldn't tell whether this was a true characteristic of Karp's or simply another way of ridiculing others. 'French bread is bad for me,' Karp said. 'One is obliged to open one's mouth too wide. But ham is first-rate. It doesn't jam in one's teeth like cheap cuts of beef.' Karp prodded a tooth with a stubby forefinger and freed a sliver of bread from a cavity. 'Why don't you ask me about Sally? Isn't that why you rushed back?'

'All right. Where is she?'

'Out for a walk. She'll be back soon, I suppose. I told her you were here. Can't you wait?'

Norman laughed.

'And your trip,' Karp asked. 'Did you enjoy yourself?'

'Yes and no.'

After a few days in Paris Norman had gone to Toulouse, where he had spent a week with Pepe Santos. Santos, formerly a colonel in the Spanish Republican Army, had been an intimate friend of Norman's father. The two men had talked endlessly about Dr Max Price.

From Toulouse Norman had gone to Madrid.

And there, leaning against the trunk of an olive tree at the University City, there, watching the indifferent young pass hand-in-hand over the indecently green meadow where, it seemed to him, the best blood of his generation had been spilled, he pondered over Nicky, his desire for a family of his own and, ultimately, the death of his father.

Max Price, the surgeon who had given up a spectacularly, lucrative practice in Montreal to go to Spain, had been killed during the defence of Madrid.

Great he was, Norman reflected, and quick to act. Not a hesitant, self-indulgent oaf, like me.

But in those days, Norman remembered fondly, the choice of enemies had been clear. Today you were no longer altogether sure. You signed the petitions, you defended Soviet art to liberals, and you didn't name old comrades. But your loyalties, like those of a shared childhood, were sentimental; they lacked true conviction.

From Madrid Norman fled to Mallorca.

A sum of lazy, sunny days on the beach helped to seal, if not exactly heal, the wound caused by Nicky's death. Norman wrote a long letter to his Aunt Dorothy thanking the Singletons for all they had done to educate Nicky. During his stay on Mallorca he also wrote three voluminous letters to Sally and then tore them up and sent her a postcard instead. But he bought her a mantilla and an album of flamenco records and a suede jacket, which he hoped was the right size. And then, even though his money was running out, he was still not ready to return to London. He took the boat to Ibiza instead.

The cracked brown island of Ibiza rises out of the calm blue sea like a blister evoked by the sun. Norman arrived early one morning when the port town itself, a hill bandaged round and round with bony white houses, was held in a haze of orange heat. For one delightful week he swam every morning in the bay and explored the Phoenician ruins. Then he began to drink a lot and had an affair with an American girl who wrote pornographic novels under the pseudonym of Baron von Kleeg.

Nina was a delightful girl, really, and she had hit on a wonderfully original idea. The hero of her novel was a teacher in a school for nubile blind girls. The teacher came to school nude every morning for he was, after all, invisible in his particular world. Nina was also compiling a definitive anthology of filthy limericks.

After Nina left his room around five a.m. one morning Norman stepped out on his balcony and there, suddenly, was the sea and the gift of the morning. The sun rose whitely from behind a clump of parched brown hills. A boat with sails whacked full of wind charged into the harbour, as below, on the quay, two peasants led a troop of eight donkeys laden with sacks of olives towards the warehouse scales and wizened men with parched trousers spread their nets wide. There was the chug-chug-chug of the fishing fleet just slipping into the bay, gulls thickening like a halo around them, and the one-eyed gaseosa vendor setting up his cart hopefully, unfolding his little deck chair, and then promptly falling asleep.

Norman's despair lifted mysteriously. He was suddenly so glad to be a part of it, so grateful for the flames that had scarred but saved him, that he wanted to carve this chunk of morning out of time for special remembrance.

He decided to hurry back to Sally.

Sally.

Sally was the answer. Sally was his hope. With Sally he could make it.

'Have you been seeing Charlie and Joey?' Norman asked.

'As little as possible. Your friend has no money. He bores me.'

'Yeah, I knew Charlie was broke. He owes me rent money.'

Norman told Karp about the deal with Winkleman. Now that he was back, he said, Charlie would be getting more money. He had spoken to Winkleman that very morning. Everything was O.K.

'Will you have dinner with me?' Karp asked.

'I'd be delighted,' he said unenthusiastically. 'But look here, I haven't told you my news yet. I'm going to ask Sally to marry me.'

Karp averted his eyes.

'What's wrong, Karp? Don't you think she's good enough for me?'

Karp shrugged his shoulders; his cane swung from side to side.

'We have a new tenant here. He's a German. Ernst, so to speak, rents the room next to Sally.'

'So what,' Norman said. 'Why shouldn't he?'

Karp's face wrinkled, his eyes squeezed shut. They opened again as his smile faded. 'When you are angry,' Karp said, 'you remind me of Anna Pauker as a young man.' Karp poked an open suitcase with his cane. Pushing aside the mantilla he revealed an album of flamenco records. 'Gifts?'

'I'll see you later,' Norman said sharply.

Karp hesitated at the door. 'One shouldn't insult one's landlord,' he said, and he was gone.

II

Norman threw a shirt over Sally's gifts, planning to uncover them as a surprise when she came. If only the jacket fits her, he thought. He prepared tea, lit a cigarette, and began to wait impatiently. An hour passed. Then, just as he was about to pour himself a drink, there was a knock at the door.

'Come on in.'

Her hair, bleached by the sun, was blonder than he had remembered it.

'Sally,' Norman said. 'Sally.'

She kissed him on the cheek, but when he tried to make the embrace more intimate he felt her stiffen.

'Take it easy,' Sally said.

Norman saw Ernst for the first time and he understood why she had stiffened. Sally was shy because of the stranger.

Sally, as though to warn Norman, took Ernst by the hand and introduced him. 'Ernst lives in the house,' she said. 'He's a refugee from East Berlin.'

Ignoring Ernst, Norman fumbled through a suitcase. 'Here, Sally, this is for you.'

'How perfectly lovely!' Sally draped the mantilla over her shoulder and, as Norman bent to reach for the suede jacket, she swung around and around before Ernst. 'Like it, darling?'

'Yes,' Ernst said. 'Of course.'

Norman dropped the jacket. He stared.

'Am I expected to say you shouldn't have done it?' Sally asked.

'No, certainly not.'

'Is there anyting wrong?' she asked.

'Of course not. Why should there be?'

'I don't know.'

'If you don't know, then neither do I.' Norman cleared his throat. He recovered sufficiently to smile. 'When do you start work?' he asked.

Sally noticed that Norman was greyer. The circles under his eyes were darker. He was tanned, he looked extremely healthy, but he appeared to have aged considerably in a month.

'Next week,' Sally said. 'I'm so excited. The school's not far from here. The Northern Line takes me directly there.'

Norman dared not look too closely at Ernst yet, but his expression, when he turned to Sally, was rich in accusations.

'Just in case you haven't been told,' she said, 'Ernst and I are living together.'

Norman wiped his greying curly hair with a clammy hand. He lit a cigarette. Looking at Sally again he saw her briefly as a shallow young girl intent on thrills; no more. But the impression didn't last long enough to help him.

Suppressing an urge to toss them both out of the room, Norman poured tea. 'Why don't you both sit down,' he said, not looking at either of them.

'Oh, Norman, I knew we could count on you. I knew you'd help us.' He shrunk from her hopeful smile. 'Why didn't you write to me more than that miserly little postcard?'

'I was very busy.'

When they sat down together on the bed Norman looked away from their clasped hands.

'I was so sorry to hear about your brother,' Sally said. 'What a shame!'

'Yes,' Norman said emptily, indicating that the subject was closed. 'It was too bad about Nicky.' He noticed that Ernst was not drinking his tea. 'Would you prefer a glass of cognac?' he asked.

'No,' Ernst said. 'Thank you.'

'What do you plan on doing in London, Ernst?'

'I—'

'We can be honest with Norman. He hasn't got any papers. He's here illegally. But Ernst can speak five languages, Norman. He's awfully intelligent.'

'I would like to be able to support myself. I don't like taking Sally's money.'

Sure, Norman thought, sure. 'I think I'll have a drink myself.' Norman poured himself a glass of cognac. 'Well,' he said coldly, 'I hope you'll like it in London.'

'Don't worry about that,' Sally said, the quiver in her voice belying her frivolous manner. 'One day Ernst is going to marry a big fat lady who'll take him to America. He's going to be rich.'

Norman ignored her. 'You describe yourself as a refugee,' he said. 'Do you mind telling me why, exactly, did you leave East Germany?'

'I'm not a bikini-ist,' Ernst said, 'or a thief or a sexual pervert. The police aren't after me, if that's what you mean.'

'You chose freedom, so to speak.'

'So to speak.'

'Let's not talk politics,' Sally said. 'I hate politics. Karp picks on him, Norman, he—'

'What do you expect? Karp spent years in their concentration camps. He has his little memories.'

'My father,' Ernst began, 'also . . .' But he stopped. Norman, like all the others before him, looked quite prepared to disbelieve him.

'No,' Sally said. 'Tell him.'

'My father,' Ernst began, 'also . . .'

But he couldn't tell Norman about his father. The anguish was too deeply felt to be cheapened by argument once more.

Looking at Norman, Ernst thought, you come from a community of friends, you have shelter, office, enemies, family, and the memories of other women, so please let me be. Go find yourself another girl, he thought. Let me stop running for a month.

'You don't know what the Russians did in Germany,' he said.

'The communist regime in Germany,' Norman began faint-heartedly, 'is probably the most imperfect—'

'Please,' Sally said, 'let's talk about something else.'

'What would you expect,' Norman asked, 'after the camps?'

'I have done you no harm,' Ernst said.

Norman did not reply immediately. He was afraid for Sally. She was so innocent, so trusting, and Ernst was so obviously worthless. 'How old are you?' Norman asked.

'Twenty-two.'

Sally bit her lip. 'Norman,' she asked, 'will you help Ernst find work?'

Twenty-two, Norman thought, and Nicky was only twenty-one.

'Will you help us?'

Norman poured himself another drink. 'Did she ever tell you why I left the United States?' he asked Ernst.

'No. She didn't.'

'I was an assistant professor at a university. They wanted to know if I had ever been a member of the communist party. I refused to tell them.'

'What's that got to do with Ernst?' Sally asked.

'I won't help him, Sally. And I prefer that you didn't bring him to my room again.'

Sally flushed. 'I certainly never expected you to—'

'Please go,' Norman said. 'Both of you.'

As soon as they left Norman drained his glass.

It would not have worked out anyway, he thought. Probably she would have wanted a Swedish Modern double bed, impressionist prints, and no love making in the mornings. Children would have been horrible. Diapers; sitters; measles; and growing up Rotarians, or worse. Better this. Better your own private place to come home to. All marriages ended the same. After five years – bickering, little affairs on the side, a resentful tolerance, no more desire.

Norman poured himself another drink.

A complaint – something terrible, something that could not be isolated – filled his body acidly. The palms of his hands sweated. He wouldn't sleep tonight. Or he would sleep and wake at five in that familiar sweat of fear. Norman rubbed his jaw, loosened his tie, and cursed softly. All his nerves tingled.

'Yes,' he had said. 'It was too bad for Nicky.'

Nicky had been so tall and splendid, a beautiful boy, and now he was gone.

Jesus, Norman thought.

There was the weight, the crippling weight, of all the things he had omitted to do. Like being too tight to befriend Hornstein, then watching him die. Like not telling Charlie he was a sensational writer, when such a small lie would make him so happy. Like avoiding Karp. Oh, so many little kindnesses withheld. So much bastardy.

If only, he thought, I could be a better, warmer man.

'You're like the sober one at an orgy,' Zelda Landis had once said. 'The one who is too decent to remind you the next morning what a fool you made of yourself the night before.'

Why couldn't he fling himself at life like Charlie? Why couldn't he make a fool of himself more often? Why had he fled Sally?

Norman felt old. Very old.

His gaze fell on the suede jacket. Maybe it will fit Joey, he thought.

III

Karp sighed; he sucked his tooth.

He didn't bring me a gift, he thought. After all I did for him, after I bathed and washed him in the hospital, he was gone all this time and he didn't bring me a gift.

Karp's apartment consisted of three rooms, and a kitchen, bathroom and toilet. All the rooms but one, the bedroom, were on the same floor. To get to the bedroom you had to climb another, inner flight of stairs. The kitchen gleamed with every modern convenience. Karp studied himself in the bathroom mirror for a while. His colour was bad. There were little circles under his eyes. Karp rubbed his face with cold cream and then dabbed his cheeks with tissue paper. He applied another lotion on his hands, made a note of the fact that he needed a manicure, and then returned to his easy chair in the living room, where he resumed his watch.

The table was lavishly set for two. It was 10.30. But Norman had yet to come for dinner.

A half hour later Karp looked at his watch again, he sighed, and went into the kitchen. Karp prepared himself an hors d'oeuvre of Portuguese sardines, tomato and carrot slices, beetroot, devilled egg, shrimp, a spoonful of potato salad, and mixed a splendid salad dressing to go with it. In the living room again he sat down with the plate of food, a glass of beaujolais, and a book of Redoutés *Roses* to study while he ate.

Karp owned a large library of books on plants, flowers,

85

trees, and animals. He was aware that people like Winkleman, Landis, and Graves said that a flower was 'pretty' or a tree was 'nice'. They never knew the proper names. This was one reason why Karp was so fond of Norman. Walking with him a comment on a tree, the breed of a dog, or the especial charm of a certain hybrid of rose was not lost.

Most Jews are remarkably deficient in a knowledge of nature. Karp was determined to remedy this and any other traits, like an emotional distaste for sea food and a tendency to tell self-deprecating jokes, that might brand him. This was neither self-hatred nor the idle fancy of a social climber. Karp had already paid an exorbitant price for being a Jew. The next time they were rounded up he wanted to get off free. He already knew a lot about Catholicism and when the going got tough again he planned to convert. This was not a repudiation of his people. It was part of his plan for survival.

Norman came at last. He stumbled into the living room, his eyes red and glassy.

'Norman,' Karp said gleefully. 'Why, Norman, you've been drinking.'

Norman slumped back on the sofa and removed his glasses.

'I read a few pages of your book earlier this evening,' Karp said, 'and I must say I found a lot to criticise.'

'I'll thank you not to go through my papers.'

'You were late for dinner. I went up to your room to see if you were sleeping and—'

'And there was my manuscript,' Norman said. 'At the bottom of a locked suitcase.'

'The key was on the bureau.'

For ten years Norman had been working on his book. *A History of John Dryden and his Times*. The book was a secret and a work of love. If it was ever published, which was doubtful, he would dedicate it to his father, but meanwhile, like Sunday painting for others, it was something he could return to with hope and again and again. Polishing, rewriting, and, most of all, enjoying himself. Norman meant to present Dryden and his period in the round. Finishing the book was of some consequence to him – more than he chose to admit – for this, however humble, or academic was to be his special contribution to scholarship. Meanwhile, the book was fun. A private world. A little source of sanity for Norman Price.

'Would you care for a drink?' Karp asked.

'I love her, Karp. I love Sally.'

Karp patted Norman's back. 'There,' he said. 'There, there.'

'How could she prefer that Aryan bastard to me?'

'Are you hungry?'

'No. I'm not hungry.'

Karp poured Norman a scotch and soda. 'You look older,' he said. 'Your brother's death has affected you.'

'Affected me?' Norman said. 'Nothing affects me. Didn't you know?'

'There,' Karp said. 'There, there.'

'Why didn't I have the courage to tell Sally how much I loved her when I had the chance?'

'Are you sure you're not hungry?'

'Jesus.'

'Then, if you don't mind. 'I'll go ahead with my dinner.'

'I'm going away. As soon as I can scrape enough money together I'm going to go to the Continent. I must keep my life free of disturbances. I'm afraid, Karp.'

IV

Norman woke late the next morning. He woke with a hangover. But once he had read his mail his head cleared and he was jubilant. His agent in New York had written to say that Star Books had accepted revisions on his thriller and that a cheque for two thousand dollars was forthcoming. Norman phoned Winkleman right away.

'I've got bad news for you, Sonny. I want to back out of that script deal.'

'The hell you do. I paid Charlie another two-fifty yesterday just because you promised to get right down to work. What happened?'

Jesus, Norman thought. He couldn't write Charlie's scripts for him. He would explain everything and lend him some money. That was the most he could do. 'I'll get you the money back,' Norman said.

'We must have a bad connection. My name is Winkleman. Is that Norman Price speaking?'

Norman laughed.

'O.K. Let's say there *is* a second flood. What about the first payment?' Winkleman asked.

'The story line was worth what you paid for it.'

'Not if you won't work on it. *Like you promised.*'

'Let Charlie rewrite it.'

'Ixnay.'

'Why?'

'Don't be an ockshmay, Norm.'

'Why?'

'Because Charlie can't rewrite it. He writes dialogue like it was for *New Masses*. Sober up, Norm, and write something that'll spark me.'

'I'm not drunk.'

'*Then get drunk.* One minute. Bella wants to talk to you.'

Norman adored Bella. He didn't want her to think that he was doing Sonny dirty. He told her about his trip to Spain. She told him about the children.

'How's your girl?' Bella asked coyly.

'My girl?'

'Sally. Isn't that why you rushed home?'

Norman stiffened. 'Well, I—'

'Who'r'ye trying to kid?'

'Nobody,' Norman said weakly.

'Bring her around Saturday night. We're having a party.'

'Sure. I'll bring her. Tell Sonny I'll be around tonight,

though. I'm serious. I won't be able to do that script. I'm going away again.'

'Tell him yourself, darling.'

Charlie, though, would have to be told first.

Norman was invited to lunch by Charlie and Joey. He bought a bottle of wine and took the album of flamenco records with him. Norman always came with gifts. Gifts were a proof against eviction. And considering the nature of the news he had for them a gift was clearly in order.

Charlie had been having a hard time while Norman had been away.

Charlie ran, he ran, he ran, he ran from television to stage to movie maker. He picked up a penny's worth of hope here, the bone of a promise there, a smile from somebody big and a cry from somebody small; an if and a maybe and a promise to call soon; he gulped down a coffee with Graves who called Houston John, waited outside Cameo Production's offices so that he could run into Pearson casually, told the director of *A Gun for Julia* a joke that the director had told somebody else earlier in the day, had a quick crap, ate a sandwich standing up, and arrived too late at the restaurant where Boris Jeremy was supposed to eat; he huffed, he puffed, he combed his hair, he slept for half an hour in a newsreel cinema, phoned his agent, phoned home, turned around three times for luck, changed a line of his play while queuing for a bus, had a drink in somebody's office, picked up some 'additional dialogue' to write for *Pirates of the Spanish Main*, read his horoscope in the *Star*, hurried home to see if there was any mail, ran upstairs to see if he could catch his wife in the act of being unfaithful to him, opened up a bottle of beer, and settled down to wait for the next mail delivery.

Charlie's favourite uncle had drifted from failure to failure. Charlie had written a play about his tragedy, but nobody wanted it.

But yesterday, beginning with Winkleman's phone call, everything had gone right for once. So Charlie was in an expansive mood when Norman arrived. 'Quick,' he said to

Norman, 'come to the window.' Norman came to the window. 'See it,' Charlie said.

There was an unmistakably new car parked downstairs. A Morris Minor.

'I bought it this morning,' Charlie said. 'We gave you as a credit reference. Do you mind?'

'Of course not. But I thought you were broke.'

'Have a seat, old chap.'

Joey immediately perched on the arm of Norman's chair.

'Yesterday morning,' Charlie began, 'Rip Van Winkleman finally came through on my script. I got another two-fifty. I'm starting on a rewrite tomorrow.'

A long ash dropped from Norman's cigarette end. As he looked around searchingly Joey indicated the ashtray held tightly in her lap, just about where her tight brown skirt creased into a V-shape.

'Winkleman is a big noise, you know. As soon as the deal came through I got in touch with Boris Jeremy and told him I had a sensational story for him. He liked the story but was a bit wary of having me do the shooting-script until I told him that I was doing one for Winkleman. My contract with Jeremy is now being drawn up. On the strength of these two contracts I went to see Cameo Productions and got three *Sir Galahad* scripts to do. Armed with all this I went to see my bank manager and there below – ' Charlie tapped the window – 'is the afterbirth. A month from now I'll trade it in and get me a new Jag.'

Norman responded as best he could to Charlie's febrile talk at lunch. He was alarmed because Joey, who usually acted as a brake at times like these, seemed to be even more excited than Charlie. But he could understand. It was hell to be a failure's wife in the *emigré* colony.

'Hey' Charlie said, 'I got a letter from Tommy Hale this morning. He heard that I had to leave the States and wants me to come back to Toronto. There's loads of work there, he says. But here's one guy who doesn't want to be a whale in that little fish pond. No CBC panel games for me, Norman. I'll make it here or nowhere.'

Norman nodded and told them they could keep the flat for a while. He was happy where he was.

'Have you seen Sally yet?' Joey asked.

'It's all right,' Norman said. 'I know about the German boy.'

'It's a shame. I thought that she was such a nice kid.'

But Joey kicked Charlie under the table and he quickly changed the subject. 'What are you hoarding all that wood in the cupboard for?' he asked.

Norman explained that he had bought the boards because he intended to build a bookcase. Charlie offered to do the job for him, but Norman said no, he was going to get a carpenter to do it.

'I think I'd better be going,' Norman said.

Joey offered a walk with him for a bit. Outside, they wandered up to Notting Hill Gate.

'I'm happy for Charlie,' Norman said.

Joey hooked her arm through his.

'Me too. This all means so much to him,' Joey paused. 'I was just about ready to accept a typing job from Bob Landis. And you know what *typing* for *him* means.'

'Bob's a boy,' Norman said affectionately. 'He wants to make every woman he meets.'

'And you?'

Norman's face darkened.

'OK.,' Joey said gaily, 'I won't tease.' But she stopped him short in front of a smart lingerie shop. 'There,' she said, pointing out a wooden blonde in the window warmed by a lacy black négligé, 'why doesn't anyone buy *me* something like that?'

'Joey,' he said, as they walked on again, 'do you think I'm a prude?'

Joey laughed. Her laughter spread. She held her hand to her mouth as though her laughter, like an egg, might fall and break, and all at once she was serious again.

'No,' she said, 'but if you ever let yourself go I'm sure you'll be worse than Bob.'

'I'm tired of being a bum, Joey. I want to get married and have children.'

91

She tightened. 'So does Charlie. He wants kids too, I mean.'

'I'm sorry, sweetie. No crack was intended.'

'I know,' Joey said, angry with herself. 'Oh, why must it always be so hard for two friends to talk without apologising to each other every second minute?' She reached up and straightened Norman's raincoat collar. Her smile was rich in tender concern. 'Norman,' she asked, 'did you ever tell Sally how you felt about her?'

'I told you,' he said sharply, 'she was just a – a girl to me.'

'Oh, Norman, really!'

He stopped and kissed her gently on the forehead. 'See you,' he said. 'God bless.'

'If you want her that badly,' Joey called after him, 'then put up a fight.'

When Norman got home Karp was waiting on his bed. He held a half-stripped banana in a little hand. One of his cheeks was swollen, like he had a bad tooth.

'How did you get in?' Norman asked.

Karp stretched out an arm mutely, a little hand open wide, as though to protect himself from a gust of wind. Norman waited while Karp swallowed his banana.

'I've got the keys to all the rooms. I'm the landlord, remember?' Karp rose wearily. 'Mr Sonny Winkleman called three times.'

Norman phoned Winkleman. 'It's O.K., Sonny,' he said. 'I'll write you your script. Would you put on Bella for a minute, please?'

Bella came to the phone.

'If it's all right with you,' Norman said, 'I'd like to bring Sally and her boy friend to your party.'

'And her *boy friend*?'

'That's right. If it's all right with you.'

'Sure,' Bella said, 'if—'

'Thanks,' Norman said, hanging up.

'An excellent idea,' Karp said. 'I was going to suggest it myself.'

'Just what do you mean by that, Karp?'

'Your friends are refugees from the West. Ernst is a refugee from the East. Once Sally sees what your friends think of Ernst she may think again.'

'Nonsense,' Norman said. 'I'm trying to make a gesture, that's all.'

'Of course,' Karp said, and he was gone.

V

'Don't you see?' – Sally flung Ernst down on the bed and jumped on top of him – 'This means that Norman wants you to be his friend. He's changed his mind about us.'

Ernst, too, was delighted. In the three days to go until the party Sally told him all about the people who were likely to be there. He helped her to select a dress and on Friday, as a surprise, Sally took him out and bought him a new sports jacket.

At night Ernst lapsed into a world of impossible dreams. Nicky, and other nightly horrors, did not drift away obligingly, but stood off like sharks preparing for a more deadly assault. Ernst was determined to make a good impression on Norman's friends and for three days he considered all possible approaches. He might even tell them about his father.

Karl Haupt.

Ernst visualised the old man wandering from zone to zone, dependent on the irregular money forthcoming from a disowned son, seeking something lost – his family and his self respect – and being suspected by both sides. The Jews had justice and their considerable dead. Karl Haupt's legacy was compounded of weakness and a dubious pride in the fact that he had objected to Hitler slightly, but not enough. Ernst recalled that when the old man had at last been picked up for questioning in Saxony the communist police official turned out to be the same one who had used to question him for the Nazis. The cell had been an old gestapo cell. Ernst

had kicked up a row about the incident at the time and there
– if he went back and put his finger on it – his doubts about
the FDJ, about communism, had come to a head and burst
like a boil.

From that day onwards Ernst was a suspected man. All
the same he had scraped some money together, taken his
father back to the Western Zone, and found him a room.

'You're with them,' the old man said. 'You're dirty.'

'Enough.'

'You're no better than a thief.'

'Foolish old man,' Ernst had said. 'What do you know?'

'*I* never joined them.'

'The Nazis, you mean.'

'The Nazis . . .'

'No, you never joined the Nazis. But neither did you ever
work for the underground.'

'I am your father. Speak with respect.'

'My group was with the underground. We are different.
We are fighting for a better world.'

'Again?'

Ernst had said nothing.

'You are with them,' his father had said, 'and you are
dirty. They are not so different.'

'Foolish old man,' Ernst had shouted, 'what do you
understand of history?'

The dazed, inconsolable eyes had hardened with an old
man's rancour. 'Don't come back to see me again. You are
no longer my son.'

Ernst had settled his father's rent for a month. Back in
the Eastern Zone a week later he discovered that he was
being followed by the SSD. He went through the gestures of
belief for another month and then all at once even one more
day would have been insufferable. So he fled. His father
wouldn't see him again, but he wrote asking for money from
time to time.

Sally warned Ernst not to repeat this story at the party. A
lot of Norman's friends were fellow-travellers; they would
not believe him anyway. A better approach, she said, would

be not to say anything about Germany. It might be best to avoid political discussions altogether.

Ernst didn't sleep the night before the party.

For years he had dreamt that one day he would be introduced into an intelligent society of artists and professional people. In this fantasy he saw himself as a man with a faithful wife and children, giving small dinner parties and being invited to others. There were no uniforms. All crimes, all hungers, and penniless days were done. People like Norman enjoyed his company. They did not think of him as a German. He was well-liked. Honourable. Another happy conformist.

And here, at last, he was going to be introduced into just such a society. Ernst calmed himself with two drinks before they left for the party.

'Don't worry,' Sally said, 'they'll adore you.'

'It doesn't matter,' Ernst said stiffly. 'I'm not interested in their opinions.'

But seated in the taxi with Norman and a smiling Karp, too anxious to take part in the small talk, Ernst, unaware that he was interrupting a conversation, suddenly blurted out, 'I'm a very good carpenter, Norman. If you like, I'll build you a bookcase. I will do that for you as a gift.'

Norman fidgeted with his glasses; he shifted uneasily in his seat.

Sally pressed Ernst's hand to caution him, but he couldn't stop talking. He turned to Karp. 'I'm a good electrician, too. From now on I will do all your electrical work free of charge.'

It was at times like these that Sally felt small and uninjured beside him. She tried not to weep.

'Here we are,' Norman said.

Ernst insisted on paying the taxi fare. He would have it no other way.

*

VI

The party was in honour of Colin Horton. Horton, a progressive journalist, was the most recent arrival in London. He was a heavy man, in his early forties, with a tight bony head, shiny black hair and flat black tack-head eyes. Norman suspected that his humility, like a panelist's groping after the right word, was a professional's mannerism. But the fact was that Horton was a highly skilled journalist and, had his politics been other than what they were, he could have been entrenched in an executive position with one of the big news magazines today.

'I had the most interesting experience in a taxi this morning,' he said. 'The driver, who recognised me from my newspaper pictures, refused to allow me to pay my fare. He said anybody who wasn't wanted in America could ride free in his taxi any day. After all the abuse that my wife and I' – he acknowledged his wife with a stab of his pipe – 'have suffered in America I was genuinely touched. I'm telling you this because I thought it would please you to know that among the working-class our stand against creeping fascism has not gone unnoticed . . .'

Norman turned away; he headed for the bar.

'I'm anxious to visit the People's Democracies as soon as possible,' Horton said. 'It would certainly be pleasant to be in a country where peace isn't a dirty word.'

'Ah,' Karp said, 'I must introduce you to Ernst later. He's from East Germany. One would think you two would have a lot to talk about.'

Sonny took Norman aside. 'O.K.,' he said, 'now tell me why you brought that little goon into my house.'

Bella joined them with her gentle smile. 'Spain seems to have agreed with you, Norman. You look wonderful!'

'Hey,' Sonny said, 'did you know that he was bringing that goon here?'

'I forced him on Bella,' Norman said. 'I wanted you to meet him. I thought maybe you could help him get some work.'

Winkleman's face flamed. 'Who do you think I am? Jesus Christ?'

'Look Sonny, you don't even know the boy. He—'

'Who wants to know him? Are you seriously asking me, a Jew, to be tolerant of a little Nazi punk?'

'He's not a Nazi.'

'You *are* asking rather a lot,' Bella said.

'Look here,' Sonny said, 'Bella loves you. You want money, you want a lay, you want I should get you the best head-shrinker in London, just ask me. But if you want me to play a son-of-a-bitch Christian, book a run for your own place, kid. This here house is one hundred per cent un-American Jewland.'

'Take it easy,' Norman said.

'Ask me a favour,' Sonny insisted. 'Test me.'

'He's teasing,' Bella said.

'Come.' Sonny took Norman into his office and gave him a cheque for two hundred pounds.

'Why did you bring me in here?' Norman asked. 'I could have waited for the money.'

'Joey was listening. You told me you didn't want Charlie to know that you were working on the script.'

'Do you think she heard anything?'

'No.'

'Joey is very penetrating.'

'The only thing penetrating about that girl is the looks she gives her husband. Listen, what's the score on Charlie?'

'What do you mean?'

'Drazin tells me he isn't even listed in *Red Channels*.'

'Charlie's o.k. I've known him for years.'

'All I want to know is why a guy who could earn a living in a civilised country would ever come here.'

'He was blacklisted, that's why. He just isn't important enough to have been listed in *Red Channels*.'

Back in the living room Sonny introduced Norman to Joyce Drazin. Joyce was having lunch with her agent tomorrow.

'Tomorrow,' Bob Landis said, 'I'm going to get myself a new analyst. This one never laughs at my jokes.'

'I'm having lunch with an important backer tomorrow,' Budd Graves said. 'If things work out you and I may have something to talk about.'

'You'd better take it easy on those lunches,' Charlie said.

Budd Graves looked like a melon ready to burst.

'Charlie's right,' Landis said. 'A few more lunches and all of Winkleman's men will not be able to put Budd Graves together again.'

'If things work out tomorrow,' Budd Graves began again, 'I—'

'Charlie,' Landis interrupted, pointing to Sally and Ernst, 'what gives? I thought she was saving that creamy white body for Norman?'

'So did Norman.'

'There's something not kosher about Norman,' Budd Graves said.

'He sells plenty of scripts,' Charlie said, 'doesn't he?'

'Ah, we're all hacks,' Landis said. 'Anybody can knock out the kind of crap we write and sell it. But Norman seems to be a kind of Jonah.'

Sure, sure, Charlie thought. Anyone can sell hack work. Thank you very much. But the reason why I can't sell so easily is because I'm not a hack and maybe another factor is my name never used to be Lipschitz.

'Tell me something about Sally's boy friend,' Landis asked.

'He's a German,' Charlie said. 'From East Berlin. "He chose freedom".'

'Who brought him here?' Graves asked angrily, 'Norman?'

Ernst was everywhere. You took out a cigarette casually and a match held by Ernst flared under your nose. You had hardly finished your drink and Ernst was there again to seize your glass and get you another . You were interrupted once in the middle of an argument or flirtation when Ernst bobbed up again, cutting you off with a plate of unwanted hors d'oeuvres.

The more hostile his reception, the harder Ernst tried to please, and the more obnoxious he appeared to others. Sally tried as gracefully as she could to get him to stop running the party like a race, but there was no stopping him. She overheard somebody say, 'Isn't his behaviour typically German,' and sat down forlorn in a chair, anticipating the collision to come.

There were other curiosities at Winkleman's tonight besides Horton. There was a captive Englishman and his wife. Sir James Digby was a film director of sorts, his wife was a starlet. The effect of their arrival at the party was much as if two sharecroppers had crashed a gathering of Southern planters.

Norman overheard Winkleman tell Plotnick. 'Take a look at the boobs on her,' and then he whispered something in Plotnick's ear.

'She doesn't, Plotnick said with appetite. 'I don't believe it.'

Valerie Digby, her tight warm breasts half unpeeled, half trapped in the black lace of her gown, tossed her smile like a hat into the pot-bellied ring around her and fetched Bob Landis, tall, tweedy, a regular writing chap, to her. Bob drove her like a moth into the corner of the room, cutting off the others with his back. Norman watched enviously from afar.

Norman had first met Bob in New York in 1939. The evening Norman had visited his flat, Bob and his girl, a bony black-haired set designer, had quarrelled fiercely. Bob had been offered a summer job as a gag writer in the Catskills. His girl threatened to leave if he took it. But Bob was badly in debt, he had a mother to support, and as he had explained over and over again two months off the novel would do the book a world of good. As the quarrel flamed brighter more and more people had slipped into the cold-water flat until, at its burning best, a full-blown party was in progress, and the quarrel, dampened by the wisecracks of outsiders, had been put out.

Of the young people there that evening three had since become famous. The rest of them, like Bob, had been moderately successful. But that spring evening in 1939, what with two survivors of the defence of Madrid in their company, what with everyone young, talented, handsome or pretty, and with fame two or at the very most three years ahead, they had all been suffused with a warm glow. The girls, the girls, Norman remembered, had been so splendid and the men so tall with promise. Somebody, at last somebody, had gone to the window and cried, 'Look. Oh my God, look.' Dawn had come even to the East Side.

The next time he had come across Bob Landis it had been in the shape of a cheque for five thousand dollars signed by him and payable to the American Labour Party. From the Catskills Bob had gone to Hollywood. The Rinky-Dinks, as Charlie called them, had been dispersed. For the third member of the group to make it – that night a dadaist and today a sophisticated Broadway playwright – had made the biggest splash of all by naming everyone who had, and a few who hadn't, passed through the flat that night at a television session of the committee fifteen years later.

'He's a former Hitler Youth leader,' Zelda Landis said.

'If you ask me,' Charna Graves said, 'sometimes Norman Price goes just a little bit too far.'

'The trouble with Norman,' Joey said, 'is that he expects people to accept one another on trust. That's why . . .' That's why I love him, she thought.

'He shouldn't have brought that boy here,' Zelda said.

'Germans,' Molly Plotnick said, 'give me the shivers.'

'They're talking about us,' Ernst said.

'Take it easy, darling. You can hardly expect them to like you at first.'

But she wished they hadn't come. Norman must have been crazy too bring Ernst here.

100

'Parlour-Bolshies,' Ernst said. 'That one with the pipe. I know the type so well.'

Norman loomed up drunkenly before them. 'Enjoying yourselves?' he asked guiltily.

'Loads,' Sally said.

Karp hovered a little way off like a storm impending, waiting for Norman to go.

'I'm sorry,' Norman said, 'I should have realised . . .'

'Yes,' Sally said, 'you should have.'

'I wish they would speak to me,' Ernst said thickly. 'I wish they would give me a chance.'

'You're both drunk,' Sally said. 'It's disgraceful.'

Ernst rose, swaying a little. His cheeks reddened, 'I would like to . . .'

Sally was astonished. She had never seen Ernst genuinely humble before. She felt as though he were exhibiting all his separate selves to her one by one, like scraps of evidence.

'. . . would like to be your friend,' he said.

'Sure.' Norman smiled as gracefully as he could. 'Of course.'

Then, as he went off to replenish his drink, Karp confronted Ernst and Sally with a swing of his cane. 'There's someone I want you to meet,' he said to Ernst. 'Come.'

Childish. Norman realised that it was childish. But once in the toilet he squeezed out the toothpaste tube and wrote it on the mirror.

Horton banged his pipe on the mantelpiece, blew into it fiercely, and then reached for his drink. 'Whatever happens,' he said, 'we mustn't lose our faith in the American working-class.'

Karp broke through the circle around him. 'Ah, Mr Horton,' he said, 'here is the boy I told you about.'

Sally found Norman talking to Sid Drazin in the hall. 'Quick,' she said, 'I think Karp is going to get Ernst into trouble.'

101

'One would think,' Karp said, 'that you and Ernst would have much to talk about. Ernst used to be an official in the FDJ.'

'Are you here on a visit?' Horton asked.

'No,' Sally said, 'he fled. He found conditions there intolerable.'

Norman squeezed Sally's arm.

'Tell me,' Horton said, 'were you a student?'

'No.'

'Because if you were a student, and a worker's son, you would be able to get a scholarship in the East, wouldn't you?'

'Yeah. But I would have to study what they wanted me to study.'

'Something useful, is what you mean?'

A rash of smiles broke out all around.

'He used to be in the Hitler Youth,' Zelda Landis said. 'What would you expect?'

'Zelda,' Bob Landis said.

'Everyone was in the Hitler Youth,' Ernst said.

'You mean everyone who wasn't gassed,' Horton said.

'Norman,' Sally said. 'Please Norman.'

'Those who joined the Nazis to get privileges are now members of the SED for the same reason,' Ernst said. 'You took off your Hitler Youth badge and put on an FDJ one.'

'That sounds like the anti-communist line to me.'

'I am not a Nazi.'

'But you were a member of the Hitler Youth. Come, come, boy.'

'But—'

'You agree that if you were a worker's son you could get a scholarship in the East. But you're against *useful studies*. I take it, then, that you believe in the utmost freedom for the individual.'

'Well, I . . .'

'Hitler held the freedom of the individual to be sacred.'

More smiles.

'People like him ought to be shot,' Charna Graves said.

'Come on now, Ernst, don't play games with me. You'd like to see East Germany "liberated", wouldn't you?'

'I'd like to see them free, but—'

'Never mind. You've explained yourself.'

'There are still big parades,' Ernst yelled. 'Still uniforms. We marched for Hitler once and now we march for—'

'For peace,' Horton said.

'Peace.' Ernst shook his fist at Horton. 'If I ever hear that word again, I will scream.'

'I don't think,' Horton said, 'that there's any need for us to go on with this discussion.'

Norman stepped between Horton and Ernst. 'How dare you judge this boy so glibly,' he said.

'Aren't you Norman *Price*?' Horton asked.

Norman nodded.

'I wonder what your father would think if he saw you defending a little Nazi—'

'I think you're a bully, Horton. I think you stink.'

'Now we know where *he* stands,' Budd Graves said.

'Oh,' Bob Landis asked drunkenly. 'Where?'

'When someone's argument is indefensible they usually resort to adolescent abuse,' Horton said. 'You've been drinking . . .'

'That's the most sensible suggestion I've heard so far,' Bob Landis said. 'Let's all have another drink.'

'Norman,' Bella said gently, 'please . . .'

'Look,' Norman said, 'you're all my friends here—'

'That's news to me,' Budd Graves said.

'—but I'm sorry to say that I'm disappointed in the lot of you. All evening I've been hearing second and third hand stories about Ernst. Most of them untrue. Of course he was in the Hitler Youth, but they all were. Sure he talks a lot of nonsense, but why hasn't one of you – just one of you taken the trouble to treat him like another human being?'

'Everybody,' Bob Landis called, 'everybody choose your partner for a Paul Jones.'

'Maybe he *is* a little bastard,' Norman said. 'I'm not sure. But at least I'm willing to take the trouble to find out.'

103

'Now that Billy Graham has spoken,' Budd Graves said, 'I—'

'Look,' Norman said, 'most of us were on the hot seat at home. Don't you recognise Horton's technique of questioning?'

'Really,' Horton said, 'this is too much. Are you accusing me of being a McCarthyite?'

'That's just what I mean. Remarks like that,' Norman said. 'Twisting my words to his own purpose.'

'You want us to go around kissing Nazis,' Budd Graves said. 'Is that it?'

'No,' Norman said, 'and I want them to stop locking up communists. But if I don't want to see any more Rosenberg cases neither do I want to see any more Slansky trials.'

'That's a very revealing remark,' Horton said.

'Maybe it is.'

'Excuse me,' Horton said, 'I'll be right back. Tell me if I miss anything.'

'After all he's suffered from the witch-hunters,' Budd Graves said, 'you had no right—'

'Oh hell,' Norman said, 'what's the use?'

'Take it easy, Norman,' Bob Landis clapped him on the back. 'Don't get so worked up.'

That's when Horton burst into the room and grabbed Norman by the collar.

'You – you—'

Norman struggled to break free.

'Are you responsible for that foul slander on the toilet mirror?'

Oh, hell, Norman thought. I forgot. 'I'm sorry,' he said feebly. 'I only meant it as a joke.'

'A joke? FBI agents. Is that what you find funny?' Horton turned triumphantly to the others. 'He wrote "COLIN HORTON IS A SPY FOR THE FBI" on the toilet mirror.'

Bob Landis howled with laughter, but, responding to a kick in the shins from Zelda, he broke off abruptly.

'Oh, Norman,' Joey said, 'how could you have been so childish?'

'How old did you say you were?' Budd Graves asked.

'O.K., Budd,' Bob Landis said, 'stop pushing him.'

Norman pulled back and swung wild and blind at Horton. Horton crashed to the floor.

'Fascist,' Horton said. 'Dirty little fascist.'

Norman stooped to retrieve his glasses. 'This is crazy,' he said. 'I don't hit people.' He tried to help Horton up, but Horton shoved him away. 'I'm sorry,' Norman said.

The others turned away from him. Norman took Ernst and Sally home.

'I'm sorry, Ernst. My friends behaved abominably.'

'You weren't to blame,' Sally said.

'I was, you know. I mean – Come on into my room for a nightcap.'

Norman poured three stiff drinks, but he didn't talk. He felt miserable and ashamed. 'Everything happened so quickly,' he said.

Restless, upset, her bosom rising and falling quickly, Sally paced up and down the room. She stopped at the mantelpiece and took down a photograph of Nicky. The photograph showed Nicky feeding peanuts to the pigeons of Trafalgar Square. 'Is this your brother?' Sally asked.

'Yes,' Norman turned to Ernst. 'I'd like to help you.'

'I have come between you and your friends,' Ernst said. 'I'm sorry.'

'Maybe I can get you some work translating, I'll see.'

'You are very kind.'

Suddenly Norman burst out laughing. 'I've been meaning to hit Horton for years,' he said.

Ernst grinned. 'Next time,' he said, 'we'll take them all on together.'

'That suits me fine,' Norman said.

'Hard as nails,' Sally said, sitting down beside Ernst, the photograph of Nicky still in her hand, 'the both of you.'

Norman exploded with laughter again. He slapped his knees. 'Jesus,' he said, 'did you see the expression on Horton's face when he hit the floor?'

'Fascist,' Sally said, mimicking Horton, 'dirty little fascist.'

Ernst leaped up and, adopting the posture of an inquisitor, shook his finger at Norman. 'Are you responsible for that foul slander on the toilet mirror?' he demanded.

Sally began to sway drunkenly. 'Everybody,' she said, 'everybody choose your partner for a Paul Jones.'

All three began to laugh helplessly. Ernst doubled over, holding his sides. Sally collapsed on the bed. Norman slapped his knees; he rubbed his eyes. As they quietened down again Norman attempted to drink his whisky, laughed as he swallowed, coughed, wiped his mouth, and started them off on another paroxysm of laughter.

When they recovered again at last Sally wiped her eyes and, discovering that she still held Nicky's photograph in her hand, passed it to Ernst. 'Look,' she said, 'Norman's brother.'

All at once Ernst looked as though the blood had been sucked out of his face. 'How did he die,' he asked, 'exactly?'

'On manoeuvres, I think,' Norman said more soberly. 'There were no details.'

Ernst got up, his body soaked in sweat, and put the photograph down on the desk. 'I think we ought to go to bed,' he said to Sally.

'Come,' Norman said, 'stay for another drink.'

'I don't mind,' Sally said.

'No,' Ernst said, 'I am too tired.'

Sally rose, displeased, and a little embarrassed. 'Maybe it would be best,' she said.

Ernst took her arm.

'Good night', Norman said.

At the door Sally kissed Norman on the cheek, held him tightly, for an instant, and then broke free. 'Good night,' she said, 'and thanks.'

*

VII

'All right,' Sally said, as soon as they were in their own room again, 'now will you please tell me why we couldn't stay for another drink?'

'I was too tired.'

'You were very rude to Norman.'

'I don't need Norman to defend me.'

'He put himself out for you before his friends. I think you should be grateful.'

'I don't want his favours.'

'He's already done you an awfully big one. I thought you wanted to be his friend.'

'You don't understand. We could never be friends.'

'Why?'

'Norman is dangerous, he – I've had dealings with his kind before. They are the first to crack up. They are—'

'Good?'

'Yes,' he said. 'How I hate a good man.'

'I don't understand.'

'I didn't expect you to. But Karp would understand. Karp knows.'

'I don't have to ask Karp. It's good enough for me to know that you hate a good man. That's what you said, isn't it?'

'You don't understand.'

'I don't understand. You said that too. If I don't understand I don't understand. Are you satisfied?'

Ernst struck her with the flat of his hand, knocking her back on the bed.

'Sally . . .?'

She crouched, silently there, her head drooping, her face splashed with hair.

'Did I hurt you, Sally?'

She hid her face in her hands.

'I'm sorry if I hurt you,' he said.

Her eyes, when she took her hands away, were not tear-filled. They were dry with shock.

'I forgot myself,' he said.

Sally got up, cleared the table, and began to undress, folding her clothes with fantastic care.

'Are you angry?' he asked.

'Let's got to bed. You're tired.'

He watched sullenly, and not without excitement, as one by one she shed her underwear, hung them on the back of a chair, and got into her pyjamas.

He sat down on the edge of the bed. 'Forgive me,' he said.

Sally continued to brush her teeth.

'I didn't know what I was doing.'

She came to him as last, forcing his head against her flat warm stomach, his scalp a pressure just under her breasts. Her fingers, running like roots through his hair, discovered the running scar in his neck. 'What about this,' she asked. 'Where did you get this scar?'

'In a fight with another boy.'

'And the other boy?'

'He's dead.'

She drew away from him.

'I had no idea that you had actually . . .'

'The first boy I killed was a Werewolf. Do you know what a Werewolf is?'

'I don't want to know.'

'During the last days of the war the cream of the Hitler Youth was organised into special battalions for a last ditch defence of Berlin. I got into a fight with one of these boys several days after the end had come.'

'Why are you trying to frighten me?'

It's true, he thought. I'm trying to frighten her.

'What will become of us, Ernst?'

'I don't know.'

'We could get married.'

'The others would say I did it for your passport.'

'But it wouldn't be true.'

'Why not,' he said, 'you have a passport.'

'But you love me,' she said. 'You've said so.'

'You have a passport. Maybe that's one reason why I love you.'

'Do you believe in God?' Sally asked suddenly.

'*Who?*'

'GOD.'

'I don't know. I never thought about it. Is it important?'

'I was brought up not to believe. My parents are socialists. But I believe in God.'

'So you believe in God,' he said, 'so what?'

'It's no use. You don't understand.'

'Yeah. That's right,' Ernst said, slipping into his jacket, 'but we will never be able to understand each other. Our lives have been too different.'

'Where are you going?'

'For a walk,' he said. 'I don't feel well.'

'Ernst.'

But he was gone.

When she woke the morning after their first night together Sally, although they had not made love, was overcome by shame. Ernst was a pick-up. Ernst had awakened that first morning with a feeling of rejection. He had not really expected Sally to allow him to spend the whole night on the floor.

'My shirt isn't dry yet,' he said. 'I'll go when it's dry.'

'I thought you had a little suitcase. I thought you were going to bring it.'

'You don't want me to stay.'

'Yes,' she had lied. 'I do.'

Ernst had washed and polished her floor as he had promised and that afternoon Sally had arranged with Karp for nim to occupy the vacant room down the hall.

When they made love for the first time three days later Ernst had employed so much technique that, even if he had with one gesture succeeded in expunging from her memory the two or three hasty boys who had preceded him, he had also aroused the fear in her. She had been startled to discover that she had been able to shout imprecations and whisper endearments to a man who was not only a stranger but a stranger who probably didn't care. But after he had begun to yield to her in little things, after they had given up the farce of separate rooms, she had recognised that his claims on her were larger than sexual. Those first few weeks, however, had been too taut with terror and pleasure and pain. Each day she had resolved to tell Ernst to go and each night they had made love more violently than the last. At times her fear of Ernst had made her physically ill. Yet there had always been the inner assurance that this could never last. This was an adventure: no more.

A week after he had moved in Ernst had come to an arrangement with Karp about doing work around the house. Two weeks after he have moved in he was doing odd jobs for other people on the street and, once again, he had been able to send money to his parents. When he had begun to share Sally's room he had contributed two pounds weekly to their living expenses.

Yet he remained an enigma. Games fascinated him, he collected stamps haphazardly and he was an addict of Westerns and the most sentimental Hollywood musicals. *Scaramouche* was his favourite novel. His insights, however, were alarming.

Once, when she had been ill with the flu, Sally had discovered something else about him. This child of violence could sing to make you weep. Somehow, somewhere, between theft and brawl and flight, Ernst had picked up the songs of Mozart and Schubert. But as the snake, perhaps, is ashamed of its beautiful colours, so Ernst was loth to admit to his gift. He made her promise not to tell anybody. But when she bought him a guitar he was hard put to conceal his delight. He sung for her almost every evening.

'You ought to take lessons,' she said.

'I can't,' he said. 'It's impossible.'

In order to survive Ernst had seemingly drawn the line nowhere. But his one beautiful possession he would not exploit. Sally understood. She stopped pushing him.

And there followed for the two of them a loud time of pleasure, discovery, foolery, and dream-castles. A time when Sally had always run the last block home from school and begun to discard her coat, unzip her skirt and quake inside, even before she had thrust the door open to kick off her shoes one-two-three and leap into his arms. A time when she had pitied the sodden unlit faces of the others in the tube. When to touch was more than she could rightly have asked of life. A time of endless, talkative nights filled with loving and shared cigarettes and fantasies and wines. A time when she embarrassed the other girls at school with sudden and unaccountable gifts of laughter that sprang from heated memories. Yet she knew it was temporary. The joy that was his and hers would have to be swiftly harvested. He was a night person, a doomed one.

When Ernst had met Sally all he had wanted was to get to America and to become rich. He had been realistic about his chances. On the one side were his intelligence, his good looks, his proficiency in bed, his knowledge of languages and, above all, his indifference to others. Against him were his lack of formal schooling, a tendency to cough that might be consumption, and the police. The one thing he had not counted on had been the possibility of his falling in love.

Ernst knew what lovers were reputed to feel about one another and so gradually he had realised that he was, so to speak, in love with Sally.

When he was with Sally he began to suspect that happiness was more than an old man's tale, like peace. He began to feel that it was good to make love, be hungry, stay up all night, rub your face against the damp belly of your loved one, sing and play the fool. He studied his songs, he learned to live with hope and appetite. But there were the times when he awoke at three a.m. from a nightmare of Nicky and contemplated her plump and dead to him in their bed with such fear that he eventually poked her awake and back to him. There were also the times to be suffered alone. As he plastered a ceiling next door or mended a brick wall down the street or waxed the floor around the corner an especially

111

beautiful posture of hers, a secret caress or taste, would come to him and suddenly his breath would falter, his legs would ache and, making one feeble excuse or another, he would run home to wait through the thirty-six hundred seconds of an hour for her when, at each tick of the clock, the police threatened to come to claim him first.

Ernst decided that he would like to give Sally a gift, so he took a photograph of her to an Australian painter who had exhibited a picture of a girl with a dog on her lap in the Hampstead Open Air Exhibition and, after some haggling, the Australian agreed to take the commission, his first, for twenty-five guineas. For ten days Ernst watched the man in his studio each afternoon, complaining, disputing the choice of colours, and criticising where the likeness was untrue. They quarrelled over the frame. The Australian wanted another ten guineas for it, but Ernst, who was not satisfied with the likeness anyway, refused to pay a penny more. Not only that, but he insisted that the Australian paint a bowl of roses in the right hand corner which, otherwise, was sort of empty. A bowl of roses, the Australian said, would destroy the portrait's balance, but Ernst came up with another five guineas and in it went. The next afternoon Ernst took the picture home and hung it above the bed before Sally came home from school.

The picture was so bad as to be beyond criticism. But Sally guessed correctly that this was the first time Ernst had ever given anyone a gift.

'It's beautiful, darling. Absolutely beautiful.'

'You are being kind.'

'Really, darling, I think it's superb.'

Ernst jumped up on the bed. 'The likeness could be better, but the eyes, I think, are very good. We can give it back if you don't like it. I don't care.'

She wouldn't hear of giving it back. That's what she told him.

When Ernst came back, about an hour after he had walked out on her, Sally was sitting up in bed addressing a letter.

112

Ernst had returned resolved to tell her the truth about Nicky. But as soon as he came in she rushed into his arms, she hugged him, she kissed him, and murmured words of endearment. 'You must never walk out on me like that again,' she said. 'I thought you'd never come back.'

Ernst sat down wearily on the bed. 'That might be best,' he said.

'I've written to my father about you. A letter a mile long. I told him that you asked me to marry you.'

'But I haven't.'

'I was anticipating.'

'Anticipating?'

'It means looking forward to. Aren't you going to marry me?'

'Yeah. Sure.'

'We'll get married,' she said, 'and go back to Montreal.'

That would mean applying for papers, he thought. If he applied for papers they would learn that he was here illegally.

They might also find out about Nicky. There must be a police record.

'Your father,' he said, 'would not be pleased.'

'All right,' she said. 'We don't have to go back. We can stay right here.'

'Yes,' he said heavily, 'we can stay here.' Then, to her astonishment, he turned on her savagely. 'If you see a dead man on the street in your Canada then you stop, a crowd collects, the police are called, but where I come from you hurry on. You don't dare look.'

'Ernst, Ernst, love. All that is past. Why must you—'

'Your people will hate me before they have even met me.'

'We don't have to go back. I told you that. As long as we're together.'

'Stay here?'

'Yes.'

Sure, he thought. Stay here. With Norman downstairs.

'We're in love, Ernst. The others can go to hell.'

'Lots of people are in love. So what?'

113

'The others can go to hell.'

'You are a child.'

'They can go to hell, I said. The others can go to hell.' Then, in a calmer voice, she added. 'We're in love. Isn't that something fine?'

'We are in love,' he said wearily.

'Yes.'

'My father wanders from zone to zone. He will not stop until the day he dies.'

'We will take him with us.'

'Yes,' he said, 'and my mother too. I think she is with a British sergeant now. He is from Blackpool.'

'And the sergeant from Blackpool.'

'Yes,' he said, 'and we'll take my Uncle Hans too. He's an idiot, Hans is. The war lasted too long for him.'

'We'll take him with us.'

'And the children,' he said. 'We must bring the children. We'll turn them loose in the fields. There'll be no youth movement or self-criticism notebooks. Just jam-trees and carrot sticks. Carrots are excellent for children.'

'*Excellent* for children? That's the beginning, isn't it?'

'You're right, darling, no carrots. But where,' he said, 'where are we all going?'

Sally made no reply.

'Where?'

She thought hard.

'It doesn't matter,' she said, 'as long as you're there.'

'As long as we're together.'

'That's it.'

'We can even stay right here,' he said cynically.

'Yes,' she said, 'if you like.'

Ernst rose hastily and was sick in the sink. Sally held his head. He was sick twice more. She made him tea.

'What is it?' she asked.

'I may have to leave you.'

'Leave me,' she said. 'What have I done to hurt you?'

Ernst rose once more. Sweat broke from every pore, then the shaking came. He tumbled on to the bed and brought his knees up to his chin and hugged himself tight. Sally held his cold shaking body close. 'Shall I call a doctor?' she asked.

'A minute,' he said. 'I'll be O.K. . . .'

An hour passed before he quietened down again.

'There is something . . . something I should tell you . . .'

'Not now,' she said. 'Tomorrow.'

She made more tea. 'Come,' she said. 'I'll brush your hair.'

'I hate myself,' Ernst said vehemently. 'Oh if you only knew how much I hate myself.'

'Sleep,' she said. 'Please sleep.'

Sally woke again at three a.m. when Ernst let out a wild scream. He had had a bad dream, he said. He was feverish with a tendency to tremble, but he gradually quietened down again. He fell asleep with his head on Sally's breast.

VIII

When he woke the morning after Winkleman's party Norman remembered enough to be deeply embarrassed. He phoned Bella and wrote letters of apology to Horton and Graves. Bella was happy to forget the whole incident, but neither of the men replied to his letters.

Norman was concerned. Although he hadn't been a party member for several years he remained a Marxist yet. This gave him the benefit of a code, a system of responses, that was of singular value to him. Helping Ernst was contrary to that code. For the first time Norman began to feel the sands shift under him.

I'm getting involved, Norman thought, and for what? Ernst is possibly everything Horton says he is. Sally will never be mine.

Sally, he thought.

The day after the party Sally and Ernst invited Norman to their room for dinner. He ate with them three more times within ten days. That week Norman was working very hard putting the finishing touches to Charlie's film script – *All About Mary* – but he was curious, glad for the diversion, and so he accepted their invitations. At first it was painful for him to see Sally and Ernst obviously making a go of it when he wanted her so much himself, but he reluctantly came to accept his position as a fellow conspirator. To begin with Ernst appeared to be uneasy in Norman's company. He hardly ever spoke. But two weeks after the party he began to relax more.

One evening after the three of them had had far too much to drink Ernst picked up his guitar and, without being asked, sang for Norman. He had a remarkable voice. Norman, taken by surprise, demanded more and more songs and Ernst obliged with enthusiasm. Norman went out for another bottle of whisky and when he returned Sally made up outrageously and came through with some hilariously shameful dances. When Karp's other tenants began to complain about the racket they were welcomed into the party. Even Karp himself, when he finally appeared at one a.m. failed to inject his customary chill into the gathering. He sang naughty German music hall songs using his cane nattily. Mr O'Brien, an otherwise dour water-works clerk, enriched the party with his repertoire of filthy limericks. Miss Kennedy, her hair in curlers, danced the Charleston with Norman. Sally sat on Mr O'Brien's lap. But Ernst, a guitar on his lap and his back to the wall, was the soul of the party. He sang again and again.

Before going, Norman took him aside. He told Ernst about the wood in the cupboard of his flat, reminded him of his offer, and asked if he would build him a bookcase.

'I'll go first thing tomorrow morning,' Ernst said.

But alone with Sally again, rejecting her tired happy smile and her embrace, he felt as though he had been judged. You'll come to hate me, he thought. Both of you will come to hate me.

'You sentimental people,' Ernst shouted. 'You make me sick.'

IX

Early the next morning, Ernst, saw and tool kit in his hand, left for Norman's Kensington Church Street flat. He was exhausted; he'd had enough. He decided as he had before, to tell Sally the truth about Nicky when he got home. This time, though, he would go through with it. No matter what.

Sally stood on a chair and emptied the wardrobe. Clothes, old magazines, socks, suitcases, were dumped on the bed. When she reached the top Sally came across Ernst's torn little black suitcase. She clutched it to her bosom affectionately. This, she remembered, had been his only possession when he had first come to stay.

Karp loomed smiling and obese in the doorway. 'What goes on here?' he asked.

'Spring clean-up.'

'In September?' he asked.

'Come in, Mr Karp. I'll give you a cup of tea.'

Sally dumped the little black suitcase on the bed.

'That would be a pleasure,' Karp said, producing a little box of pastries.

Sunday morning tea had become something of a ritual for Karp and Sally. Karp came when Ernst was out and spoke to her of his flowers, the other tenants, and sometimes asked her advice on a choice of patterns for new wall paper. He was fond of Sally. Of his other new friend, Charlie Lawson, he was not fond. With Charlie he played the tease. He delighted in telling him dreadful stories about Norman, most of them fantasies, just to arouse him. Charlie he found an amusing fool. Sally was a comfort.

'Oh damn, I'm out of milk. Look,' she said, 'the milkman just passed. You wait here and I'll catch him.'

As soon as he heard the downstairs door slam Karp rose

and licked the cream off a chocolate eclair. He began to poke at things with his cane. The little black suitcase, he saw immediately, was of a German make.

X

Ernst missed Charlie. A half hour earlier Charlie had driven off to pick up Winkleman's two boys and, incidentally, a final copy of *All About Mary*. This morning Charlie was taking Winkleman's boys, Jeremy's little girl and Bob Landis's boy and girl out for a trip to the zoo.

Charlie was worried.

Even though he had work, taking into consideration that if *All About Mary* was produced he would get his first screen credit, he still felt that he was not accepted by the group on the same level, say, as Bob Landis. He and Joey were only invited to the big parties. Charlie would have given almost anything to be able to say that he had been invited to all the more intimate dinner parties, get-togethers, and at homes. That, he thought, was a measure of your success.

Joey was worried too.

Although Charlie hadn't enough cash for a second payment on his car, although Jeremy was far from pleased with Charlie's work and Cameo had yet to accept one of his scripts, he had gone and bought a television set, a record player, and a tape recorder: all on hire purchase. His bank manager wanted to see him on Tuesday morning about his overdraft.

Joey, looking forward to a morning alone, had laid out a pattern for an autumn suit on the rug and, a pair of scissors in her hand, she sat cross-legged on the floor in her black lace slip. When the door bell rang she cursed. Wasn't it just like Charlie to forget something? It was Ernst, tall and resolute. Joey brought her hand to her mouth and said, 'Oh!'

Norman had phoned earlier to say that Ernst was coming

and that he would be round for dinner himself, but she had forgotten. Ernst waited while she ran off and slipped into her pink, quilted dressing gown. Then he set down his saw and tool kit and took out his tape measure. 'Where are the boards?' he asked.

'In the cupboard. But wouldn't you like some coffee first?'

Ernst followed her into the kitchen and drank his coffee like a duty.

'Charlie's taken the kids out for the day,' she said. Then, annoyingly aware of the implications of what she had said, she added. 'Why didn't you bring Sally with you? We could have gossiped while you worked.'

'I didn't think of it.'

'Are you and Sally planning to get married?'

'Perhaps,' he said. 'We'll see.'

Joey stooped to refill his cup. 'That would be nice for you,' she said, 'wouldn't it?'

'I beg your pardon?'

'Marrying Sally. You could go to Canada if you married her.'

When Joey joined him in the living room a minute later he did not look up. 'Am I intruding?' she asked sarcastically.

'Would you mind if I cleared the floor. I have to saw.'

Joey cleared the rug hastily. 'I'd better spread paper on the rug before you start,' she said.

'If you don't mind.'

Once he had begun to saw Joey sat down to sew in a chair by the window. Much as she tried to avoid it her gaze kept returning to the young, muscular body bent so purposefully over the boards.

'Norman is very good to you, isn't he?'

Ernst nodded.

'I hope you appreciate all he's done for you.'

'What do you mean?'

'He's alienated a lot of his friends for your sake.'

'Alienated?'

119

'A lot of people have turned against him because he hit Mr Horton.'

'I didn't ask him to hit Horton.'

Every time he looked up at her he was confronted with a lip of black lace and a pair of crossed slender legs.

'Have you built many bookcases before?'

'No.'

'Do you like building bookcases?'

'It's a job.'

'But you're something of a carpenter?'

No answer.

'Would you rather I left the room?' she asked.

Ernst ceased sawing in mid-stroke. His shirt was soaked in sweat. 'Do as you like,' he said, 'It's your flat.'

Joey's brown bony face hardened. 'Mr Lawson is a damned good carpenter. He would have built the bookcase for nothing. But Norman insisted on you.'

Ernst returned to his work sullenly.

'I didn't mean that as an insult,' she said.

'I ain't insulted.'

'I was just trying to illustrate how eager Norman is to help you.'

Once he was through with the boards Ernst reluctantly asked Joey if she would hold up one end of the tape measure while he checked the wall measurements. Their bodies touched once or twice before the work was done.

'Why don't you take a break,' Joey said. 'I'll get more coffee.'

When she came in with more coffee Joey sat down on the sofa and held out a cup to Ernst. He sat down beside her.

'You're a quiet one,' Joey said.

No reply.

'*Aren't you?*'

'What is there to talk about?'

'Norman was really so sweet on Sally – before you showed up, I mean – that we rather thought they might marry.'

120

Ernst cleared his throat. 'I'd better clear up the mess,' he said.

'Norman must be fifteen years older than Sally. They never would have been happy together.'

Ernst tried to get up, but Joey pulled him back on the sofa. 'Finish your coffee,' she said.

Joey wanted him to make a pass. She would have liked Ernst to give her cause to slap him.

Ernst showed her his empty cup. 'I'm finished,' he said.

'Oh, go ahead. Get back to work.'

Ernst noticed the script lying on Charlie's desk. 'That's a very funny story,' he said.

The only script on the desk was an early copy of *All About Mary*. 'How do you know?' Joey asked.

'Norman let me look at it.'

'I didn't know that Norman had a copy.'

'I don't understand you. Norman wrote it.'

'Wrote *All About Mary*? Don't be stupid. This just so happens to be a script by Mr Lawson.'

'You are mistaken. I know Norman wrote this script.'

Joey laughed at him.

'He took a finished copy to Mr Winkleman this morning,' Ernst said. 'I know.'

All at once everything became agonisingly clear to Joey. Norman was 'the hack' who had been called in to touch up the script here and there. The day he left for Paris he asked Charlie not to tell Winkleman that he was going away, because Winkleman would not commit himself to anything as long as Norman was gone. Norman was the reason for Charlie's 'success' in London.

'You're lying,' she said.

Ernst guessed that he had been indiscreet. 'I could be mistaken. Come to think of it Norman's script had a different title.'

But Joey was not prepared to accept a kindness from a boy like Ernst. 'Are you finished?' she asked.

'I have hardly started. I would like to come back after lunch.'

121

'Nobody will be here after lunch.'

'Couldn't you give me a key?'

'No.'

'I wouldn't steal anything.'

'How much do I owe you?' Joey asked sharply.

The room that swirled around her no longer held Ernst. She saw the car unpaid for, the television set, the record player, the bank manager who would have to be faced. She saw Charlie broken.

'Nothing,' Ernst said.

'Will a pound do?'

'You owe me nothing.'

'I'll give you two pounds; no more.'

'I'm doing this for Norman. I don't want any money.'

'Look here, we happen to be the present occupants of this flat. Not Norman Price. *I* can do without his charity.' She squeezed two one pound notes together. 'Here.'

'Is it O.K. if I leave my tools here?'

'Take the money!' She threw the money at his feet as Ernst bent over his tool kit. 'Take it you little Nazi bastard!'

Ernst placed his things by the door, the money he left where it was. 'Have you a broom?' he asked. 'I will sweep up.'

'*I'll* sweep up.'

Ernst shook his head sadly.

'Get out,' Joey said.

'Why do you hate me?'

'Please go.'

'Tell me what I've done to you first.'

'GET OUT, PLEASE!'

Joey crumpled up on the sofa, but no tears came. Remembrance came.

An hour passed before the phone rang. Rang and rang. She picked up the receiver wearily. 'Hello,' she said.

'Hullo, darling. All alone?'

Bob's joke was smeared with purpose.

'Yes,' she said, 'I certainly am.'

He had to get a script out in a hurry, he said, and he

wanted to know if she could come right over and type it for him.

'Oh, Bob, you're such a child. Won't you ever give up?'

No answer.

'Bob, Bob, what's going to happen to me? I can't bear to see other people happy.'

'Come over,' he said. 'We'll talk about it.'

XI

Stout, red-haired Sonny Winkleman, his desk spreading like a shield before him, put aside his blue-bound copy of *All About Mary* and smiled as Bella entered the room. 'I thought it was Norm,' he said, his smile lapsing. 'O.K. Shoot.'

The Winklemans had a rule. Bella never interfered with business. But they both knew that she was going to upset that rule now, which upset Bella even more than it did Sonny.

'I want you to be gentle with Norman,' she said.

It was only because of her that he had used to give old, has-been actors work in his films. The last one had turned informer. 'Sure,' he said, 'I'll be nice.'

The doorbell rang. 'That must be him,' she said.

'Maybe it's Lord Moustache and Sir Mild & Bitter.'

It was a private joke. An old one. For Winkleman had a permanent residence and the men from the Home Office didn't call any more. But the joke worked. Bella leaned over and kissed him on the cheek before she went to answer the door.

Norman came in. 'Are we going to sit in the office?' he asked.

'Business,' Sonny said uneasily, 'is business.'

Business, however, was usually conducted much more informally.

'O.K., Sonny. The office it is.'

It suddenly struck Norman that he hadn't been invited to the Winklemans' for dinner or a party ever since the incident with Horton.

'Last week,' Norman began with a smile, 'a complete stranger came up to me at a party and warned me to keep an eye open for a chap named Price. This Price, he said, was mentally unstable, he had beaten up Colin Horton, and was rumoured to be an FBI informer.'

But Sonny didn't even smile.

'I haven't seen Horton around since your party,' Norman said. 'What's become of him?'

'He's gone to Rumania for a youth conference.'

'Youth conference. He must be forty-five.'

'All right,' Sonny said sharply, 'but I'll bet he'll talk a lot more sense than the kids there.'

'But a *youth* con—'

'Maybe he's a chaperon,' Sonny frowned. He seemed anxious to repudiate his joke. 'Horton's a brilliant man. He's had a fine education.'

Sonny had first been drawn to Norman because he had once been a professor. Horton he admired because he wrote incomprehensible articles like '*The Error of the Historical-Relativists*' for Marxist journals which Sonny, and others like him, did a lot to subsidise. It hurt Norman to think that Sonny had probably been touched for a tidy sum before Horton had left for Rumania.

'Well, Sonny, what about the script?'

'You've done a first-class job as usual Norm. Charlie was in earlier to pick up the kids. I gave him a copy of the script to take home.'

'You didn't tell him that I worked on it.'

'Of course not.' Sonny scratched his head. 'Look Norm, I've made a deal with Graves. We've got an excellent property; a book. Graves has been able to bring in a big chunk of New York money. Would you be interested in working on the script?'

'What's the book?'

124

'We'll come to that.'

Winkleman, Graves, and the other *emigré* producers spent a good deal of their time in the public libraries reading books – books that were in the public domain – but nevertheless books and not synopses for the first time in their lives. They were as secretive about their reading lists as uranium prospectors are about their trips out of town.

'Come on, Sonny, you can trust me.'

'There's a rumour going around – and please don't ask me where or how I heard it – that you told Charlie you never would have given up fifteen hundred a week for friends and ideas you didn't believe in any more. Is that true?'

'Not quite,' Norman said, startled. 'What I told Charlie is that it was certainly a lot to ask of a guy.'

'O.K.,' Sonny said, 'so now I've got your version of the story.'

'Somebody's been twisting my words. What in the hell's going on, Sonny?'

Sonny cracked his knuckles. 'You were seen coming out of Canada House three days ago,' he said timidly.

Norman guffawed. 'Jesus,' he said, 'did you think I was filing my report with the RCMP?'

'Nobody said anything like that.'

'What are you saying, then?'

'Look Norm, these are crazy times.'

'Yeah,' Norman said. 'Tell me about them.'

Sonny flushed. He knew that Norman had left the University because he wouldn't say whether or not he was a communist. That was the story anyway.

'Take Graves, for instance. He worked in association with a guy for *fifteen years*. They were like brothers. Then one morning Graves wakes up and sees in the paper that his partner has named him as a Red. Jeremy, Plotnick – all of us – have had somewhat similar experiences,' Sonny took a deep breath. 'What were you doing at Canada House?'

'Getting my monthly pay cheque.'

'Ho, ho, ho.'

'It's the truth,' Norman said. 'It so happens that I get a monthly pension from the RCAF. Since I move around so much I have it mailed to me care of Canada House.'

But even as Sonny breathed easier Norman added:

'That wasn't why I was there, though.'

'Oi.'

'I'm not telling you why I was there. It's none of your business.'

'How come,' Sonny asked, 'you're seeing so much of that little Nazi punk?'

'That's my business.'

'Not when you go around hitting people like Horton, it isn't.'

'Is that why I'm not invited here any more?'

'People are talking,' Sonny said more meekly. 'They're saying things about you.'

'I'm not trusted any more.'

'No.'

'Do you trust me, Sonny?'

'Forgetting that this Ernie stinker is a former Hitler Youth, overlooking the fact that he probably fled the East because he was wanted for rape or worse, how come you're so anxious to help the kid who stole your girl? It's not normal.'

Norman stood up. Sonny rose hastily and blocked his way to the door. 'I'm sorry,' Sonny said. 'I forgot myself.'

'You certainly did.'

'I said I'm sorry.'

Norman sat down again. 'She loves Ernst. There's nothing I can do to change that. I'd like to see her happy.'

Sonny spoke in a calmer, softer voice.

'Look, Norm, in this world you've got to make a choice of enemies or you just can't live. The boy stands for everything you and I are against. Haven't we suffered enough for our beliefs without bending over ass-backwards to help the other side?'

'I don't want to discuss Ernst here,' Norman said. 'What

126

about your book? Do you want to work on the script?'

'*I* do. Certainly *I* do. But Budd Graves—'

'You mean you don't want Graves to know I'm working on it?'

'Does Charlie know that you worked on *this* one?'

'If, I'm going to write a picture for you and Graves then Graves has got to know. Understand?'

'Be reasonable, Norm. *I* trust you. It's only that Budd is bringing in the backing and that because of his unfortunate experience with this guy he worked with for fifteen years he—'

But Norman was on his feet again. 'Get Charlie to write your script,' he said. 'Still better why don't you get Horton?'

Norman slammed the door and hurried out of Winkleman's house. Bella pursued him down the street. 'Norman,' she called. 'Norman.'

He stopped. 'Yes, sweetie.'

'What happened?'

'I've just been blacklisted,' he said, walking away again.

'Wait,' Bella said. 'Don't go away like this, Norman.'

He walked back to her.

'Don't be too hard on Sonny,' she said. 'He could have been in charge of production at a big Hollywood studio today, but he refused to give them names. He gave up everything, Norman – everything – all for a principle.'

'Yeah,' Norman said. 'I know. But would you mind telling me what that principle was?'

'Freedom of speech. Freedom to believe in what you like.'

'From where I stand it looks like his principle is the same as theirs. Freedom for Winkleman to speak. Freedom for Winkleman to believe what he likes. I'm beginning to see for the first time that the argument was not one of principle but of power. Right now they're inside and Sonny's out.' He hesitated. 'I'm sorry, sweetie!'

'All right,' she said in a fury, 'be an intellectual. All I know is that my husband has given up more than you'll ever have to give. *All for a principle.*'

'You're a very silly woman,' Norman said. Then, embarrassed, Norman turned away from Bella, walking towards Swiss Cottage. The sands began to shift under him again. Soon he thought, I will no longer know where I stand. Or how to stand, he added, turning the corner.

Bella found Sonny in the living room. A slumping, disconsolate man with a head of shaggy red hair and a wart the size of a dime on his neck and a stiff drink of whisky in his hand. In all their twenty years of marriage Sonny, despite his tall talk, had never been unfaithful to her. He had laid his money aside for her and the children. For as long as she had known him, he had never raised his hand to anyone. He had a reputation for being a hard, shrewd dealer – that was true – but otherwise he never would have survived. Sonny had given more money to the Spanish Aid Fund. He had sat on platforms. His name had appeared on innumerable letterheads.

Bella came up softly behind him and kissed his head. Sonny started. 'O.K.,' he said miserably, I'm a stinker. Maybe Norman should be trusted. Probably the talk is all crap. But why did he have to hit Horton? Tell me that?'

'You're not a stinker,' Bella said. 'Norman is a fool.' A principled, cold-hearted fool, she thought, who thinks he's too good for us. She saw Norman in the guise of an intruder, a threat to the whole structure of their happiness, for the first time. 'He thinks that just because he's been to Cambridge and all . . . You're good, Sonny. Don't feel badly about what's happened.'

She hadn't failed him, for that he was grateful, but somehow this only served to heighten Sonny's resentment. Norman had got the better of him, he wasn't sure how or why, but that Sonny would never forgive him.

'Horton's forty-five if he's a day,' Sonny said. 'Why in the hell does he have to go to youth conferences?'

128

Bella went into the kitchen to see about lunch for her family.

XII

When Ernst got home around one o'clock his little black suitcase lay open on the bed. Nicky Singleton's army identity papers were on the table. Sally was waiting.

'Sit down, Ernst. I want to ask you something.'

Ernst sat down on the bed.

'Why did you tell me that Norman could never be your friend after we came home from the party at Winkleman's?'

'Don't ask me questions like that. I have been questioned like that too many times before.'

But her questions were not meant to be answered. She spoke out of a miasmal haze.

'Why were you so ill that night?'

'Don't make me hate you,' he said. 'Come to the point.'

'Did you kill Nicky Singleton?'

'Would you like to hear the story from the beginning?'

'You killed him. Why didn't you tell me before?'

'I tried. You wouldn't listen.'

'You couldn't have tried very hard, then.'

'I told you that I had killed.'

'Yes. But those were like stories. I didn't know them.'

'I see,' he said, 'it's only wrong to kill somebody *you* know.'

'That's not what I meant.'

Ernst squeezed his hands together. He stared at her.

'I was going to tell you the whole story this afternoon anyway.'

'Do you expect me to believe that?'

'No,' he said, 'of course not.' He leaped up. 'Open your eyes, damn you, when I was thirteen I was already a soldier. What were your problems at that age?'

Sally began to whimper.

'Will you let me tell you how it happened?'

'You killed him. The story doesn't matter . . . and Norman,' she said suddenly, 'how could you – Oh, Ernst, Ernst, Ernst.'

'You,' he shouted, 'you haven't even been born yet. What right have you got to judge me?'

'There's still such a thing as right and wrong, you know.'

'Don't make me laugh.'

'Laugh,' she said. 'Laugh?'

'A brother and sister in Munich distributed pamphlets against Hitler during the war. They were shot as traitors. After the war they were resurrected as heroes. Today they are traitors again.'

'I'm not listening.'

'When your Ike came into Germany and saw the camps he said we shall never forget this. Ten years later the same Ike said—'

'I don't care,' she said, 'I don't hear a word.'

'There is no right or wrong. There are conditions, rewards, punishments, and sides, but that's all.'

Sally, her voice unnaturally thick, asked: 'Are there many like you?'

'Many.'

'You're perverse, Ernst.'

'Oh, am I? What about you?'

She didn't answer.

'You are not crying because I killed. You are crying because I killed Norman's brother.'

'Will you please, please, please shut up!'

'You are no better than me, Sally, but you have had more privileges.'

'No, Ernst. If circumstances meant that much there would be no sense in living.'

'Is there?'

Sally glared at him, like one insulted. 'I can't take any more just now,' she said. 'I'm going out for a walk.'

'O.K.,' he said. 'I understand.'

'What do you understand?'

'You've had enough. The game is up. I'll be gone when you get back.'

'He understands.' She slipped into her mackintosh. 'Perhaps I'm privileged. Maybe I'm still unborn . . . Possibly you're right about everything . . . But I'm trapped, you see. There is no game. I can't love you on and off. But, listen here, don't you run away either. I expect you to be here when I get back.'

XIII

Charlie came home early that afternoon and found a note on the kitchen table:

'Can't make it for lunch. Sorry. But Bob L. called and asked me to do a rush type job for him as a favour. Please don't forget to buy salad. N. coming for dinner at 7. Will be back 6 latest.

J.'

Charlie sat down in the living room, within reach of the phone, and poured himself a glass of beer. The least Ernst could have done, he thought, was to sweep up after he had finished work. He would have to speak to Norman about that.

When Charlie had gone to see Sonny there had been no trouble – and trouble is what Charlie anticipated – but, instead, a blue-bound copy of *All About Mary*. The hack, the other slob on the script, had completed his job. Sonny told him that a deal was being set up with a British studio and Charlie was going to get the sole film credit, more money when the film went into production, and a percentage of the producer's profits. I'm on my way, Charlie thought. He opened another bottle of beer and began to read the revised script Sonny had given him. The changes that had been made astonished him.

XIV

Sally walked.

It was a fine autumn day. Haverstock Hill was loud with Sunday afternoon strollers. Time out this way, reprieve, two hours liberty from the bed-sitters. Tomorrow the battle; this afternoon the sun was a fact. There was the Heath, Tynan's column to read, and always the possibility that somebody might offer you a drive. Next week was plenty of time to start looking for a room where one could have guests after eleven. This evening at the Duke of York Beasley might turn up with the fiver he owed you. Later, if you were lucky, you might bring back a girl for tea and chocolate digestives.

Sally joined the crowd working up the hill to Hampstead Heath. There were corduroy boys with girls nicer than candies. A bearded man with a red fez spoke against Christ in front of Mence Smith's. Young-marrieds pushed prams before them. Thick, square Eastern Jews passed in groups of five and three. At every other corner a poky little man watched over a wide sweep of Sunday papers. Gilbert Harding will, for just a thru'pence, tell you the most embarrassing incident of his life. Hitler's valet reveals all for the same price. So will Sabrina. At the next corner a West Indian in a shapeless fedora knelt tenderly over his little girl and gave her a lick of vanilla ice-cream under an arrow which said: 'To Keats' House'.

Sally stopped off at the Duke of York and ordered a whisky and soda. Ordinarily she and Ernst avoided this pub because of the people who gathered there, but today Sally found the crowd reassuringly gay. She watched one group in particular, pretending to be one of them. There was a high man with a chalky British face and a silk scarf knotted round his neck who Sally was sure had contributed at least one poem to *Time and Tide*. He was talking to a girl who wore her hair in a pony-tail. Wendy was her name, and she had turned in a bloody good performance on I.T.V. last night. There were three others in the group. A squat red-faced bore, who, had he been Canadian would have been put down for an insurance salesman, but, being British, had probably won the M.C. for his part in organising the partisans in lower Albania. The third man had obviously cultivated his Oxford stammer like a garden. The other girl, who had warned Dylan repeatedly that drink would be the end of him, was a spare blonde in toreador pants. All five pretended to abhor the pub and the people who frequented it. They gathered there, because like everyone else there, they found it droll to watch the others.

Sally squeezed out of the pub and continued up to the Heath. She felt numb. Something was dying inside her. A hope, perhaps, or a child's faith in the impossible. She watched for almost an hour as a man sailed an exact replica of the *Queen Mary* through the gales and lesser traffic of Hampstead Pond while his chauffeur leaned against the waiting Rolls Royce. The man, who sat on a canvas stool by the shore of the pond, controlled his ship by an electronic box. He often brought the Queen perilously close to the concrete shores before he made her turn sharply to the oohs and ahs of an apprehensive audience. Before long he shamed the adult owners of punier craft away from his sea. When Sally turned to go only the children's sailboats were left to dispute with the *Queen Mary*.

She descended into the Heath proper and counted all the boys with scarves and all the girls who wore glasses. She subtracted one sum from another, multiplied them by three and divided the new sum by two, and then she sank to the grass and wept long and bitterly. When she woke the first evening star was out. Walking down Haverstock Hill again she didn't realise that her eyes were red and that many of the passers-by, particularly the older ones, eyed her with a not unkind concern. Running out on him, she thought, was a cowardly thing to do. Her steps quickened. But outside the house she experienced a moment's grief. She could hear Norman typing. Sally lowered her head and tip-toed past his door. Her room was empty. The little black suitcase was gone.

'Ernst!'

Sally rushed out into the hall.

'Ernst!'

Norman came out of his room.

'Ernst! No. No, Ernst!'

Norman caught her as she began to sway and dragged her back to her bed. He slapped her cheeks. Gradually she came to.

'Are you all right?' he asked.

'Yes,' she said. 'Please don't make a fuss.'

He brushed back her streaky blonde hair from her forehead. Sitting so close to her, longing to take her in his arms, he recalled once more, the evening he had told her about Hornstein. 'This is Europe,' she had said. 'I want things to happen to me here that could never happen to me at home.' Yet again the phone robbed him of her embrace. 'A telegram came for you,' Joey had said. Nicky, he thought. Nicky.

'I had a quarrel with Ernst,' Sally said, 'that's all . . . He stormed out of the house.'

'I'm supposed to go to the Lawsons' for dinner. But I can stay with you, if you like.'

He came with gifts, Sally remembered, and a month in Spain had aged him so much. Norman was even greyer now. Nicky's death, she thought, that's what did it to him. And me, perhaps.

'Norman, I . . . I don't . . .'

He kissed her tenderly, soothingly, and then – unable to restrain himself – sympathy widened into passion. A hand on her breast, his other arm tight around her waist. Norman kissed her long and fierce. Sally succumbed. She responded with heat, and then remembering, alarmed, and even a little hysterical, she broke free of him. 'Norman,' she whispered. 'Please Norman. We mustn't.'

Norman withdrew, his embarrassment huge. 'I'm sorry,' he said. 'I didn't mean to . . . I'm sorry.'

'Norman,' she began, 'if you . . . if you did love me then why—' Her voice broke. 'Never mind.'

'No,' he said thickly. 'Go ahead.'

'Why didn't you write me from Spain? I was all alone in London. All alone, Norman. I had no idea how you—'

'I did write,' he said, 'but I tore up the letters.'

'But why?'

'I was so much older than you. It seemed unfair.'

'Norman, there's something—' Norman, she thought, only Norman could advise her, and he was the only one she couldn't turn to ' – never mind. I'll be all right. You'd better go,' she said. 'You'll be late for dinner.'

He hesitated at the door. 'I've got some good news for you,' he said. 'I meant to keep it a secret, but – look, I've been on to an old friend of mine at Canada House. He's going to see what he can do about getting Ernst into Canada.'

Sally tried to control her voice. 'Will there be some sort of check on him?' she asked.

'Oh, I told Atkinson he's here illegally. Everything's unofficial so far. Atkinson's O.K. He was in the RCAF with me.'

'But there will be a check?'

'The usual sort of thing, I expect. You're not worried, are you?'

'Of course not.'

'Would you like me to stay until Ernst gets back?'

'No, thanks. I think I'll try to sleep.'

XV

Ernst had begun to pack as soon as Sally left. He had only four pounds and some change, but his clothes were in good shape, his cough had all but disappeared, and his English was better than ever. He had planned to take the train to Liverpool, pick up a seaman, rob him of his papers, and sign on the first ship bound for Montreal. Later, perhaps, he would slip across the border to the United States.

Outside, Ernst was overcome by his old sense of purpose. Again he was watchful. Again he no longer had to account to anyone for his actions. Passing Collet's Bookshop on his way to the tube station he remembered that he had forgotten to pack his English-German dictionary. Let her keep it, he thought, I'm not a sentimentalist. But crossing to the tube station he found himself hoping that Sally would see him, that she would stop him, and take him home again. He ejected that thought from his mind like a splinter. That kind of life, he thought, is not for me. When he next recalled his interlude with Sally, this time as he got off the train at Liverpool Street Station, he was able to look on it as an adventure that had happened to someone else.

The black station was thick with sandpaper faces. Searching for a likely victim in the crowd Ernst sensed that the pockets of those about him would probably yield nothing more than crumpled betting slips and ten shilling notes carefully folded into wallets between mildewy photographs. So he took the train to Leicester Square. The West End, it seemed to him, would yield better pickings, but once loose on the streets again Ernst was immediately struck by the brutalised faces of the spivs and whores who worked the different corners. Berlin, London, Paris, it was all the same: squalor under the winking neon. These were his people. Night squeezed them like blackheads out of the face of the city. In spite of his fine clothes nobody bothered to proposition Ernst. He recognised them; they recognised him. Another week, two at the most, and he would be coughing again. One of these days his luck would break and, like the rest of them, he would do his stretch in prison. Soon, he thought, I may have another murder to account for. *Account for*, he thought, what's got into me? *Damn her*.

Ernst sat down to rest on a bench in Soho Square, his hands bunched in his pockets and his eyes moist with remembrance.

*

136

Charlie was just going to phone Sonny to tell him what he thought of the script when Norman arrived.

'I'm sorry,' Norman said. 'I think I'm a little early.'

'Come on in,' Charlie said. 'Joey should have been here ages ago.' He was still carrying the script. 'This is the last time I ever do business with Winkleman.' Charlie poured Norman a glass of beer. His round face reddened with anger. 'I give him the most exciting comedy he's seen in years. He puts it through the sausage machine and out it comes a hunk of crap. Wait till I get that bastard on the phone.'

'Don't phone him now,' Norman said.

'Sure, sure. Maybe I should wait until the damn thing gets produced with *my* name on it. That would be the end of me here.'

'Is it that bad?'

'I wouldn't even put Landis's name on it. More I can't say.'

'There's a lot of money in it. You can use the money.'

'Sure, sure. I can use the money.'

'If it's your name you're worried about why not use a pseudonym?'

'There's principle involved. *I* would know who wrote it.' Charlie stepped back from the phone. 'I know what you're thinking. I've never had a film script credit before. You think I'd be crazy to jeopardise the deal. Look, darling, a lot of guys think I'm a bust, but I've got my pride too, huh? If my name is going to go on a script I want it to be my script. Whichever of Winkleman's boys hacked this one up has changed my original so that nobody'd recognise it.'

'But nobody's seen your original. Nobody would know.'

Charlie half-shut one eye and beat his fist against the palm of his hand again and again. 'Of course, I could wait until the picture was made. If it was a success I could – I'm not that kind of worm. Sorry.' Charlie fixed that half-shut eye on Norman. 'Besides, you'd know . . . Sure, sure, I know.

Norman is the quiet one.' Charlie flipped through the script thoughtfully. 'It's not that bad, you know. It might go. I mean whoever hacked it up was a pro. All the imaginative work is mine, of course.' He rolled up the script and tapped Norman's shoulder with it. 'You know my trouble's always been that I've got too much vitality. My stuff overflows. Smaller guys, like you or Artie Miller' – Charlie laughed and winked – 'have better control.' He unrolled the script again, and read a page to himself. 'This hack, whoever he is, knows his stuff. Maybe he cut a bit too much here and there, but—' Charlie frowned – 'If it's a smash, though, wouldn't he want some credit too? I mean if after I let on that this was my script completely – and that's true, you know – it would be pretty embarrassing if this hack turned up and . . .'

'It's your script,' Norman said. 'You said so yourself.'

Charlie began to bang his fist into the palm of his hand again. 'What would you do? In my position, I mean.'

'You need the money.'

Charlie stood pensively by the window again. 'There are other things beside my pride. Joey, for instance. Maybe I should be practical for once.'

'I think so.'

'If you hadn't come in when you did I would have been on the phone to Winkleman already. Isn't that true?'

'Yes.'

'O.K. I'll do it. I'm grateful to you, too, for the idea.'

'Stop worrying,' Norman said. 'Where's Joey? I'm starved.'

Charlie outlined two plots and an idea for a comedy series to Norman. 'Hell,' he said, I've got all the faults of genius. I'm poor like O'Casey. I'm dirtier than Balzac. I'm just as crazy about women as Byron ever was. Why, I've even got piles as bad as Marx ever had them, so why am I so emotionally unsuccessful?'

Joey arrived before Norman could reply. 'Hiya,' she said, waving a bottle of whisky in the air. 'Hiya.'

'I guess you and Bob have been working pretty hard,' Charlie said coldly. 'You must be tired.'

Joey flopped into a chair and kicked off her shoes. 'Pour me a big one, lover,' she said to Norman. 'Pour yourself one too.' Then she turned to Charlie. 'Let's eat out tonight. Bob gave me a bonus for working late. I'm rolling.'

'I bought salad,' Charlie said. 'You left me a note asking me to buy salad.'

'We can eat salad tomorrow,' Joey said, 'for breakfast.'

'Big joke.'

'I think Joey's got a good idea,' Norman said. 'Let's eat out.'

'We're going to eat at home.'

'Home is where you hang yourself,' Joey said. 'That's one of Bob's jokes. I typed it three times.'

'Ha, ha, ha,' Charlie said.

'Charlie darling,' Joey seemed genuinely surprised. 'What is it?'

'The Winkleman deal went through. We're sure of a production. I also sold a half-hour to Cameo today.'

'Aren't you the big success,' Joey said ambiguously.

'I came rushing home to tell you and you weren't here. I had intended to start work on my play this afternoon. Instead I had to go out and do the shopping.'

'Not another word, I'm going to make dinner.'

'We can eat out,' Charlie said. 'We can celebrate.'

'Celebrate? No,' she said, 'we'll eat right here,' and turning to Norman she added, 'with our patron.'

Charlie had a lot to drink at dinner. Always a gifted story-teller tonight he really shone. Norman and Joey did not see a fat balding man with foxy brown eyes before them. Once more they were in New York. Once more the cold-water flat and the hack work were, as Charlie put it then, fodder for the sensational autobiography he would write afterwards, like Sean O'Casey. They had believed him at the time becaue he had been laughing at himself when he had given his letters catalogue numbers. But when younger men had begun to make their reputation the jokes had ceased and, instead, when somebody wrote a hit play Charlie had asked. 'How old is he?' Tonight, however, Charlie was happy and successful.

Norman, a little drunk himself, remembered the Charlie of the old days. Looking across the table he saw an angry young man shaking an empty Chase & Sanborn coffee tin, crudely labelled 'SPAIN', under the faces of first-nighters on Broadway, where someone younger than him had just opened with a smash.

'You're good, Charlie,' Norman said. 'Very good.'

Charlie wiped back his horseshoe of hair. 'I've just made a decision,' he said. 'No more hackery. First thing tomorrow I'm getting down to my play.'

'Wonderful,' Norman said.

'Wonderful. Sure, sure. You're convinced I'll never write it. You too, Joey. You don't think I've got the talent. You think Norman is more intelligent than I am.'

Norman rubbed the back of his neck uneasily.

'We've known each other for nearly twenty years now,' Charlie said, 'but we've yet to sit down and speak frankly. You wrote my wife love letters, but she preferred me to you. You've never forgiven me that. And you,' he said to Joey, 'you're probably sorry now. Take tonight, for instance. This will sound petty to you, I know, but it's pretty significant. Norman's steak was twice the size of mine. Go ahead, laugh. But you do that every time he comes here.'

'Please,' Joey said, her voice severe, 'let's not always make a spectacle of ourselves. If you—'

'Better this,' Charlie said, 'than scrabble.'

'—if you must have this out, Charlie, let's wait until we're alone.'

'Look here, Miss Daily Worker Bazaar of 1932, Norman isn't above patronising a little Nazi thug for the sake of a girl, so I'm sure he won't lose his virginity if he sits in on a quarrel which concerns him.'

'Charlie,' Norman said, precisely polite. 'if you don't stop this I'm going to get up and go. You won't see me again, either.'

140

'You're both afraid of the truth,' Charlie said, 'that's what.'

'Please, darling. We have more to thank Norman for than you know of.'

'And just what do you mean by that?'

Norman looked sharply at Joey.

'Nothing,' she said.

Charlie glared, he coughed and then suddenly he smiled widely and winked. 'I'm a choice son-of-a-bitch,' he said, 'aren't I? Trouble is I should have been a great artist. A big, primitive power, like Agatha Christie. Instead . . . ' He got up and filled their glasses. '*All About Mary,*' he said, 'is the most sensational property Winkleman ever mortgaged. Landis here, Landis there. I'm the guy who's putting Rinky-Dinky back on his feet as a producer here.'

'Let's talk about something else,' Joey said.

'Why? Aren't you pleased?'

'I'm thrilled,' Joey said coldly. 'Honestly darling.'

'Why that tone of voice, then?'

'Ask Norman.'

Norman's face darkened.

'Go ahead. Ask him.'

'Joey's making a joke,' Norman said, 'and it's not a very good one.'

'Well, she ought to be thrilled,' Charlie began meekly. 'I told her on the ship coming over, Norman. London is going to be lucky, I said. I had that feeling.'

They drank some more. Joey moved to the arm of Norman's chair and gradually, as though by accident, she slid on to his lap.

'There must be more comfortable—'

'Go ahead,' Charlie said with forced cheerfulness, 'help yourself.'

'Joey,' Norman said. 'Come on. You're not that drunk. Get up.'

'One morning I'll wake up and discover that Charlie's only interested in young girls. Like you.'

'Joey!'

141

'Don't "Joey" me, brother.'

Charlie laughed desperately. 'That would be a plot,' he said. 'That would make a fine half-hour. Friend of the family cuckolds the—'

'It's too corny,' Norman said sharply.

'The corny plots,' Joey said, 'always sell. Ask Charlie.'

Joey embraced Norman.

'Hey,' Charlie said, 'stop that. You're humiliating me.'

Joey held on to Norman with a frightening force.

'I know this is only a joke,' Charlie began, 'but . . .'

Norman struggled with Joey. She was unmovable.

'Hey,' Charlie said, 'hey . . .'

Charlie seized Joey by the arm and pulled her off Norman. Joey stumbled.

'Oh, I'm sorry,' Charlie said.

Joey banged against the wall and then sank like a wreck to the bottom of the room.

'I'm sorry.'

Charlie's face was coming undone.

'Ask Norman about the script.'

'What's going on here,' Charlie yelled. 'Will somebody please tell me what's going on?'

'I was the guy who worked on the script for Winkleman,' Norman said wearily.

'Winkleman told Bob Landis that he never would have bought your script if Norman hadn't promised to work on it. He overpaid you – that's exactly what Winkleman said – because of Norman.'

Stuck again and again by their bandilleras Charlie shook his head thickly, he glared, he coughed, but, even as the other two waited for his last long bellow, all he did was to sigh deeply.

'I want you to go, Norman,' he said in a small voice, 'and never come back here again.'

Charlie's pride, Joey thought – the fear bursting like a boil inside her – means more to him than I do. He never would have thrown Norman out because of *me*.'

'I want to die,' she said, 'I want to die.'

Charlie couldn't resist it. 'Go ahead and die,' he said.

Norman got up. His back ached where Joey's finger-nails had cut deeply.

'Now I know why you tried to talk me out of phoning Winkleman,' Charlie said. 'You betrayed me.'

'Your wife's forehead is cut. Why don't you attend to it?'

Charlie's laughter came out solid like a stone. 'I should have guessed that you were a bum,' he said, 'when you started running after Joey behind my back.'

'You should have, but you didn't.'

'Before I even knew that it was you who had worked on the script didn't I say that it had been ruined?'

'Joey's going to be sick in a minute. Get her into bed.'

'My friend Norman.'

Joey passed out.

'If you needed money so badly,' Charlie said, 'couldn't you have come to me instead of plotting with Winkleman behind my back?'

'She's fainted.'

'Keep your filthy hands off her.'

Norman put on his jacket.

'Just one thing before you go, Iago. Do you understand why you did it at least?'

'No. You tell me.'

'You wanted to belittle me before my wife,' Charlie applied his hand to his forehead like a poultice. 'I'm sending Winkleman his money back in the morning. It's your script. You take the credit and the money.'

'This is all a bad dream,' Norman said. 'I'll wake up and none of it will have happened.'

'Bring in the violins. Go ahead. Try to put me in the wrong.'

Joey began to groan.

'Jesus,' Norman said. '*Good night*.'

'Good night and goodbye.'

*

XVII

When Ernst got home around eleven that night Sally was still sitting up in bed. Her eyes were burnt dry, and she was pale. Ernst kissed her streaky blonde hair and then rested with his head on her lap. She kissed the scar on the back of his neck again and again. She lay with her hot cheek against his head. Ernst kissed her fingers one by one.

'Mrs Buller phoned. She wants you to build some book-cases. She asked if you could come round early Monday morning.'

'What did you say?'

'I said I thought you were free.'

'She's nice.'

'Mrs Buller? Isn't she the one who complained about your work?'

'No. That's Mrs Hellman.'

Norman was typing late. They could hear him.

'Tired?'

'Yeah. I'm tired.'

'Me too.'

He went to the window and took down the curtains. 'They're dirty,' he said. 'I think I'll wash them.'

The noise of the tap briefly drowned out the typewriter downstairs, but soon the rat-tat-tat was with them again. Ernst hung up the curtains to dry over the back of a chair.

'Are you hungry?'

'No,' he said. 'I ate.'

Norman's door slammed, but he had only gone to the toilet. The typing started up again.

'Play something on the guitar,' she said.

'What will we drown him out with tomorrow night,' he asked, 'the record player?' He sat down on a pillow with his guitar. 'I didn't intend to come back.'

'You're here. I'm glad you're here.'

'You are beautiful,' he said. 'I love you.'

'The world outside,' she said. 'Their world. It's not much

good.' She told him about the old man, and his electronically controlled ship. 'I went up to the Heath,' she said.

'I was in Soho. I looked at all the movie posters.'

'Oh, my darling love. Oh, my darling.'

'It's not fair to you, I shouldn't have come back.'

The typewriter stopped, stopped for five full minutes, and then began again.

'Tap on the floor,' she said.

'No.'

'He said we should do that any time he disturbed us.'

'No.'

'Go ahead. He won't mind.'

'NO.'

'I would have died if you hadn't come back.'

'I would like to tell you about it. I want you to know exactly how it happened.'

'No,' she said. 'Some other time.'

He told her that he had run away from the refugee camp at Sandbostel with the idea of robbing an American soldier of his identity papers and making his way to Paris. He had met three soldiers in a bar in Munich. One of them, a Jew had not liked him. The second he could hardly remember. The third had been Nicky. The trouble, he said, had started when the four of them had gone to the jazz cellar.

'I liked Nicky,' Ernst said, 'and I was looking for a way to show him how I felt. When the other boy – not the Jew – began to feel sick I took him down to the toilet with me. I took his wallet. But I wasn't stealing. I thought that I would return it to Nicky later and tell him that one of the whores in the cellar had stolen it from him. I thought it would make a good impression. But the Jew—'

'Don't keep saying the "Jew". The boy must have a name.'

'I forget it.'

'Call him Harry.'

'No. I'll call him Lester. That was more like it.'

'Anything, but not the "Jew".'

'O.K. But Lester found out about the wallet first. When I

145

returned it to Nicky later he didn't believe my story; he turned against me.'

He told her about the party, Nancy, and the room upstairs.

'I didn't want to fight with Nicky. I swear it. I just wanted to get out before the M.P.s came. But he wouldn't let me go. He came at me with a broken bottle in his hand. I didn't want to be scarred. I'm handsome, it is one of the few things I have, and I need it.' Ernst averted his eyes. 'So I took out my knife. He came at me like a madman and—'

'Never mind the details.'

'. . . afterwards I stole his identity papers. That's all. That's the whole story.'

Sally made no comment.

'Perhaps,' he said wearily, 'it would be best if I left.'

'No,' she said, 'I—'

'I would understand. Please don't try to make me stay if . . .'

'How can I let you go?'

Norman stopped typing. They heard him go out.

'I'll sleep on the floor tonight.'

She protested.

'Please,' he said, 'don't argue. It's just something I feel.'

'But – '

'The floor will be fine. I'll spread my coat under me.'

'All right,' she said. 'If you insist.'

Both of them were still awake when Norman returned about an hour later. He was quiet, he seemed to be walking on tip-toe, but they both heard him.

'Ernst, I just remembered something awful.'

Sally told him that Norman had been to Canada House. There would be a check on him, she said.

'We'll have to leave here,' Ernst said.

'We'll give Karp our notice tomorrow afternoon,' she said. 'As soon as I get home from work.'

'It has been a long day,' Ernst said.

They would have to flee to another country, Sally thought. They would have to hide. 'What?' she asked.

146

'It has been a long Sunday.'

Fugitives, she thought. 'Ernst,' she asked, 'do you remember our first day together?'

'Of course,' he said. 'I slept on the floor that night too.'

'Do you know why I asked you to stay?'

'No' he said.

'It was because of the way you came up from behind to kiss me when I was washing my blouse. I had never been kissed like that before.'

'Good night,' he said. 'I love you.'

'Good night, my darling.'

XVIII

With manifest skill Karp injected a ham with a hypodermic of brandy, massaged the ham's surface with honey, stuck cloves in here and there, and eased the pan into the oven. He hadn't had anything to eat all day; he was famished. Karp decided to begin his meal with an artichoke and to eat the ham with sweet potatoes and corn fritters. Following that, perhaps, he would have a chinese lettuce with lemon sauce and cheese cake and coffee. Karp washed his hands and rubbed them with cold cream. He slipped into his dressing gown and sat down in his living room with a glass of sherry. Then there came a loud knock at the door.

'I've been expecting you,' Karp said.

Ernst nodded. Sally managed a sour smile.

'Come,' he said, 'one should feel free to call on one's landlord at any time.'

They sat down uneasily as Karp filled their glasses.

'You must come to visit more often.' Karp directed his smile at Ernst. 'You ought to take better care of her. Only the other day I was saying to myself what a lovely creature Sally is.'

'Thank you.'

'I hope,' Karp said, 'that there has been no repetition of last night's fainting spell.'

Ernst looked surprised.

'Oh, I feel fine,' Sally said. 'Really I do.' She looked down at the thickly carpeted floor. 'We've come to give you our notice.'

'We've found a little flat for ourselves.'

'How come,' Karp asked, 'that you have the army identity papers of Nicolas Singleton?'

Ernst turned accusingly to Sally.

'He came in for tea while you were out yesterday morning. I ran out to get milk and he must have—'

'You see,' Karp said, 'when Norman heard of his death there were no details. We presumed that he had died on manoeuvres. An accident, perhaps . . . One minute. I'll be right with you.'

In the kitchen Karp opened the oven and ran a finger over the ham and licked the honey off it. He lowered the gas a fraction before he returned to the living room.

'It was foolish of you not to burn the papers,' Karp said, 'if you killed him.'

'I bought the identification papers from a dealer in Munich. That's how I happen to have them.'

'And is that,' Karp asked, 'why you are both planning to run away?'

'We have found a flat.'

'You know, of course, that Norman isn't well.' Karp leaned back and sighed. 'A very tricky business it is. Although he has not had an attack of amnesia for some time he is still not supposed to be exposed to over-excitement.' Karp rose. 'Excuse me.'

He poured a little more honey over the ham. It had begun to crackle. In the living room again he noticed that Ernst had moved his chair closer to Sally. They had been holding hands.

'When I first met Norman Price I was a hospital orderly. This house, everything, I owe it all to him. He has never asked for a favour in return.' Karp adjusted himself more

148

comfortably in his chair. 'What would you do in my position?'

'In your position,' Ernst began, 'I would have spoken to Norman immediately.'

'But he's sick,' Sally began. 'You said that over-excitement...'

'Supposing,' Karp said, 'I didn't tell him. Then what?'

'We would speak to him ourselves,' Sally said.

'Supposing one didn't believe you?'

'There's nothing we could do about that,' Ernst said.

'Frankly speaking,' Karp said to Sally, 'he is not the most trustworthy person in the world, is he?'

The aroma of baking ham filled the room sweetly.

'Why haven't you offered me money?' Karp asked. 'A person of my race, I mean. That, one would have thought, would have been your first move.'

'How much do you want?' Sally asked quickly.

'Don't be a fool,' Ernst said. 'He's making fun of us.'

'Am I?'

'How much *do* you want?'

'Why is it,' Karp asked, 'that people will believe anything of me – and my kind – and not,' he said, pointing at Ernst, 'of his?'

'Ernst had done you no harm.'

'Look at me,' Karp said, 'and what do you see?'

'Stop bugging her.'

'Potatoes! A short, fat Polish potato-eater. We're all marked with the same grey puffy face.' Karp laughed a deprecating laugh. 'Don't you think that I, too, would like to be tall and – and have a mistress as pretty as her?'

Sally shuddered. 'Aren't you a homosexual?' she said.

Karp smiled acidly at Ernst.

'I'm sorry,' Sally whispered.

'She doesn't care what you are. Neither do I.'

Karp spread out his hands and bounced the fingertips of one against the other. 'The young,' he said, 'how I despise the clumsy young people. 'I'll be rightback.' Opening the oven he saw that the ham was doing splendidly. He lowered

149

the gas and put the sweet potatoes in to bake. Then, after he had wiped each of his fingers individually, he returned to his guests. Ernst and Sally had risen from their chairs. 'Are you going?' he asked. 'So soon.'

'Sally is tired.'

'I upset her?'

'She's tired.'

'But Norman won't be here for another—'

'Are you going to tell him?' Sally asked.

Karp eased himself into his chair again and sipped his sherry pensively.

'Mr Karp, please . . . It wasn't Ernst's fault. Not exactly . . .'

'Where were you,' Karp asked Ernst, 'when I was in the camp?'

'His father was in a camp, too.'

'Certainly.'

'I was in the Hitler Youth.'

'Why didn't you run away before she found out,' Karp asked. 'Why didn't you spare her?'

'I love her.'

'So,' he said wearily, 'he loves you.'

'We love each other.'

'Is that funny? Sally asked. 'Do you find that so funny?'

'I won't tell Norman,' Karp said severely. 'Not tonight anyway. But don't you dare run away from here. If you run away I'll find you.'

They went back to their room and unpacked. Sally wept.

XIX

Joey came to see Norman later in the afternoon. 'If you let me in,' she said, 'I promise not to throw another tantrum.' She wore a tight green woollen dress. Her brown face was itchy with panic.

'Anything wrong?' Norman asked, taking her coat.

'It's Charlie. You must help me, Norman. I'm going crazy.'

'He sent me a post-dated cheque for two hundred pounds this morning,' Norman said, 'and a note saying that he didn't want his name to appear anywhere in the film credits. That's stupid, Joey. It's his money; he earned it. Will you take it back to him?'

'It's no use. He won't have it.'

'Are you broke?'

'Worse. But we've been broke before – Tell me the truth, Norman, do you think I've stood in his way all these years?'

'Is that what he says?'

'He's always supported my family, you know. It adds up to a hell of a lot.'

'You've been terrific for Charlie at any price. I mean that.'

Joey hastened to the window. 'He thinks I'm having an affair with you.' She looked up and down the street anxiously. 'I'm afraid he may have followed me here.'

'Easy.' Norman circled her waist and stroked her head gently. 'Charlie wouldn't do a thing like that.'

'Did you know that he meets with Karp now and then?' Joey asked.

'Karp?'

'Charlie didn't have to leave the States. He was still in the clear.'

'Let's take one thing at a time,' he said, leading her to a chair. 'Why is he seeing Karp?'

'They talk about you a lot. That's all I know.'

'Karp's condition is psychotic, Joey. He teases people the way a boy pokes at snakes with sticks. He's a kind of provocateur. I'm telling you this because it would appeal to Karp's malign sense of humour to abuse me to Charlie.'

Joey's laugh came out a catch, a stab, an ache at a time. 'I learn new things about you every day,' she said. 'I used to believe you were the one person who didn't give a damn what people said about you. Now, in your devious way, you're trying to tell me not to believe the horrible things Karp must be telling Charlie about you.'

'All right,' Norman said, annoyed, 'look at it this way. If Karp walked in right now he'd be quite capable of making all three of us feel that he had interrupted a seduction scene.'

Joey rushed to the window again. 'Please draw the curtains,' she said.

'Joey, sweetie, he's not following you.' Norman pulled on his jacket. 'Let's go to the pub.'

In the pub they were forced to stand very close together, her dress was very tight, and he found it increasingly difficult to concentrate on what she was saying.

'There was a time,' she said, 'when I believed in every one of Charlie's schemes. He was leaner then. And at twenty-one, I guess, you think that every hopeful is going to make it. There seems to be so much time.'

Norman looked down into his glass, but from there his gaze went, inevitably, to her wide capable hips, so he quickly looked up at her face again and smiled inanely.

'But I'm glad he never did,' Joey said. 'Because if Charlie had made it, Norman, he would have left me. Not that he isn't going to leave me anyway. Probably sooner than you think.'

'What are you talking about?'

'I'm the girl Charlie promised everything to. Don't you think he's got a heart? Last night he saw it all. He was never going to do any of the things he had always counted on. Do you think he wants me around for the rest of his life to remind him he's a failure?'

'Last night was an aberration. He'll be O.K. yet.'

Norman ordered two more whiskies and a bottle to take home with him.

'He's dying to have a child, poor man, and I'll never be able to give him one.'

'You could adopt one.'

'Damn it, Norman, why is it the bastards who always have the talent? Tell me that.'

152

'I remember,' Norman said, 'that when they were all drawing cheques from WPA, Charlie was the envied one. He could tell a story better than most of them.'

'Where will he go from London? There's no place left for him to go.'

'There are other things,' Norman said self-consciously.

'Not for him, there aren't.'

'What about you?'

'I don't matter.'

'Come on, Joey.'

But she was serious.

'I love him. In my own bitchy way I always have. I could forgive him for not ever making it, but that's just what he doesn't want.'

Norman paid for the bottle of whisky and they returned to his room.

'What will I do when he leaves me?'

'You're being morbid. He's never going to leave you.'

Joey sat down beside him on the bed. 'None of us have amounted to much,' she said, 'have we?'

Norman was hurt. 'I guess not,' he said.

Joey gave him the full benefit of her body in profile.

Norman coughed. 'We seem to belong to a world of broken promises and angers valued like valentines. A world that's done. But Ernst – you know – is struggling to be born. We came from an ordered world, Joey, and out of that order we made chaos, and out of that chaos came Ernst. So in a sense we're responsible for him. Or that's the way it seems to me anyway.'

'Are you in love with Sally?'

'Yes,' he said, 'I am.' But he was startled. He had not expected to say that.

Joey began to tremble. 'Norman. Oh, Norman.' He held her cold, shivering body close and stroked her hair. A knife-like sob cut through her. 'Oh Norman.' He led her to the bed, her body boneless, submissive, feverish, and pulled back the blankets and covered her. As she lay there sobbing brokenly he poured two stiff drinks and then, as an after-

153

thought, he drew the blinds. Joey whimpered. He kissed her cheeks. He took off her shoes and rubbed her ice-cold feet.

'What will I do if he leaves me, Norman?'

'He'll never leave you,' he said, handing her a drink.

'You say that because you think he's second-rate. You've never taken Charlie seriously, have you?'

'Of course I have.'

'A word of praise from you would mean so much to him, but you never mention his writing at all . . . Ernst seems to mean more to you than Charlie.'

Norman didn't reply.

'He works so hard at it,' Joey said. 'He's always leaving himself open to rejections and ridicule. He's not a coward like you. All these years working away on an academic biography the size of an insect. Polishing and polishing and polishing. Too frightened to expose it to the light of day.'

'I happen to enjoy working on it.'

'You're not dirty like Charlie. Your hands are clean,' she said, shivering.

'Would you like a hot drink?'

She shook her head.

'More blankets?'

'All his life Charlie had had to do with second-best. Like me.'

'Come off it, Joey,' he said, covering her with another blanket.

'Did I ever tell you how we met?'

'No.'

'I was working for—' she named an important left-wing magazine of the 'thirties '—when Johnny Rubick came back from Madrid.'

Rubick, who had talked to the committee since, was one of Hollywood's most gifted directors.

'He was working on his novel then – it was before you knew him – and all the girls in the office were after him. He was so glamorous, Norman, and – Charlie was writing for us too then and he was always asking me out, but I never had time for him. Not in those days. I – You see, I became Johnny's mistress. One of his *innumerable* mistresses I should say...'

She told him how after he had impregnated her, Johnny had told her not to worry, he had a friend who would fix her, and the two of them had gone to a cheap hotel with Johnny's friend, a disbarred doctor, and the job had been done there. But Joey shouldn't have gone to work the next day, that was her error.

'I bled badly...' Johnny, she discovered, had driven off to Mexico with an actress. He was gone. 'When Charlie looked up from his typewriter he saw that I'd fainted...'

Joey would always remember the young doctor with the bad teeth, who sucked the shell-frames of his glasses, as he told her that she would never be able to have children.

'And when I awoke, Norman, there was Charlie. He had been sitting with me for two days... When I woke in the public ward, wishing myself dead, Charlie was there holding my hand and smiling. He had come with flowers and a proof of his latest short story. He came, Norman, when nobody else would have me.'

'I'm sold,' Norman said. 'He's a great guy.'

'When the war came Charlie didn't become a P.R.O. like the rest of them. He could have had a soft job with the army shows, like Bob, or been attached to a film unit like so many others. But not Charlie. Old and flat-footed as he was it was still the infantry for him. Four years of it, Norman, with all those people offering him soft jobs.'

Norman bent over Joey and kissed her forehead.

'Help him,' she said. 'Tell him he's good. Coming from me it doesn't mean much to him. But from—'

'I'll try,' he said, smoothing down her hair. 'I'll try to help.'

The phone rang.

'Don't answer it,' Joey said.

'Joey,' he said, 'please'. He picked up the receiver, his smile reassuring.

'I know she's there,' Charlie said. 'Don't pretend.'

155

Norman was too stunned to reply.

'Tell her that if she's not home in fifteen minutes she needn't come home at all.'

Norman hung up. 'It was Charlie,' he said. 'He must have followed you here after all.'

Joey leaped out of bed, hurried into her coat and shoes, and left without a word.

XX

A little later Norman climbed the stairs to Karp's flat for dinner. Karp wasn't there. There was a huge ham, untouched, in the garbage pail. The kitchen reeked of burnt potatoes. In the living room Norman noticed the empty bottle. The door to the upstairs bedroom was shut. Norman put his ear to the door and, although the sound was muffled, he could tell that a man was crying out in pain. This had happened before. The last time Karp had not emerged from his bedroom again for three days.

Norman stopped off and knocked at Ernst's and Sally's door.

'Ernst?'

He thought he heard someone move quickly inside.

'Sally?'

No answer.

Outside, he hailed a taxi. He wondered idly whether there was a party at Winkleman's tonight. He thought of going to visit Jeremy, but he was afraid. Wherever he went tonight he wanted to be sure of a kind reception. Landis? Bella had certainly phoned Zelda by now and he was probably not welcome there too any more. Graves? Certainly not.

At that moment Norman realised something that should have been obvious to him before: he realised that all his friends in London were aliens like himself.

Proud they were. They had come to conquer. Instead

they were being picked off one by one by the cold, drink, and indifference. They abjured taking part in the communal life. They mocked the local customs from the school tie to queueing, and were for the most part free of them by dint of their square, classless accents. Unlike their forbears, they were punk imperialists. They didn't marry and settle down among the natives. They had brought their own women and electric shavers with them. They had through the years evolved from communists to fellow-travellers to tourists. Tourists. For even those who had lived in London for years only knew the true life of the city as a rumour. Around and around them the natives, it seemed, were stirred by Diana Dors, a rise in bus fares, test matches, automation, and Princess Margaret. The aliens knew only other aliens. It was reported occasionally that the men in bowler hats had children and points of view, that, just like in the movies, there were settlers in Surrey, miners in Yorkshire, and workers who – aside from being something you were for like central heating or more gin cheaper – were bored with their wives, suspicious of advertisements and, just like you, inclined to wonder at three-thirty in the afternoon what it would be like to come home to Sophia Loren.

Norman felt stupid.

Around and around him men clocked in every morning at 7.30 a.m. and girls sat down after an eight hour shift at Forte's to write letters to Mary Grant. Clocks, cars, pyjamas, and railways ties were produced. Around him the real £. s. d. world existed. The only sons of white fathers went out to Malaya to murder the only sons of yellow fathers in the interests of national prestige. At eleven every morning pimpled boys went from office to office with luke-warm tea in tall chipped white cups for girls who took letters from their bosses beginning, 'In reply to yours of the 23rd inst.'. Middle-aged couples failed to see the latest Martin and Lewis at the local Gaumont because they couldn't afford it. High-strung boys from Wapping failed their eleven-pluses. Old age pensioners were admitted free to the public baths. Around and around him people had already realised that they would never be able to sleep in until after eight on a Monday morning or go for a walk in the park on a Wednesday afternoon or see Paris. Around him moved a real city where Sally's choice of a lover, Charlie's script, Winkleman's chance of a production, and his own loneliness were of no bloody account.

Norman's thoughts turned to Thomas Hale in Canada and he wondered how it looked to him. Hale came over every year like a kafka with office to mark you down either in the book of sales or the book of rejection slips. Again and again he discovered the would-be author of the Great Canadian Novel and shipped him off to London, often at his own expense, only to discover that his hopeful had taken to gin or television writing by the time he got round to him again. But Hale was indefatigable. He didn't know that the British didn't care a damn about Canada. That, as far as they were concerned, somewhere out there between lost India and them lay the loyal Dominion of Canada, where Lord Beaverbrook came from. He also didn't know what it was like to live in London.

The Canadians had come to conquer. They were the prodigal offspring of a stern father. Coming home again, however, they had not counted on the old man having grown feeble while they had prospered overseas. They were surprised that the island was great only in terms of memory or sentiment. The choice of coming to England, where the streets were paved with poets, rather than to the United States bespoke of a certain spiritual superiority, so they were appalled to discover that this country was infinitely more materialistic than their own, where possessions were functional, naturally yours, and not the prize of single-minded labour. They were surprised to discover that they had arrived too late.

Norman looked at his watch and wondered again where he could go.

I'm a bum, he thought. I have no more friends. Norman laughed at himself. In a few days this will all have blown over, he thought. Everthing will be O.K.

158

He got out of the taxi at Curzon Street and found a girl who pleased him. They went to a small hotel together.

XXI

There was something doing at the Winklemans that evening. Charlie was there, and so was Colin Horton. Horton had just returned from his tour of the People's Democracies.

'They're all familiar with the present climate of hysteria in the States,' he said. 'People in Budapest were amazed at the way the FBI has been able to hoodwink the American public.'

Bella served hors d'oeuvres.

'Time and again I was asked why people like myself had left. I told them that there was such a drive towards conformity in America these days that not going to church was enough to brand you as a Red. The breadth and success of the witch-hunt astonished them. But when I explained that most of the informers were psychopaths and that one never got a chance to face one's accuser, they began to understand.'

Horton, who had to address the Anglo-Hungarian Friendship Society at nine-thirty, left early. As soon as he was gone the others got down to business.

Boris Jeremy was in trouble.

Tall, affable Boris Jeremy had been considered to be one of those on the way up in Hollywood until he had been called before the committee. At the hearing it had come out that Jeremy had not only contributed to the Spanish Aid Fund, but that his brother-in-law had died at Guadalajara and, what's more, that Jeremy's wife was a former Y.C.L. member. So Jeremy had come to England. Here, after much determined work, he had once more been considered to be a man on his way up. But when – after seemingly interminable negotiations – he was supposed to have signed a contract last week to direct his first big-budget film for a British studio, the deal had suddenly, inexplicably, gone ice-cold. This morning his passport had been revoked; he had been given six weeks to return to the United States. There was no doubt that, unless he was willing to become a 'friendly witness', he would not be able to get work there. Boris Jeremy had a wife and three children.

Sonny Winkleman toyed unhappily with his glass. 'Tell them what you told me, Charlie,' he said.

Charlie hesitated.

'Come on. Don't be embarrassed.'

'Karp,' he said, 'has told me in so many words that Norman Price is mentally unstable.'

'Come again,' Bob Landis said.

'Do you know how many times they opened up Price's head in the hospital?' Graves asked.

'No,' Bob said, 'do you?'

'Go ahead, Charlie'.

'Karp says that Norman feels he's wasted his life – as he puts it – getting mixed up in headlines and ephemeral angers. He told Karp that the fight we put up for the Rosenbergs was vitiated by the fact that we shut our eyes to the grosser injustices of the other side.'

'Is he a Trotskyite?'

'How should I know?'

'Hey, what *are* Norman's politics?'

'Charlie?'

'I dunno. Not any more.'

'Didn't he go to Spain recently? I mean a guy who would give Franco dollars . . .'

Landis grinned avidly. 'Let's get him down here,' he said, 'and make him tell us what his politics are.' But the others didn't see the joke.

'What else, Charlie?'

Charlie shifted uneasily in his chair.

'Tell them what you told Sonny,' Graves said.

'What I told Sonny was private.'

Winkleman explained. 'I bought a story from Charlie

here – a real cute comedy – and hired Norman to work on the dialogue here and there. This afternoon Charlie comes roaring in here to tell me that he doesn't want anything more to do with the picture. All this, mind you, after we've set up a production. He tells me that I can have my money back and that Norm can take all the credit for as far as he's concerned.'

'That was something else,' Charlie protested weekly. 'There's another reason for that.'

'Come on.' Winkleman slapped Charlie on the back. 'Stop trying to protect him.' He told the others something of the history of *All About Mary*. 'They're old friends,' he said.

'That's not why I want my name off the picture.' Charlie said. 'I—'

'There's loyalty for you.'

'Mr Chairman,' Bob began drunkenly. 'A point of—'

Jeremy slapped the table. 'I've got it,' he said. 'I can easily figure out why Norman didn't want Charlie to know that he was the other guy on the script. He was afraid that someone with Charlie's guts never would have agreed to work with an informer.'

Charlie rose swiftly from his chair. 'I never once said Norman was an informer,' he shouted.

'A point of order,' Bob insisted loudly.

'What's with you, Bob?'

'Why isn't Norman here to defend himself?'

'*I never once said that Norman was an informer.*'

'But he's a bit screwy, Charlie, isn't he?' Graves asked. 'How do you know that when he has one of his lapses he doesn't . . .' Graves tapped his head and drew quick circles with his finger. 'He, you know . . . You know, like – Ask any psychiatrist.'

'Maybe Bob's right,' Plotnick said. 'Let's call Norman.'

Winkleman took Bella by the arm. 'Tell them why Norm isn't here,' he said.

'When I told him that Sonny had given up everything he had in Hollywood for a principle he actually asked what that principle was.'

'Really,' Bob said.

'When she insisted on it,' Winkleman added, 'he told her that she was a very silly woman.'

'Maybe,' Bob said. 'But I don't like the tone of all this. Norman should be here.'

'Bob's right,' Charlie said.

'Why,' Graves asked, 'so that he can hit somebody again?'

'Or get more information for the FBI,' Jeremy said.

'I never said that Norman was an informer.'

'Here,' Winkleman said, passing Bob the phone, 'call him.'

Landis hesitated.

'I guarantee you that he won't come,' Graves said. 'He doesn't want to have anything more to do with us. *We're mediocre.* That's what he told Karp.'

Charlie scratched his head furiously.

'Look,' Winkleman said, 'don't you think we were fond of him too? But he couldn't do enough to help that little Nazi bastard. He—'

'Sure, but—'

'Obviously somebody here has informed on Boris. Was it me?'

'No, but—'

'Maybe I'm an informer,' Graves said.

'No, but—'

'Charlie's living in his flat. The shelves are crammed with people like Trotsky and Koestler. Do you know what Charlie found in his desk? Three back issues of the *Intelligence Digest*. That's a fascist magazine that you can only get by subscription.'

'How do we know,' Landis asked, 'that anyone here did inform on Boris in the first place? Maybe the passport people just happened to get around to him . . .'

'Yes,' Charlie said hopefully, 'that's it.'

Graves embraced Charlie affectionately. 'I know you don't like this, boy. It's a shock for you. We understand. I worked with a guy for fifteen years . . .'

Graves told him the story of his partner who had testified

against him.

'I feel sick,' Charlie said.

'Go home, boy. We understand.'

Charlie rose shakily. As he slipped round-shouldered out of the living room he just had time to hear Jeremy say, 'How come there isn't more work for a guy like Charlie?'

'If things work out for me tomorrow,' Plotnick said, 'I'll be able to use him myself.'

I should go back, Charlie thought, and explain. Explain what? That Norman had cuckolded him? He wasn't going to be made a laughing-stock for Norman's sake.

'Well,' Graves asked, 'what are we going to do about Norman?'

But with Charlie's departure they had all been purged of their fury. Everyone except Graves was ashamed.

For an hour they had created the illusion that they were back in Hollywood. For an hour they had been powerful executives once more, for an hour they had been resurrected as creative gamblers, as men with functions and offices. But then Winkleman had looked out of the window, where there was no studio lot below, and Plotnick had leaned on his desk, where there were no buzzers to summon obsequious aides, and Jeremy had walked past the window, which looked out on no swimming pool, and Landis had rested his hand on the phone, which could summon no starlets, even though he was bored. So the illusion had been destroyed.

'I dunno,' Plotnick said.

'Come to think of it,' Jeremy said, 'maybe we're making a mountain out of a molehill.'

Winkleman sighed. 'Norman's coming here tomorrow afternoon. I'm supposed to see him about his contract.'

One by one they said goodbye. Nobody paired off. They drove or walked home one by one.

Charlie drifted towards Swiss Cottage. I never once said that he was an informer, he thought. They twisted my words. They drew their own conclusions. But somebody, he thought, must have informed on Jeremy. How do I know that it wasn't Norman? Could I swear to it? Norman *is* a bit

163

odd. Then there's that story about Graves's partner. Maybe they're right.

Charlie stopped off at the nearest pub and ordered a double whisky. There he realised for the first time that the post-dated cheque he had come to return still lay on Winkleman's desk. Nothing had been settled about *All About Mary*. He was still broke. He still had to see his bank manager in the morning.

Where am I going to get some money, Charlie thought, where?

XXII

Norman came round to see Charlie early the next morning. Charlie came to the door in his dressing gown. He looked shocked. 'I thought it was the milkman,' he said, holding the door half-open. 'It's not even nine o'clock yet . . .' He gathered up his newspapers anxiously. 'Joey is still in bed.'

'I came to see you.'

They sat down together at the kitchen table. Charlie put aside his copies of the *Manchester Guardian* and the *Daily Worker* and scanned the headlines of the *Daily Express*. 'What do you want?' he asked sharply.

Norman, who had come directly to Charlie's flat from the small hotel off Curzon Street, risked a friendly smile. 'I've had a hard night,' he said.

Joey moaned something inaudible from the bedroom.

'You might as well come in,' Charlie said. 'He's *your* friend.'

'I'd rather speak to you alone,' Norman said.

Joey came in, yawning, and rubbing the nape of her neck drowsily.

'I've come to apologise,' Norman said.

'For what?' Charlie asked.

Norman smiled inanely. 'I'm not quite sure . . .'

'First you make a shady deal with Rip Van Pinkleman

164

behind my back and then, as if to prove that it wasn't a fluke, you hop into bed with my wife at the first opportunity.'

Norman took out the cheque Charlie had sent him and laid it on the table. 'This is yours,' he said, 'no matter how you feel about me.'

'Keep it.'

'You're upset, Charlie. You have every reason to be angry with me. I shouldn't have gone ahead with the Winkleman deal without speaking to you first. But nothing happened last night. Joey hasn't been unfaithful to you.'

'I know that you two went to bed together.' Charlie reached for Joey's hand. He clasped it warmly. 'But it doesn't really matter any more. You can't harm us now. We're going to make a fresh start.' Charlie winked desperately. 'Like Abelard and Heloise.'

Norman looked inquiringly at Joey.

'What makes it doubly sad,' Charlie said, 'is that I was about to forgive you the Winkleman deal. I thought to myself we've been friends for years so what the hell. As a matter of fact,' he added, 'I was going to ask you to lend me two hundred pounds. Now it's out of the question . . .'

Norman pushed the cheque towards him again.

'No,' Charlie said, '*this* cheque I could never take. Borrowing would have been different. But I couldn't even do that now. I'll just have to manage as best I can.' Charlie rustled his *Daily Worker* nervously. 'Look at this,' he said, 'our old pal Waldman is the latest to sing. Son-of-a-bitch. If I,' he said, watching Norman intently, 'had as little integrity as these guys I could be pulling down two grand a week on the coast. No thank you, Daryl.'

'I'll lend you two hundred pounds.'

'I need it badly. But I couldn't take it.'

'I'll mail it to you,' Norman said. 'You don't even have to see me.'

'It's something I just couldn't do.'

'Look' Norman said, 'we didn't make love last night. Or any night. I swear it.'

'I hate saying this,' Charlie said, 'but you aren't well. I wouldn't blame you for not wanting to remember.'

'What?'

'I'm sorry, Norman, but you've been known to suffer from lapses of memory before.'

'Why, that's absurd,' Norman said, but his voice was slivered with weakness.

'I tried to tell him,' Joey said, 'but he wouldn't believe me.' She looked from Charlie to Norman, her eyes filled with tears, and rushed out of the room and slammed the bedroom door after her.

Charlie smiled helplessly. 'Another cup of coffee, huh?'

'No.'

I hate you, Charlie thought. You make me lie. You make me cheat. You're no better than me any more. I hate you.

'Hey,' Charlie said. 'I've been offered a picture deal. They'd like me to do a story with a mining background.'

'Oh.'

'Would you like to work on the story line with me?'

'No.'

Charlie passed his sweaty hand over his forehead.

'I'll write you a cheque for the two hundred pounds,' Norman said.

'I'd be able to pay you back in a couple of months. But I couldn't take it. Not now.'

Norman wrote out a cheque. This would mean another overdraft at the bank, but there was nothing he could do about it.

'I couldn't,' Charlie said. 'Really I couldn't.'

'It would make me feel better.'

'Would it?' Charlie asked. 'Are you being sincere?'

'Yes.'

'O.K.,' Charlie said, 'but it's a loan. Remember that.'

Norman got up. 'So long Charlie,' he said.

'Hey, what do you mean "so long"? We've known each other for years.' He followed Norman into the hall. 'I'll call you.'

'Sure.'

166

'You ought to get married. You need someone to take care of you.'

'Yeah.'

Charlie laughed nervously. 'See you soon,' he said. Then, on impulse, he chased after Norman. He caught up with him outside. 'Wait,' he said. 'I'd like to speak to you.'

They went to an espresso bar around the corner. The place was choked with boys in duffle coats and girls with pink polished faces.

'Don't you think I know deep inside that I'll never make it?' Charlie asked. 'Don't you think I know?'

'Why don't you pack it in then?'

'I'm forty years old, Norman. I haven't got a trade or a cent in the bank or anything. I haven't even got a son. Sure, sure. I know. I'm a failure.'

Charlie looked up at Norman hopefully. He seemed to expect praise, a friendly gesture, the gift of a lie.

Help him, Joey had said. Tell him he's good. Norman felt sympathetic, he wanted to lie whitely, but he couldn't. Charlie, he felt, had been waiting for Lefty all these years. He was forty. Godot had come instead.

'I'm a failure, O.K., but don't you think that if I wanted to I could have been a successful executive or lawyer or agency man?' He leaned closer to Norman. 'Don't you think. . . ?'

Norman's head ached. 'I guess so, Charlie,' he said.

Charlie's laughter spilled out humourlessly, like bile. 'Sure I could have,' he said. 'Only I decided early that I wasn't going to get into the rat-race. Maybe I'm a failure, but *I* never squeezed out a smaller competitor or squirmed to a boss or worried about keeping up with the Joneses. I've always been free.' Charlie leaned back; he cleared his throat. 'I'm a non-conformist.'

'A beautiful person bashed to bits by the soul-destroying machine of American capitalism.'

'Something like that.'

'Charlie,' Norman said. 'Charlie.'

Charlie bit his lip. 'I'm a bum,' he said, offering his

confession to Norman like a cake. 'You look at Hale, though. A big cheese he is in Toronto. He's a frustrated artist, that's what he is. He sold out.'

'So what?'

'I thought you didn't like Hale?'

'Why did you leave the States, Charlie? You weren't black-listed.'

'In another month they would have deported me. They – I've always wanted to come to London. I love the British.'

'How many do you know?'

'Here,' Charlie said, leaning still closer and offering his cheek to Norman. 'Hit me.'

'Charlie,' Norman said, 'please . . .'

Charlie hid his face in his hands.

'Why don't you take Joey back to Toronto with you?' Norman asked.

'I wanted to be famous.'

'O.K.,' Norman said, 'but you're not. A few—'

'Oh, I wish I was like you. I wish I was a stone and didn't feel anything.'

'A few minutes ago you told me that you didn't have enough talent. Are you going to go back on that now?'

'You don't like me,' Charlie said. 'You never have. Admit it.'

'Charlie. Come on, Charlie.'

Charlie's eyes wavered. Again and again he wiped the table clean with his hands. 'I could never go back and face them there, Norman. Before I left for Hollywood I told them exactly what I thought of them in Toronto.' His voice rose to a hysterical pitch, 'The CBC presents . . .' and cracked.

'Go back to Toronto, Charlie.'

'I used to be so sure of myself. I would go to bed with a magazine that had a picture of Humphrey Bogart on the cover and I would be sure that I'd meet him some day and that we'd like each other. I could imagine him phoning me. "That was a sensational script, Charlie. Why don't you write me something one of these days?" I'd dream about

168

spending weekends with Arthur Miller and phoning Ava Gardner long distance from Paris to say she'd just have to forget me. Go ahead, laugh. Tell me I'm a child. But I saw myself an intimate of Hemingway and Houston and telling Louis B. Mayer he could go shove his millions, but I wouldn't change a line of my last script for him. I was so sure I was going to know all those people. And I'll tell you something, Norman, even now I know that they would have liked me. Even you have to admit that I'm very amusing at parties. Everybody says I'm witty.'

Charlie sighed; he cracked his knuckles.

'I thought I would go back to Toronto occasionally and maybe even buy a house in the suburbs – I would never drop names – but famous people would come to my house for weekends from New York and London and I would be at the station shooing away photographers, but getting in the papers anyway . . . I'm being honest with you.'

'I know, Charlie.'

'How can I go home like this? A failure.'

'Don't go home,' Norman said, irritated. 'Stay here.'

'I'm nothing. A bum. Even in Toronto they used to turn down most of my scripts.'

'If you're so anxious to be famous why not turn informer? Like Waldman. That'll get you in the papers.'

'Look here,' he said, 'all my life I've been a man of integrity.' Charlie cast a cold eye. 'If I had to do it to save my life,' he said, 'I could never inform.'

'Good for you.'

Charlie half-shut one eye. 'I used to hope,' he said, 'that I could always say the same thing for you.'

'You and I, Charlie, have different problems.'

That, Charlie thought, is as good as a confession. He began to feel a little better.

'You're a cold one,' Charlie said. 'I've never been able to understand you. Nothing seems to affect you.'

'Not even that weather,' Norman said.

'Haven't you ever looked through the ads in the *New Yorker* and wanted the girl, let's say, who models slips for

169

Vanity Fair? Wouldn't you like to be invited to one of those Hollywood parties where naked girls jump into the pool? Haven't you ever longed to go to Nassau or the opening of a Hilton Hotel?'

'We've got different problems. I want to get married and have children. I'd like to finish my book.' Norman got up. 'I've got to go now. Ernst ought to be around this afternoon to do more work on the bookcase. Will you tell him to phone me, please?'

'I'm afraid we've decided not to allow Ernst into the flat again.'

'I hate to remind you of this, Charlie. But that's my flat. You and Joey are only there temporarily.'

'You want it back. Take it. We'll move out next week.'

'All right,' Norman said. 'If you like.'

Charlie left the coffee bar without bothering to say good-bye. Look at them, he thought, look at all those bastards walking up and down the street. I'm bleeding, he thought, and nobody cares. Charlie began to walk more quickly. Maybe, he thought, there's a contract or a cheque in the mail. Today may be my lucky day. You can never tell.

XXIII

Norman trudged slowly home in the rain. What, he thought, if Charlie was telling the truth and I have been to bed with Joey? No, that's crazy. But I do suffer from lapses of memory...

Norman felt like one of those animals in an animated cartoon who had been shot up into the sky and stood there amazed and treading air desperately.

His head ached, and he felt feverish, and turning up Edgware Road he was suddenly consumed by a fierce, choking sadness.

Oh, damn this dying capital, he thought.

Think of it. Think of all the shifting, homeless people of

170

London, scrabbling over each other's backs and just about making-do. All those tweedy, slap-footed girls reqd. at a starting sal. of £10 wk., long hopeful ladies with commercial knowl. & exp. and a shorthand and typing speed of 100/50 w.p.m. being offered canteen facilities, a pension scheme, chilblains, a divan-sit. with a gas ckr. of their very own – Comf. musical/lit interests – and, once yearly, a chance to chase the sun to Sorrento or Southend, for two more weeks of chastity. Norman bent into the rain, his back hunched as though from every window these girls were peering down at him accusingly. Oh, give a moment's thought please to the librarian, Grade IV, with some practical exp. of classifying, cataloguing, and rolling his own cigarettes, off tonight to hear Donald Soper and other prominent speakers protest at Caxton Hall, and to look left, right, and centre, only to come home alone again to an X cert. dream. A thought, too, if you don't mind, for Mayfair Social Appointments, who will find you the Right Partner for all occasions. A second's silence, please, for the elderly lady who hawks *Peace News* in the wind and the rain of Edgware Road.

Think of the pain, Norman thought, the pain of all these people in their damp, ill-lit individual cells. Add it up.

What, he thought, am I doing in London?

Sometimes those animals in the animated cartoon managed to walk across the sky to the roof of the nearest skyscraper. Other times they suddenly realised where they were and came crashing down to the pavement.

Norman hurried home in the rain.

XXIV

Karp was waiting for him on the bed. 'I'm sorry about last night,' he said. 'I meant to serve you a stupendous dinner.'

171

Karp rose, and leaned forward on his cane. 'Everything is going to be perfect,' he said.

'What do you mean?'

'Tell me the truth, Norman. Do you still love Sally?'

Norman's face darkened. He glared at Karp.

'Ah,' Karp said, 'just as I thought.'

'What do you want?'

'You're my old friend, Norman. You're the only person I care about.'

'Come to the point.'

'I live vicariously, so to speak.'

'Karp!'

'Objectively speaking,' Karp asked, 'is my walk very feminine?'

'Not very.'

'But *I* have no dignity; have I?'

'What's happened?'

'Supposing,' Karp said, 'your brother Nicky had not been killed on manoeuvres?'

Norman shook off his fatigue.

'Supposing,' Karp said, 'he had been killed quite by accident in a brawl?'

'Give me the letter, Karp.'

'What letter?'

'Don't pretend. I got a letter from my Aunt Dorothy. You opened it. Give it to me, Karp.'

'There was no letter.'

'Then what—'

'I would not like to be in your position.'

'What do you mean?' Norman asked weakly.

'Because it was not Ernst's fault. I know the story. Your brother brought it on himself.'

'Brought what on himself?'

'Ernst killed him.'

'My brother,' Norman said. 'Are you sure?'

'Absolutely.'

Norman seized Karp by the shoulders and shook him.

'Who told you?'

172

'She did.'

Norman let him go.

'*She* knows?'

Karp nodded.

'You're mad, Karp. I don't believe it.'

'They might run away,' Karp said. 'What are you going to do?'

Norman took the stairs three at a time. Karp pursued him.

'She's out,' Karp said. 'She won't be home from school for hours.'

'Where's Ernst?'

'Wait.' Karp took out a key. 'There you are.'

The room was intact. They hadn't fled.

'I'll kill him.' Norman shook his fist under Karp's face. 'I'll kill that little bastard with my own hands.'

Karp sucked his thumb. He smiled lasciviously.

'I'll kill that little Nazi,' Norman shouted.

Karp clapped his hands together. 'Then Sally will be yours,' he said.

Norman turned furiously on Karp.

'Sure,' Karp said, 'don't you want the girl?'

He slapped Karp hard.

'The best ones were killed, Karp. Only the conniving, evil ones like you survived.'

Norman collapsed on his bed and lay there for a long time before he got up and undressed.

I'll kill him, he thought, that's for sure.

Norman emptied his pockets as he intended to take his suit to the cleaners when he woke. Once in bed he fell into a deep, untroubled sleep.

Part Three

I

Norman woke shortly after noon with a headache and a shapeless feeling of disquiet. Something more alarming than the bad taste in his mouth was hounding him, but the nature of his complaint was elusive. Norman rose warily, like one who expected his right to rise to be challenged. But this wasn't the air base. Neither was it the hospital. This was his own room in Hampstead. The clock on the floor, his desk, his books, even the cigarette burns in the rug, were exactly as they should be. Norman put on a clean shirt, got into the suit that he had meant to take to the cleaners, and shoved ten one pound notes into his pocket. The rest of his things he left on his desk.

Outside, he wandered down to Swiss Cottage. Something was bothering him. But whatever it was would, he felt, reveal itself to him around the next corner, like the fires he had chased as a boy. But around the next corner and the one after that it was all the same: rain.

In the tube station Norman began to suspect that he was being watched. Eight times he read a poster urging him to bring the *Evening Standard* home to his wife. Somebody, another bachelor perhaps, had blackened the teeth of the wife in the poster. Norman started as the train came thundering into the station. Someone could easily have pushed me in front of it, he thought. He boarded a non-smoking car. The watchful strangers saw that he had no newspaper to read. He could tell from their smiles that they also knew that he, unlike the others, had no destination.

Norman fiddled with his glasses.

At Oxford Circus he got out and on again a couple of cars back. Next thing he knew they were at Waterloo. Norman wandered up to the air terminal. He bought an *Evening*

Standard and sat down near the arrivals stairway. But even armed with a newspaper he felt restless, and so he drifted up to the bar. A hard, barely feminine voice announced over the loudspeaker that passengerss from Zurich had just arrived in the terminal. That's when Norman first realised that he had lost his memory. He was astonished. This is ridiculous, he thought. Norman watched as some, who had been listening intently to the voice over the loudspeaker, slumped back in their chairs while others hurried off. He was not sure what was expected of him. He waited as the passengers began to emerge.

Last up the stairs was a woman with two children. An attractive brunette, probably French and an official's wife, she held hands with both her boys. The younger one was blond with rosy cheeks and must have been about four years old. He held an orange balloon in his free hand. Nobody met them. The woman looked right and left severely, not disappointed but irritated, as though being beyond public displays of affection herself, she could forgive her husband's thoughtlessness and even promiscuity, but never a lapse in efficiency. As a steward rushed to her aid the four year old boy lost his grip on the balloon. He began to wait as it floated lazily upward. Norman followed the orange balloon's twisting course until it became lodged in a corner of the ceiling, then he jumped up in a panic and walked round and round under it. Laughter, albeit gentle in tone, rose in proportion to the child's screeching. When Norman looked around again the woman and the two children were gone. Norman grabbed the steward by the arm.

'Hey,' he said, 'what about the balloon?'

The steward laughed good-naturedly.

'You may consider this a joke, but I don't. Norman seized him by the shoulders. 'What are you going to do about the kid's balloon?'

The steward broke free. 'Easy, guv.'

'I asked you a straightforward question.'

Norman caught the look of astonishment in the other man's eye.

'I'm sorry.' Norman drew back, terrified. 'I didn't mean . . .'

Norman's clothes clung to him damply. At the bar he ordered a whisky and soda.

'That'll be three and six, sir.'

He found some money in his pocket – a lucky thing, he thought – and paid for his drink. 'One moment,' he said.

'Yes, sir.'

'Judging from my accent where would you say I was from?'

'That's easy, sir. You're an American.'

In the mirror Norman saw that he must be between thirty-five and forty years old.

'Were there any planes in from the States today?'

'Flights from overseas arrive at Victoria, sir. This is Waterloo, this is.'

In the toilet, Norman went through his pockets. No papers, no baggage slips. Nine pounds and some change was all he had on him. He checked his suit jacket lapel. Meakers of Piccadilly. It had been bought in London, but it was at least a year old. Looking in the mirror he saw that he didn't need a shave. He was reassured. I haven't been wandering around like this for long, he thought.

Outside, he got on the first bus headed for the West End. But he took the bus on the wrong side of the street. He was at Clapham before he noticed it. They drive on the left side here, Norman thought triumphantly. I know. He boarded a bus going in the other direction.

A long trip it was. The longest. For the first part of the journey there was the London poor. Short, beefy people with grey teeth who bore their soiled raincoats like skins. Outside and forever a charred, broken sky and the rain. Black trees and blacker sidewalks. Rain, rain, rain. The people of the Thames were shaped by the rain, he thought, and what a sodden bunch they are. From Clapham to Lambeth there came some of the most forlorn houses he had ever seen. Brown and grey and red brick all uniformly blackened now. A child's pink face in the third story window of a hunched, fractured house. Flaking public houses wedged between shops, and in every block at least one sweet shop with a faded display of Players in the sooty window, as though for a race of Puritans only the mildest of vices would do.

As they approached the West End the fastidious ones with the big briefcases assumed their seats on the bus. Not next to the big Greek lady. Stand better than share a seat with the dustman. They were taller than the workers; whiter too. There was a semi-detached cottage and a dead man's job in their futures. Not a 'good address', though, because that was saved for the still taller ones. Norman rubbed the back of his neck. It occurred to him that after forty endless years of HP and subservience one of these fastidious men might, at last, get his semi-detached cottage only to find that the repudiated dustman, a pool's winner, had moved into the bigger one next door. Norman smiled. Everything will work out, he thought.

At the desk of the Regent's Palace Hotel the clerk asked him, 'Have you a reservation, sir?'

'No, I'm afraid not,' Norman said, 'but any single room will do.'

'We might just have something on the fifth floor.' Peering over the counter the clerk saw that Norman had no baggage with him. 'Are you an American, sir?'

'Yes.'

'Will you fill out this form please. You put your passport number here.'

'I've been travelling all night. May I fill this out after I've had some sleep?'

'Regulations, sir.'

A couple began to jostle Norman from behind.

'I'll come back. I've just remembered something.'

Norman sat through *Commanche Warrior* two and a half times before he woke. Outside, it was raining again. Norman walked quickly, as though he was being pursued. He walked down the Strand and from there to the river. He followed the river as far as Cheyne Walk, then he turned up to the King's Road. His head pounding, his legs aching, his

180

feet burning and tender, Norman stood at the bar in the Lord Nelson for more than an hour before he noticed the girl beside him. She was alone. An unassured, sensibly dressed girl with her black hair clipped boyishly short.

'May I buy you a drink?'

She told him her name was Vivian.

'I don't know what my name is,' he said. 'I've lost my memory.'

II

Karp came into their room, sat down and took an apple out of his pocket. His face was puffed. 'I've just been to Norman's room,' he said. 'Something is wrong.'

Ernst rose. Sally, who had been washing her hair, wrapped a red towel round her head like a turban and pulled it tight. She was wearing a pink slip. 'Are you sure?' she asked.

'All the papers he usually carries with him are spread out over his desk.'

'I don't understand.'

'He didn't show up for his appointment with Winkleman this afternoon,' Karp said. 'That's not like Norman.'

'Have you told him about Ernst?'

Karp rubbed his apple against his jacket until it shone. 'How was one to know that you would not run away?' he asked.

'Thank you for being so helpful.' Sally put the towel tighter round her head. 'What do you think has happened to Norman?'

'One cannot be sure. But his memory has failed him before.' Karp bit tentatively into his apple, as though he expected to find a worm there. 'But don't hope for too much. It is certainly very temporary.'

'We must find him,' Ernst said.

'Yes,' Sally said weakly, 'of course.'

'Perhaps we should send for the police,' Karp suggested.

'Aren't we being just a little big hysterical?' Sally asked.

181

'Norman left all his things on his desk and didn't turn up for an appointment. So what?'

Karp bit into his apple savagely; he smiled knowingly at Ernst. 'She has changed,' he said. 'She has come under your influence.'

'We will not send for the police,' Ernst said. '*If* Norman has no memory we will find him ourselves.'

'How?'

'I still think you're taking a lot for granted,' Sally said. 'For all we know Norman is drunk somewhere. He's probably perfectly all right.'

'If one were to find Norman,' Karp began, 'if Ernst, for example were to find Norman in his present state and was able to convince him that he was indeed somebody other than Norman Price. That would be interesting, wouldn't it?'

Karp dropped his apple into a wastepaper basket, wiped his fingers with an initialled handkerchief, and left.

Ernst slouched thoughtfully silent on the bed. If he could find Norman, he thought, and help him, if he could be the one to restore him to his friends, then Norman would be obligated to him. He might even have to forgive – He told Sally of his idea.

Sally, remembering the results of Ernst's last 'good turn' – the episode of the stolen wallet – was struck stupid with horror.

'Anyway,' she said, 'there's probably nothing to it. Norman's out on a binge; that's all.'

III

It was three a.m., or nearly that, when Vivian noticed that he was sitting up in bed.

'It's here,' Norman said. 'It's in the room.'

'What?' she asked, hardly awake.

'I can feel it in the room.'

'Don't look at me like that.'

'Turn on the lights,' he said.

There were twin beds in the room. Three of the walls were painted yellow. A North African rug was tacked up against the other wall. Vivian owed three more payments on the Swedish lamp. The bureau, rescued from a Camden Town junk shop, had been scraped and painted flat black. The wardrobe came from the same shop.

Vivian leaped out of bed. 'There,' she said, turning on the lights. 'Feel better?'

'Open up the cupboard door.'

I never should have brought him here, she thought.

But he seemed so troubled in the pub, and once he had told her his story there had been no decent alternative.

The basement flat on Oakley Street consisted of an immense living room, a double bedroom which she shared with her cousin Kate – Kate was off for a fortnight's holiday in Juan les Pins with Binky Thomas and the Hillarys – and a kitchen. She and Kate shared the toilet with Roger and Polly Nash upstairs. Roger had papered the toilet walls with *New Yorker* cartoons. He was not a bad sort.

'Open up the cupboard door, please.'

'You're frightening me,' Vivian said.

'Open – the – cupboard – door.'

She did as he had asked.

'You're a grown man. What's here? What's hiding in the wardrobe?'

'I don't know.'

He stared; he said nothing more.

'It's chilly,' she said. 'I'm cold standing here like this.'

She was also embarrassed. All she was wearing was one of Kate's diaphanous blue négligés. The lights were on, too.

'I'm afraid.' Norman held his hands to his temples and then dropped them to the blankets as though he was done with them forever. 'I'm so afraid.'

'Afraid of what? First you go on and on about a child's balloon and then you wake up in the middle of the night and—'

'Have you a flashlight here? A torch, I mean.'

183

She got the flashlight out of the bureau drawer and handed it to him. His fingers were cold, clammy.

'It's here.' He shone the light into the wardrobe. 'I'm sure it's in the room.

'What's in the room?'

'Move the clothes about. Shake them.'

'I won't do it.' Whimpering softy, she began to prod the clothes with a hanger. But from a distance. 'I've never heard of anything so silly.'

Next he shone the flashlight under the bed.

'Stop that. Please stop.'

Norman sat up on the edge of the bed and held his head in his hands.

Vivian stripped her own bed of a pillow and two blankets. 'You ought to see a psychiatrist,' she said. 'Other people have gone through worse, I dare say, and they're not—'

'Crazy?'

'Don't put words into my mouth.'

He began probing the room with the flashlight again.

'What could a psychiatrist do? It's here, here in the room.'

'I've never heard such—'

'You've got a blanket,' he said. 'You're going.'

'I'm going to sleep on the couch in the living room. That's what I should have done in the first place, but . . .'

'But what?'

'. . . I didn't want you to think that I was afraid.'

'Admit it then,' Norman said. 'Admit you feel it too.'

'Feel *what*?'

'Scared.'

'Of course I'm scared,' she said, relieved. 'You're scaring me.'

'It's here. Here in the room.'

'I refuse to discuss it any more.'

'Why did you wake then,' he asked. 'What made you wake?'

A shiver ran through her.

'You see,' he said.

'I don't *see*. But if you like,' she said, 'I'll stay. I'll sit up with you.'

He had forgotten about her. He was exploring the room with his flashlight again. So Vivian went into the other room.

Norman examined one corner of the room intently. Satisfied that there was nothing there he sat down on the floor in the corner with his back to the wall, where it couldn't get behind him. Then, pulling his knees up, he began to go over the room with his flashlight, over and over again, until he fell asleep. He woke shortly after seven in the morning because of the sun. The sun shone into his eyes. Vivian woke when he came into the living room.

'Feeling better?' she asked.

Her cheeks marked from the pillow, her black hair stuck to her forehead, Vivian flung back her blankets drowsily. Her brown back made a delightful curve as she brought up her knees to her chin, hugged them, and smiled. She had very small breasts. Her legs were a bit heavy and her ankles were thick.

'Yes,' Norman said. 'I feel fine.'

Vivian rose, embarrassed, and slipped hastily into her dressing gown. 'I'll make you breakfast,' she said.

'I haven't time,' Norman said evasively.

'What's your hurry?'

'I have to go to Waterloo Air Terminal.'

'The balloon?'

'Yes,' he said.

Again he was the severe, greying, troubled man who had picked her up in the pub. Vivian smiled sadly, concerned. 'Is it that important?'

'I have to find out if it's still up there.'

'And if it isn't?'

'What do you mean?' he said angrily. 'How could they get it down?'

'Look,' Vivian said in her most reasonable tone of voice, 'you're not well. Why don't you stay here with me for a bit? I could ring the office to tell them I'm not coming in today and—'

185

'I must get to Waterloo.'

'All right,' she said, 'but you're going to have breakfast first.'

Norman reluctantly agreed to stay for breakfast.

While he went into the bathroom to shave – she told him that he could use Binky's shaving equipment – Vivian prepared breakfast.

Looking out of the kitchen window Vivian saw a taxi pull up in front of the house. Kate stepped out, dipping one lovely leg first and then a thoughtful pause, like a child trying the water, before she risked the other one. Kate was a model. A tall, healthy blonde, with quick blue eyes. Lugging her bag across to the bedroom, she took the situation in swiftly. A man's jacket had been tossed clumsily over the Windsor chair. There were two glasses and an open bottle of gin on the coffee table.

'Come into the kitchen with me,' Vivian said urgently.

Kate kissed Vivian on the forehead. 'It's perfectly all right,' she said. 'All I hope is that he's nice.'

'But you don't understand—'

'Mind you don't burn his bacon,' Kate said. 'That would be a bad start.'

Kate was wearing a cloche hat, a thick, extravagantly striped turtleneck sweater and a mustard yellow skirt that was very tight around her hips. She propped herself up on the kitchen table, swung her legs out and inspected them dispassionately, like she was seeing them in a nylon ad.

Vivian felt wrinkled and very much in need of a bath after a largely sleepless night. 'How come you're back so soon,' she said.

'The trip turned out to be an absolute horror,' Kate began. 'The Hillarys began to fight the moment we crossed the Channel. Barbara went on *and on* about Dickie's drinking and Dickie saw black every time a wog smiled at her. Once we got to Juan les Pins Dickie was hardly ever sober. He took Binky out on the town every night and Barbara and I were left to fend for ourselves. Well, I didn't mind *that*. There was the sweetest little Indian at our pension. The son of a maharaja or pasha or whatever it is they're called. Anyway the night before last Binky burst into my room madly drunk at three a.m. and asked me to lend him ten quid. That was the first time I'd seen him in two whole days, mind you. I lost my temper. One thing led to another and I gave him back my ring. What a kerfuffle!' Kate's bosom swelled indignantly. 'The marriage is off. I'm quite relieved, actually. Have you ever met Binky's mother?'

'No, I—'

'She thinks I'm fast because we all went to Davos together last Christmas. I'm through with the Hillarys too. Dickie's a frightful bore, actually. If Barbara had any sense she'd leave him. What's your young man like?'

'He's an American.'

'I say, he's not one of those airmen, is he?'

'No, Kate. He isn't.'

'I've got the *cafard*,' Kate said glumly.

Vivian told her that she had met Norman at the Lord Nelson. He was suffering from amnesia, and had no place to go, so she had brought him home. They had slept in separate beds.

'Please, darling, you don't have to tell *me* a story. I'll pop upstairs and have tea with Roger and Polly. We can chat after he's gone.'

As Kate started up the stairs Norman came out of the toilet in his shorts. 'Oh,' Kate said, 'you gave me a fright. I'm Vivian's cousin.' She hurried past him to the Nashes' flat.

Roger and Polly Nash were eating breakfast. The kitchen smelled of bacon and drying nappies.

'Kate,' Roger said, 'I thought I recognised your hard shrewish voice.' He cleared a chair of towels and poured her a cup of tea. 'I say, has Horse-Face actually got a man down there?'

Polly saw that Kate was annoyed. 'Roger,' she said. 'Stop that.'

Polly had been a little frightened of Kate ever since Kate

187

had caught her out mistaking a *bidet* for a foot-bath when she had been telling John and Edith Laughton about her trip to the Midi.

Kate told them the story Vivian had told her.

'If she's going to have a thing with this chap,' Roger said, 'maybe you'll be able to have the flat for yourself again.'

Being on her own again, she thought, would be nice. 'I just happen to like sharing the flat with Vivian,' she said.

'Certainly,' Polly said. 'I'm frightfully fond of her myself.'

'Balls,' Roger said. 'You're afraid of losing a baby-sitter.' He smiled thinly at Kate. 'I think it's been jolly good of you to put up with Vivian for so long, but—'

'I *like* sharing the flat with Vivian.'

Roger grinned. 'What's the chap like?' he asked. 'No. Don't tell me. He's a graduate of the London School of Economics, he works for the coal board. He's from Manchester, he is. Calls poor Vivian ducks and once came first in a weekend competition in the Staggers & Naggers.'

Polly giggled.

'*He's an American*,' Kate said.

'I say, she *is* a fallen women now, isn't she?'

'He's not an airman.'

Vivian served Norman another cup of coffee.

'I must get to Waterloo,' Norman said.

'Wait till I get dressed and I'll go with you.'

Norman looked dismayed.

'Is there anything wrong with that?' she asked.

'Why do you want to come with me?'

'I'd like to help you.'

'I don't know who I am,' he said shyly. 'I've lost my memory.'

'I know,' she said. 'You told me last night.'

'Why are you so anxious to help me?' he asked.

'You're in trouble. Somebody's got to help you. Wait,' she said, getting up hastily. 'I'm going to make more coffee. I'll only be a minute.'

But Vivian had not been in the kitchen very long before she heard the front door click.

Roger and Polly and Kate rushed to the window just in time to see Norman turn the corner hastily. Only a few seconds later Vivian appeared on the pavement in her dressing gown. Kate pulled Roger and Polly back from the window.

'I'm warning you,' Kate said. 'You're not to say a word to her. You're not to say a word to anyone about this.'

Kate found Vivian in the bedroom. Her cousin was dressing hastily.

'Where are you going?'

'Waterloo Air Terminal,' Vivian said.

'But, darling, you mustn't chase him. This will never do.'

'He's sick,' Vivian shouted impatiently. 'He doesn't know who he is.'

'You can't go out like this. You haven't any make-up on. Oh, look at your hair, Vivian.'

Vivian laughed hysterically. 'Get out of my way,' she said.

'Wait. I'll go with you.'

'You certainly will not.'

IV

'What's this,' Ernst asked, as he entered the room. 'I don't understand.'

'I've packed all our bags.'

'Where are we going?'

'Anywhere,' Sally said acidly. 'I don't care.'

Ernst sat down on the bed. He was exhausted. 'There was nobody home at the Lawsons',' he said, 'but I've been almost everywhere else. Nobody has seen Norman.'

'Ernst. Look at me, Ernst.'

He lifted his head heavily. Sally was thinner, there were circles under her eyes, and a kind of fright, something

189

altogether new, in her manner. She no longer curled up sleepily satisfied in the easy chair; she sat stiffly on the edge.

'Yes,' he said.

'Do you love me?'

She noticed yet again how bony he was, how much like a fox. She would have liked to hit him.

'What's wrong, Sally?'

'I asked you a question.'

'Of course I love you.'

'I've had enough, Ernst. Every time that door opens I think they've come to take you away from me. Now you listen to me. I've taken all my money out of the bank. I've got enough to last us for a while. I want you to come away with me this afternoon.'

'No, I can't.'

'Why?'

'That's just what Karp is waiting for me to do,' he shouted.

'Karp? Don't tell me you're worried about him.'

'I said no.'

'*You* said. You said.'

'And Norman. There's Norman too. He was a big help to us.'

'Aren't you the moral one suddenly?'

'Yes,' he said, '*suddenly*.'

'Would you rather hang?'

'I'm not going to run away,' he said.

Sally sat down, suppressing nausea. 'Tell me why,' she said.

'I already told you.'

'Tell me again.'

'Oh, leave me alone. How do I know why? I can't, that's all. Norman is the first friend I ever had. He – stop trying to make a fool out of me!'

'You owe it to me to run away.'

'No.'

'I hate you,' she cried passionately. 'Oh, I hate you. I hate

190

you and Europe and I hate Karp. I think you're sordid. I wish I'd never met you.' Sally began to weep. He went to her and she hugged him very tight and said, 'Let's run away. Please, please, darling, let's run away. I don't want to see you killed. I love you.'

'I can't,' he said. 'They – all of them think I'm rotten. I'm after your passport. I'm a Nazi or – if I was Norman or Landis I could run away,' he said. 'People would be understanding. But I'm Ernst Haupt, so I can't.' He laughed bitterly. 'It's like . . . It's almost like I was a Jew myself and had to take care. I – I can't run away. I'm trapped.'

V

At Waterloo Air Terminal Norman spotted the balloon at once. It had moved a little to the right, but outside of that there was no change.

Norman sat down beside a square, chubby American, who was reading *Look*, and told him the story of the balloon.

'A damn shame,' the man said, studying the trapped balloon.

'How do you think they'll get it down?'

'A ladder would do the trick.'

'Maybe,' Norman said, 'they'll just leave it there.'

The square, chubby man returned to Norman Vincent Peale's column.

'Aren't you interested?' Norman asked.

'Sure thing.'

'Did you notice the balloon before I sat down to tell you about it?'

'Nope.'

'What do you think they ought to do about it?'

'I don't want to sound unneighbourly, but frankly speaking, son, I've got bigger worries.'

'That's not the point.'

191

'Look,' the man said, 'why not be a good fellow and let me read my magazine in peace?'

Norman rose and walked out of the air terminal.

VI

After all these years of waiting and broken half-promises, tomorrows, maybes, nearly sold scripts and knowing the people who knew the right people, Charlie felt the doors beginning to creak open.

Charlie was going to get work.

Charlie knew, he was sure, that the phone was going to ring. There had been nothing in the morning mail, no bills and no rejection slips, and that was a sign. Sure it was. Somebody, Charlie felt sure, was going to ring this morning: and he would make a sale.

The phone was poised blackly inscrutable on the little table under the window in the living room. Outside, the buses passed one after another. The clock over the electrician's shop across the street read 3.12. Charlie, standing by the window, bet himself a double whisky that the phone would ring before three more 31s passed.

I never once said that Norman was an informer, he thought. I didn't say that he was mentally unstable either. That was Karp. I was quoting him, that's all.

Charlie usually took the phone off the hook when he went to the toilet, but the Chairlady of the Bitcher's Club would soon be back and if she found the receiver off the hook with him in the toilet again she would be furious. The fifth 31 bus passed. Maybe, he thought, I'll take a chance and go. No. better wait.

When Charlie had finished college and told the old man that he didn't want to go into the business the old man had been hurt, but, all the same, he had said, 'O.K., it's your life. Live it any way you want.' So Charlie had told him that he wanted to be a writer and the old man, who read Dickens and Balzac for his own amusement, had asked to see what his son had written. Afterwards he had said, 'You're not good enough, Charlie. I think you ought to try something easier.'

He had sat in the first row when Charlie's play, *Factory*, had opened off Broadway in '48. When he came round to see him the next morning he had said, 'You're never going to be famous, Charlie.'

'I'm a progressive. That's why the critics panned me.'

'You're no longer a boy, Charlie. You haven't got it in you. Don't kill yourself.'

'Did you identify yourself with the capitalist in *Factory*?'

'A man as stupid as the one in your play could never have run a business. I do. Does that answer your question?'

'The director made me change certain scenes, I—'

'I'm an old man, Charlie. I'd like to have a grandchild.'

'Everytime you come to see me I'm not famous and you want a grandchild. She can't have children.'

Charlie cracked his knuckles. The phone, black on the table, was silent. He wanted to call Landis, maybe Jeremy, Plotnick perhaps, he wanted somebody, anybody, to talk to – he wanted to say that Norman was O.K. but he was afraid to keep the line engaged.

Factory had run for two weeks. For two weeks, every night, Charlie had sat in the balcony of the cold and all but empty theatre and watched the spiritless actors misquote his lines. One night thirty-five people and the next twenty-two. Eighteen, forty-three, thirty-seven. Every night for two weeks Charlie had come to watch his play. And little by little whatever it was in him that had been sensitive, hopeful, resilient, and generous had hardened and cracked like clay in a too quickly heated kiln.

As soon as the clock across the street read 4.05 Charlie lifted the receiver off the hook and rushed down three flights of stairs to see if there was any mail. The postman hadn't passed yet. Charlie climbed the stairs back to the flat two at a time and replaced the receiver on the hook before he collapsed, breathlessly, in his armchair. I could have

193

been to the toilet four times, he thought. But Charlie knew, he was sure, that the phone was going to ring: and he would make a sale.

The door opened. It was Joey. 'Have you heard about Norman?' she asked.

'One minute,' he said. 'I've got to to to the – I'll be right back.'

Joey was waiting for him when he returned. 'Norman has disappeared,' she said. 'I think he's suffering from amnesia.'

'Oh no,' Charlie said. 'That would be dreadful.'

'It's happened before, you know. He—'

'Oh, no. To think that I—'

'I don't think you have any reason to feel guilty, Charlie.'

'But I'm his friend. He seemed so sick when he left here. I should have made him stay.'

'You had no way of knowing.'

'He could be lying dead in a ditch now or—'

'Stop it, Charlie. I thought *you* had decided that Norman had proven himself to be something other than a friend.'

'Sure, sure. But all those years together. I'm worried about him. I – What have you got there?'

She had two letters. The first one was from home.

'How much do they need this time?' Charlie asked.

'Dr Schwartz says Dad must go to Arizona again this winter or he will not hold himself responsible for the consequences.'

'Me,' Charlie said, 'I am not holding Dr Schwartz responsible.'

'Selma is doing fine. She sends her love.'

'For that I'm mighty grateful, Mrs Browning. You can quote me.'

'What's got into you?'

'I'm worried about Norman.'

'Norman will be O.K. This has happened before.'

'What else have you got there? A bill?'

'It's an invitation to dinner at Winkleman's,' Joey said.

'Jeepers-creepers, where'd you get those peepers?'

'Are you ill?'

'I want to adopt a child,' Charlie said.

'Can we afford it?'

'If we can afford Arizona we can afford a child.'

'It seems to me we can afford neither. What's ailing you?'

'Age,' Charlie said. 'I want a son.'

'Even an adopted one?'

'Yup.'

'Charlie – Charlie, I—'

'Charlie, Charlie, somebody callin' Charlie? HEY CHAR-LIE!'

'Oh, God.'

'Here it comes; the Joey Wallace haymaker . . .'

'Charlie, what is it?'

'Remember the first night we spent together in this flat? You burnt a letter. What was in it?'

'I told you.'

'Yeah,' he said, 'but today I want the truth.'

'Do you?' Joey's voice shrivelled like burnt paper. 'Really?'

'That's what the man said. The man said that.'

'I wanted to run away with Norman in New York. *I* wrote *him* love letters.'

Charlie made a fist and bit it. His eyes filled. He coughed.

'You wanted the truth,' Joey said. 'That's what you said.'

A long time later he said, 'I know what I said.'

'I was infatuated with Norman,' Joey said in a constricted voice. 'It was silly, I know, but it was a long time ago.'

'*Long ago*,' he sang, '*and far away*— He wouldn't have you?'

'He wouldn't have me,' she said.

Charlie got up and began to walk up and down the room. 'What a life.' He read and re-read Winkleman's invitation. 'Charlie,' he mumbled, 'Charles Lawson, you're a success. People want your company.' He tore up the invitation. 'The world is such a filthy place,' he whispered, 'such a dirty, filthy place.'

'Are you going to leave me?'

'For months and months I've been dying for this lousy

little card,' he said, 'and now—' Charlie had the sensation that his heart like a match had burned, curled, and died. '—and now,' he faltered, '*Now is the hour when we* . . .'

'I would understand if you left me. I wouldn't blame you.'

Charlie turned to her sorrowfully. 'You poor kid,' he said. 'Norman wouldn't have you. Nobody would have me either.'

'We could make a fresh start,' Joey said.

'That's supposed to be my line. Then you're supposed to look into my eyes deeply as we walk off together into the technicolour sunset . . .' He laughed. 'But I'm fat and forty, darling, and, I've got news for you, you're nobody's dreamboat yourself any more.'

'I'm serious. We *could* make a fresh start.'

'It never works.'

'We have a lot in common,' she said emptily.

'Misery, failure, and lies. Don't tell me. I know.' Charlie smacked one hand into the other. 'Such a dirty place,' he said. 'The world is such a dirty place.'

'Remember,' she said, 'when you came to see me in the hospital with the proof of your short story. You were so shy in those days, Charlie.'

'I'll never forget that officious young doctor,' Charlie said. 'And you were so – You wrote me every day when I was in the army!'

'It worked once,' she said. 'Don't you see?'

'Yeah. But it would never work again.'

Joey embraced him fervently and dug her head into his chest. 'Please,' she said, 'please, please, please, don't leave me. I couldn't bear it.'

'You couldn't – But I always thought that was what you wanted most. For me to leave you, I mean.'

Joey shook her head.

'I always thought you hated me for being such a fat, funny failure.'

'Oh, no. No Charlie.'

'But—'

196

'I love you, Charlie. I always have.'

'You love me,' he said. 'I don't understand.'

'How vulnerable,' she said, 'how vulnerable we both are.'

'About Norman,' he said. 'The other night, I mean. I—'

'Don't. Let's not go into that.'

'No,' he said, 'I know you never went to bed with him, but – I hated him then. You and him. There was the script, you see. Oh, he's always made me feel so inferior. Big, honest, principled, Norman. If he had made love to you – Oh, if you only knew how much I wanted to have something on him . . . Why doesn't Norman ever do something wrong or vulgar or stinking? What a cruel, remote bastard he is. Nothing affects him . . . You know, sometimes I wonder if he's human.'

He took Joey in his arms and stroked her head.

'You love me,' he said. 'Imagine that.'

'We could try,' she said. 'Couldn't we try?'

Joey clung to him, not seeing a fat middle-aged failure, but remembering the man inside the others didn't know or had forgotten. The young, hopeful man who had wanted to write beautifully. Here he was; Charlie Lawson was his name. He had been scorned, pummelled, and lied to, he had been knocked down, pulled apart and pitied, he had been used, and only she still retained an impression of the unfulfilled man inside. Charlie, she thought, Charlie, Charlie. They sank down on the bed together and, almost with reverence, helped each other to undress. When he considered her hard bony face, the breasts that had begun to sag and the thickening waist, it was with a fondness sprung from proprietorship.

'Oh, help me,' he cried. 'Help me to live.'

VII

Norman met them in a flat in Soho. The fat, rosy-cheeked man's name was Morley Scott-Hardy. He wore a white monogrammed shirt and a purple corduroy jacket and grey flannels and brown suède shoes. His pale pulpy flesh gathered in knots about his face and body so that he was not so much fat as threatening to break out here and there. He had very little hair, a round wet mouth, and soft damp eyes. Scott-Hardy carried a gold-tipped walking stick. Yet behind the foolish façade there seemed to lurk a serious shrewd intelligence. His young friend was called Pip. A darkly beautiful boy, he was, it seemed, an illustrator of children's books.

When Scott-Hardy and Pip invited him back to the flat they shared on Sloane Street he quickly accepted; he had no place else to go.

A framed picture of Sugar Ray Robinson hung over the fireplace. The parlour was dense with pillows and drapes. Scott-Hardy poured Norman a vodka-and-tomato-juice and excused himself. Meanwhile Pip, who wore a black turtleneck sweater and pre-faded blue jeans, spread himself out on the rug like a sacrifice.

The table placed like a counter before the bookshelves was laden with little magazines rich with Scott-Hardy's pronouncements on literature. From the back pages of one of these journals Norman learned that Scott-Hardy was thirty-one, a critic, and the author of two small volumes of poetry.

When Scott-Hardy returned he rubbed himself into the sofa like a cat pushing against a man's leg and poured himself a drink. 'I'm afraid I'm a little tipsy,' he said with pride.

Pip stared at Norman, his eyes big and bothered.

'You're an American,' Scott-Hardy said. 'That's something to go on.'

'What do you think he does, Morley?'

'I haven't a clue.'

'Perhaps he was a truck driver.'

Scott-Hardy's rosy cheeks quivered. '*Tu pense?*' he asked.

'Or a wrestler?'

Norman rubbed the back of his neck anxiously.

'Here,' Scott-Hardy said kindly, 'let me get you another drink.'

'He should have been here last Wednesday night,' Pip said.

'Pip!'

'What did I say now?' Pip turned and smiled wickedly at Norman. 'Henry James was here Wednesday night.'

Norman turned inquiringly to Scott-Hardy.

'He's a writer,' Scott-Hardy said.

'Oh, Oh I see. *Last* Wednesday night?'

'Um.'

'We hold seances,' Scott-Hardy said.

'What did James have to say?'

'Not very much.'

'Go ahead. *Tell him*.'

Scott-Hardy hesitated.

'*Come on.*'

'I asked James if he was the protagonist of *The American* and he replied, "Tut-tut, young man." I thought that was frightfully clever.'

Norman drained his glass of vodka.

'Last week,' said Pip, 'we had a boy here who died of tuberculosis in Manchester in 1892, but he was illiterate and rather a bore.'

'Do you hold seances often?'

'Rather.'

'No. Not any more.' Scott-Hardy turned his glass round and round in his damp pink hand. 'My confessor forbids it.'

'Tell him about Vanessa.'

'Pip!'

'Go ahead. Don't be a bitch. Tell him.'

'Vanessa can make tables fly through the air.'

'He doesn't believe you.'

'Pip!'

'*He doesn't.*'

'Please tell Pip you believe him.'

'I believe you.'

Pip looked like he was going to purr.

'Morley's turning Catholic.' Pip rolled over on the rug, played the dead dog, and then sprang upright swiftly. 'May I have a drink too?'

Scott-Hardy hesitated too long. Pip grabbed the bottle and poured himself a quick one. One sip and the giggles broke from him like glass.

'I spy something with my little eye,' he said, 'that begins with the letter Q.'

Scott-Hardy flushed. 'Pip, that's enough.' Ignoring the boy's giggles he turned to Norman with a warm, milky smile. 'You must be tired. Would you like to go to bed now?'

Norman shifted uneasily on the sofa.

'Ask him if he knows how to play botticelli?'

'Ask him yourself, you brat.' Again the warm, milky smile. 'You won't be annoyed, I assure you.'

'But—'

'Where would you go?'

'I have to get up early. I have an appointment at Waterloo Air Terminal.'

Scott-Hardy led Norman into the spare room.

'This is very kind of you,' Norman said.

But there was little sleep for Norman in the spare room. I can't go on much longer without a name, he thought. His head ached. It occurred to him for the first time that the woman with the two children may have been waiting for him. He had gone to the air terminal without a ticket, hadn't he? Obviously he had gone there to meet somebody. *Those two boys might be his.* Zurich. She had come from Zurich with the children. Yesterday it was. Surely they would be able to give him her name. That would be the key, he thought. Her name, if she was his wife, might be enough of a jolt to restore his memory. But if she wasn't – He would ask to see all of yesterday's arrival lists. On one of them there must be a name he would recognise.

Norman started at the sound of giggling like breaking glass. When he opened his eyes he was amazed to see Pip squatting at the foot of his bed. He seemed thinner in his pyjamas and rather like a bird. Norman felt sure that a little shake of his blanket would be enough to send Pip fluttering up to the ceiling.

'Morley has passed out,' Pip said.

'That seems to please you.'

'Um.'

'What time is it?'

'Almost four.' Pip, his knees protruding left and right like wishbones, made himself more comfortable. 'What fun it must be to lose one's memory.'

'I'm not enjoying it.'

'Silly clod. Think of it. Maybe you were unhappily married. Maybe your boss gave you the sack. Maybe all your life you've wanted to make a fresh start. Some people have *all* the luck.'

'What if I was happily married?'

Pip clamped his nose tight with one hand and pretended to pull a long chain with the other.

'You think that's unlikely?' Norman said.

'Um.'

'Perhaps you'd better go and see if Morley's come to.'

'Do you like Morley?'

'Yes. I think I do.'

'He sends me up the wall, he does.'

'Why?'

'He's not one.'

'He's not "one" what?'

'Oh, really, don't try to take the mickey out of *me*.'

'I'm serious.'

'*One*. He's not one.'

'I don't understand.'

'I didn't believe all the talk myself at first. Gay people are such dreadful gossips, actually, and I had his word of honour that his relationship with Vanessa was strictly platonic. But she stays the night here occasionally and once I caught them at the funny stuff.' Pip held his nose. 'Ugh!'

'You mean—'

'He's a nasty normie, actually. The rest is all a pose.'

'A pose?'

'Um.'

'But why?'

'Isn't it obvious?'

'Not to me, it isn't.'

'Morley is madly ambitious.'

'What's that got to do with it?'

'Coo – Aren't we naïve?'

'Perhaps.'

'He's trying to pass because he thinks it'll help him in certain circles.'

'I don't believe it.'

'Cross my little.'

VIII

Again.

The best ones were killed, Karp. Only the conniving, evil ones like you survived.

With that the whole intricate structure of Karp's plan for survival had toppled. No good the books on plant life, the acquired taste for sea food, and the cultivation of Gentiles. You were always a Jew. A blight if you perished, a blight if you survived. Norman, as sure as fire, had branded him again.

Karp wiped his eyes and bit through another cube of nut milk chocolate.

And there, in the outer darkness, was the gaunt face of Obersturmfuhrer Hartmann. Karp shut his eyes, swallowed his chocolate cube, and the face became Norman's face, smiled, and was Hartmann once more.

Hartmann.

Hartmann, the ace shot of the camp, had once tumbled a hundred men without even stopping for a smoke, but the worst, the most vividly remembered agony of Karp's days as a Sonderkommando, was the young girl. Thousands, every day thousands by gunshot and fire and gas, and in all that time only the young girl had survived the crematorium.

202

When the lights were turned off she breathed in a few lungsful of gas. Only a few, however, for her little body gave way under the pushing and shoving of others. It must have been by chance that she fell with her face against the wet concrete. Cyclon gas doesn't work under humid conditions: she was not asphyxiated.

While Karp and the other Sonderkommandos prayed, while they hoped, wept and waited, the doctors worked on her. They brought her back to life. A miracle. Someone had survived. But even as they gathered round the frail, frightened young girl Hartmann came to claim her. 'It's impossible,' he said. 'She would tell the others what she had been through. Discipline would collapse.'

A miracle, someone had survived, but – objectively speaking – you had to admit Hartmann was right. If the girl was sent to any of the women's work camps, and told them what she had been through, discipline *would* collapse.

Obersturmfuhrer Hartmann took the girl outside and shot her.

The next day Karp asked the doctor for a sure quick poison, but that was a standard Sonderkommando request, and of course it wasn't granted.

Thousands, Karp remembered, every day thousands but all that seemed to matter was the young girl who was brought back to life only to be shot.

Again.

The best ones were killed, Karp. Only the conniving, evil ones like you survived.

After all I did for him. Karp thought, after I bathed and washed him in the hospital, this is my reward. All right, Norman. Splendid. Now I'll show you a thing or two. You need a lesson.

IX

As soon as Norman saw what had happened he rushed right over to the information desk. 'Where is it?' he asked.

'I beg your pardon, sir?'

'The balloon,' Norman said. 'It's gone.'

'Balloon?'

'How did you get it down?'

'If you'll just calm down sir, and try to speak more slowly perhaps we can—'

Norman seized the clerk by the collar and shook him. 'The balloon is gone. I want to know what happened to it. Is that clear?'

Somebody tried to grab him from behind, but Norman shook him off. 'All I want to know is what happened to the balloon.'

Suddenly Norman's arms were pinned behind his back. He struggled, but it was no use. There were too many of them.

'Is he drunk?'

'I wish 'e were, mate.'

'Barmy?'

'You have no right to hold me,' Norman said. 'Just tell me what you've done with the balloon . . .'

A crowd gathered around him.

'John! Come quickly, John!'

'*Hélène! Vite, cheri. Un Anglais fou. Regarde. Il porte la mine d'un cochon.*'

A short beefy man poked Norman in the ribs. 'Use your loaf, mate. Don't admit anything until you've spoken to your solicitor.'

'*Wolfgang! Komme hier.*'

'That's how it all starts,' a bearded man said to another. 'First they build a few airbases. Next thing you know decent women aren't safe on the streets any more.'

'Is he a rapist?'

'I dare say.'

A woman with a spilling bosom pushed through for a closer look at Norman's ashen face.

'Act dumb.' The short, beefy man poked Norman harder. 'Otherwise you 'aven't 'alf a chance.'

Norman was immensely relieved to see Vivian pushing through the crowd towards him. He smiled weakly.

'It's you,' she said. 'Thank God you're all right.'

'You know him?'

'Let him go at once,' Vivian said. 'He's sick.'

'Sick? He's barmy, he is.'

Two men helped Norman over to a chair in the corner. Vivian followed behind with a senior official.

'How do you feel?' she asked.

'Please,' Norman said, 'please make them tell me what they did with the balloon.'

'Balloon?' the senior official asked.

Vivian pressed Norman's hand. 'Relax,' she said.

'Balloon?' the senior official repeated. 'What's your name?'

'He's suffering from amnesia,' Vivian said in a hushed voice.

The senior official frowned.

'He was in some sort of accident,' Vivian said. 'In the war, perhaps.'

''Ere you are, mate. I think this might help.'

Vivian took the glass of brandy from the porter and made Norman drink it. 'If one of you gentlemen would be kind enough to call a taxi . . .' Vivian shook Norman gently. 'Please,' she said, 'let's go.'

'Your taxi's waiting, Miss.'

Norman froze when they passed under the spot where the balloon had used to be. The woman with the spilling bosom hit him with her umbrella. 'Shame,' she said. 'Shame.'

'*Who took the balloon?*' Norman asked.

The bearded man confronted him. 'If you were a Negro,' he said, 'and this was your country, you would have been lynched by now.'

The senior official was obviously dismayed. 'Perhaps we ought to send for a doctor,' he said.

'No,' Vivian said. 'I'll take care of him.'

'He might be D-A-N-G-E—'

'Nonsense,' Vivian said.

'If only someone would explain,' Norman began. 'It's a simple question . . .'

They got him as far as the door.

'Why does he go on and on about a balloon?'

Vivian told the senior official what she knew.

'A bit thick, that.'

'Tell them to stop staring at me,' Norman said.

'Murdoch would know,' the senior official said. 'He was on duty last night. Leave me your phone number and I'll give you a tinkle after I've had a word with him. He'll know how they got the – the B-A-L-L-O—'

'Don't be an ass,' Vivian said. 'He can spell.'

The senior official helped Norman into the taxi.

Vivian gave him her phone number. 'Thanks for being so kind,' she said.

'I know this may be like trying to teach my grandmother to suck eggs, but one thing more.' The senior official smiled self-effacingly. 'If you're taking this chap home with you don't leave any sharp instruments around.'

Vivian slammed the taxi door. As they drove off she lit two cigarettes and passed Norman one.

'I think I'm going to be sick', he said.

She loosened his shirt collar. Norman opened the window on his side. His mouth open, he breathed deeply.

'Feel any better?'

He leaned back and shut his eyes.

'Why is the balloon so important to you?'

He didn't reply. But a couple of minutes later he opened his eyes. 'The Thames,' he said.

'Yes,' she said, looking briefly out of the window, 'that's right.'

'I've been here before.'

Vivian saw the dull, leaden river for what seemed to be the first time. 'It froze up one winter,' she said. 'During Elizabethan times.'

'What?'

'The Thames. It froze up.'

'Oh,' he said, 'when?'

'During Elizabethan times. I read it in a book.'

X

'Any news?'

'Nothing,' Ernst said.

Sally took off her coat and sat heavily down on the bed. 'Teaching is a nightmare these days,' she said. 'I'm always afraid you won't be here by the time I get home.'

Ernst sat by the window, mending a patch in his work trousers. 'Maybe,' he said, without looking up, 'we should inform the police.'

'Absolutely no.'

'He's been gone three days, Sally. What chance have we got of finding him?'

'He'll come back. Don't you worry.'

'Perhaps it would be best . . .'

'No,' she said. 'No police.'

Ernst smiled wistfully. 'After the *Zusammenbruch*, the surrender,' he said, 'I got into trouble peddling black market stuff in the cafés around the Bayerischeplatz, and a British Youth Officer gave me a talk. He told me a man needs a hobby to keep out of trouble. So you see,' he said, holding up his needle and thread, 'I took his advice.' Sally didn't seem to be listening. 'You didn't sleep last night,' he said.

'Neither did you.'

'I was thinking that if I had left when you tried to throw me out of your room that first day maybe it would have been better.'

'Are you sorry?'

'If not for me,' he said, 'you and Norman . . .'

'I doubt it.'

'Are you sure?'

'How can anyone be sure? Maybe we would have – but this kind of talk is senseless. Don't you think *I'm* sometimes sorry? But look here, Ernst, we met, we . . . Well here we are.'

'Norman is a good man.'

'Are you sorry, Ernst? Have you been happy with me?'

'Happy for the second time in my life,' he said.

'And the first?' Sally asked warily. He had never mentioned another girl before.

'In the *Jungvolk*,' he said.

'The Hitler Youth?'

'At the *Heimabend* every Wednesday night we used to sing stirring songs.'

Around the nocturnal campfires on the banks of the Nuthe, Ernst told her, he had learned about the myths, manners, and customs of ancient Germans, and about the characteristics of inferior races. He had also been given a dagger inscribed 'Blood and Honour'.

'That's horrible,' Sally said.

'I'm sorry.'

'If you hadn't met me,' she said, 'you never would have run into Norman. You might have been in America already with your rich fat lady.'

'It is no longer possible.'

'Oh,' she said petulantly, 'why?'

'It's like you have given me a—' He turned away from her. 'I can't express myself.'

'What you are saying is that you are no longer free.'

'No, no. I am free for the first time.' He sat down beside her on the bed and stroked her hair. 'Maybe you are right. Maybe we should run away.'

'Let's go, darling. Please let's. They'll never find us.'

'What do you think Norman will do?' he asked.

'Are you afraid?'

He didn't answer.

'Norman has no right to judge you.' She held him close. 'You have a duty to me too, Ernst. Please let's go away.'

'We can't have it both ways,' he said.

Sally flushed angrily. 'Oh, how you've changed,' she said. 'You sound like a priest.'

But she was not dissatisfied. She didn't want him to run out; she didn't want the others to have that pleasure. Norman, she thought, Norman, her heart told her, would understand that it was all a tragic accident. It would work out. You thought you'd never learn to do long division or ride a bicycle, you never really believed you'd get to Europe, but you did, you thought you were surely pregnant *this time*, but you were late, that's all. In the end everything worked out. Norman would come to understand. It would be difficult. But he would respect Ernst for not having fled when he had had his golden chance. Norman was like that.

'You have changed too,' he said. 'Once you were shocked that I had killed. Now you are begging me to run for it.'

'Oh, shut up. Please shut up for once.'

'To you the fact that I killed Nicky is no longer – It has become an inconvenience, no more. But me,' he shouted, 'I'm the Hitler Youth scum. Oh, you big, wonderful moral people. Is this what I've been missing?'

XI

Once in the flat with Vivian again Norman had begun to shiver.

'Would you like a drink?' she asked.

'I'd like to get into bed.'

She helped him undress.

'I'm getting the shakes,' he said.

Vivian kicked off her shoes recklessly and flung her dress over her head.

'Oh, please,' he said huskily, 'do something for me.'

She jumped into bed with him and hugged him as tight as she could.

'It's terrible,' he said. 'Oh, it's terrible.'

His hands dug into her back. The pain made her wince.

'I've got the shakes.'

'Please,' she said. 'Please. Oh, please.'

'I'm going to cry.'

'Cry,' she said ferociously. 'Go ahead.'

His hand went instinctively to her small bosom and Vivian stiffened. Please be nice, she thought. Please.

'Your knee,' she said.

'What?'

'Your *knee*. Please, you're hurting me.'

He moved his knee. 'Jesus,' he said. Then, as he succumbed to another seizure of violent shaking, she hugged him still closer.

'Cry,' she said. 'Go ahead.'

He wept. A great, rock-like sob split and broke inside him, another, another and another, he gasped, he jerked, his arms quivered, then his body loosened sweatily at last and his head on her breast became a dead weight. She whispered soothingly to him and in a remarkably short time he was asleep. He talked some through his sleep, but she could not make out what he was saying. At last she slipped out from under him and set his head down gently on the pillow. Her slip was wet and wrinkled. Like we had a battle, she thought.

Kate was waiting in the living room. 'You found him', she said enthusiastically.

'Kate,' Vivian said wearily. 'Kate.'

Kate smiled tenderly. Some six months ago, after she had discovered that her cousin occupied a bed-sitter at Earl's Court in a house where everyone else was elderly, she had promptly insisted that Vivian move in with her. Vivian had been working for an historical society at the time. She had known no men other than the kind who took you to the proms and brought you gifts of Penguins when you were ill. Kate had taken her in hand swiftly. She had landed her a job with a fashion magazine, and helped her to select a clever wardrobe. At first the two cousins had got on splendidly. Then, inevitably, they had begun to get on each other's nerves. The men who visited Kate's flat had been put out by the presence of a distinctly extra and rather hostile, sharp-tongued girl. Vivian, on her side, had poked merciless fun at the intellectual limitations of Kate's friends. Kate hoped that the present crisis might help to bring them closer to each other again. She got a blanket out of the wardrobe and covered Vivian. 'I'm going to stay with

210

Nancy tonight,' she said. She wrote out the phone number. 'Promise me one thing, darling. If you need me you'll call immediately. You can call me at any hour. Promise?'

'Ta,' Vivian said gratefully.

'I'm going upstairs now to warn Polly not to come snooping around.' Kate paused in the middle of the room. Once more Vivian envied her grace. 'He could have a wife, you know.'

'I know.'

Kate stopped again at the foot of the stairs. 'If you want to use my – I mean it would be silly to take chances, wouldn't it?'

Vivian's cheeks burned.

'It's in the kitchen,' Kate said quickly, 'second drawer, under the—'

'I have one of my own.'

'You know how to—'

'Certainly,' she said with defiance.

Vivian smoked another cigarette before she went shyly into the kitchen hoping, all the while, that Kate was mistaken, and that it wasn't in the second drawer as she had said. But there it was, wrapped in a towel, with the tube and injector alongside. Vivian took it into the bathroom with her, laying it down quickly behind her, just on the odd chance that she might go through with it. Then, pretending not to know what she was about, she washed under her arms and dabbed perfume behind her ears and brushed out her short black hair. Applying lipstick to her mouth she made it appear larger, the way Kate had taught her. She brushed out her hair again. Then, happily, she found something else to do. She squeezed a blackhead out of her nose. She brushed her teeth. When she turned round again, however, the old precautionary equipment was still there. Vivian read the instructions twice, not understanding a word. She felt dizzy. I might as well, she thought, taking a deep breath, just in case.

Vivian lay stiffly and alarmed beside him in the single bed for some time before he stirred. He took her in his arms

211

half-consciously at first, almost like a reflex, but little by little there came small gestures of recognition and love. Vivian embraced him with a store of passion that had been unwillingly hoarded for many years – since, in fact, that insane Italian holiday – and then, only then, did she realise that he had fallen away into a deep sleep again. She lay back, the man tangled up with her under the blankets, and waited for the dark and then for the light again with her eyes open and moist.

Norman snored.

She was getting breakfast ready in the kitchen when he came running in 'I remember, Vivian. I can tell you my address – my name – everything. I remember. I'm Norman,' he yelled, 'Norman Price. My name is Norman Price. Can you beat that?' He took her in his arms and spun her round and round. 'My name is Norman Price. Honest to God it is!'

They ate breakfast together excitedly, but by the time they had washed and dressed, when they next sat down with a coffee table between them, a change had taken place. Norman studied the stuff on the table critically. Back issues of *Vogue* and the *Spectator*; Mr Balchin's latest novel from Boots and a book of cartoons by Ronald Searle.

'I guess you're anxious to get back to your family,' she said.

He thanked her profusely for her help, but that only seemed to double the width of the table between them.

'I work for a fashion magazine,' she said.

'Oh, how interesting.'

'What do you do?'

'This and that.'

What, she thought, if he *was* an airman. He might even be a worker. His hands were rough.

'I write thrillers, I'm afraid. Scenarios too. I used to be an assistant professor in the States. But I'm a Canadian, really.'

Vivian was overjoyed. Binky had tried to write thrillers; he failed. Roger Nash was mad keen to get into films. She

212

filled the tea cups again with more spirit. 'Am I keeping you?' she asked.

'Oh no. Am I keeping you?'

'No.'

He picked up the *Spectator* nervously and put it down again and began to flip through *Vogue*.

'My cousin's a model,' she said. 'I share the flat with her. Will you have both?'

'Oh, yes. Of course.'

The tea was luke-warm.

'Perhaps you ought to phone your family.'

'I'm a bachelor.'

Vivian's cheeks reddened. 'Oh,' she said, 'I didn't mean to pry.' She folded the *Daily Telegraph* in four and tried her best to conceal Kate's copy of the *Astrologist* under another magazine. The clock ticked intolerably loud. 'Do you think Ike will run again?'

'It doesn't much matter, does it?'

'Oh, I somehow thought Stevenson would make a much better president.' Her voice shrunk. 'Not that I know much about it.'

Norman cleared his throat. 'There's not much to choose between them,' he said.

He's a former professor, she thought. Perhaps he's one of those fifth amendment people she'd heard Roger talk about. Maybe he was a communist. 'The witch-hunt there is dreadful, isn't it? I mean,' she continued guardedly, 'lots of people are being persecuted.'

Norman swiftly conjured up a picture of Winkleman and Co. Horton. 'Serves them right.' He regretted having said that immediately.

'Oh,' she said, 'some of them *are* communists, I'm sure and . . .'

'Don't you think communists have as much right to their opinions as other people?' he asked sharply.

'Certainly,' she said in a small voice. 'I mean of course . . .'

Norman noticed the thick legs, the small breasts, he took

213

in the parched little mouth. 'I didn't mean to jump at you,' he said.

'You didn't jump,' she said.

Norman rose. 'I don't want to seem ungrateful,' he said, 'but there are some people I must see now that I'm o.k. again.'

'Of course.'

But at the door she asked what she had been struggling against bitterly. The words opened like a wound. 'Will I see you again?'

Norman noticed – and despised himself for noticing – that there was no ring on her finger, 'Sure,' he said. 'Of course.'

As he turned to go, she said, 'In that case don't you think you ought to write down my address?'

He made a note of her address and phone number.

'Look here,' she said, her voice unnaturally high. 'I would have done the same for anyone. I don't want you to think that you owe me anything.'

'I understand.'

They kissed – Norman shy; Vivian stiff, resistant – and then he was gone.

Vivian stumbled to the phone. 'Kate. Come quickly, Kate. I've made an awful fool of myself.' Vivian dropped the receiver back into place and began to laugh. She laughed in spurts. A little bit of laughter at a time.

XII

Karp didn't bother to knock. He came in and sat right down in the armchair. 'I will come right to the point,' he said. 'Norman just phoned. He is all right. He's on his way over.' Karp looked haggard; his shirt was soiled. 'He wants to see Ernst.'

'Did he say anything else?' Sally asked.

'Nothing.' Karp took a fat envelope out of his pocket.

'There are two hundred pounds in here. I want you to take it and leave at once. Norman called from Chelsea. He won't be here for another ten minutes at least.'

'I don't understand,' Ernst said.

'Neither do I.'

'Don't even try to understand,' Karp said. 'Take the money.'

'You want us to flee?'

'Yes.'

'But you told Norman in the first place,' Sally said. 'If not for you—'

'There is little time.' Karp gave them an exasperated look. 'Yes. I told him. But one – Take the money. Go.'

'Why do you want to help us?' Ernst asked.

Karp's corpulence seemed an appalling burden for the first time. He breathed heavily; his eyes were dim with exhaustion. 'You and I,' he said to Ernst, 'we too, we're survivors.'

'Sally,' Ernst said softly, 'please make Mr Karp a cup of tea.'

Sally put the kettle on the gas ring.

'Norman,' Karp said, 'never really understood about people like us. The night before – before his illness struck he abused me because I – Never mind that. That, so to speak, is finished. Take the money.'

Two hundred pounds, Ernst thought. That would be a fine start.

Karp told them the story of the young girl. 'Thousands,' he said, 'every day thousands by gunshot and fire and gas, and in all that time only the young girl survived the crematorium.' He shook a white little finger at Ernst. 'You too have been brought back from the dead, Ernst. I don't want to see you murdered a second time like—' He turned angrily on Sally. 'Make him go.'

'He won't listen to me any more.'

'Ernst. *Hor zu, Ernst. Norman wird Dich* – He'll turn him over to the police.'

'No.' Sally said. 'Norman won't—'

215

'He won't inform on me,' Ernst said. '*Er ist nicht die Type.*'

Karp rose and confronted Ernst, his face red and swollen, his eyes bulging. 'I'm a German,' he yelled, 'like you.' Exhausted by his effort, he stumbled back into the chair and rocked his head in his hands. 'If you love the girl,' he said, 'take her and go. Get out of my house.'

Ernst rested his hand gently on the old man's shoulder. 'O.K.,' he said. 'I'll take your money.'

A taxi door slammed outside. Sally rushed to the window. 'It's Norman,' she said. 'He's come.'

Karp raised his head. 'Don't worry,' he said, 'I'll detain him.' And he hurried out of the room and down the stairs, his steps short and quick and angry, like bites.

'We'd better hurry,' Sally said.

'We're not going anywhere.'

'Why did you take his money, then?'

'Because he wants to be a German,' Ernst said, 'like me.' He flung the envelope of money against the wall. 'A German,' he said. 'A survivor.' Ernst laughed shortly. 'I'm going downstairs,' he said, 'to Norman's room. You wait for me here.'

XIII

'Well,' Ernst said, 'here we are. At last.'

Norman lit a cigarette.

'We were worried about you,' Ernst said.

'This kind of thing happens to me sometimes.'

'Can't anything be done?'

'It's not organic. The doctors say I suffer from – from an inability to deal with reality.' Norman smiled ruefully. 'The longest it has ever lasted is three weeks. I guess I should try psychotherapy, but I don't trust those kind of people. They have a dirty vocabulary.' Norman was aware of the sweat beginning to soak through his shirt. He poured out two

216

drinks of whisky. 'I met a nice girl,' he said. 'She helped me through it.'

'I'm glad for you.'

'Oh, it's nothing like that. But she's nice.'

'Would you like to get married?'

'Sure I would like to get married. I want to have children.'

'I hope it works out for you.'

'Why didn't you run away?' Norman asked.

'It didn't seem like such a good idea.'

'Sally wouldn't have gone with you. Is that it?'

'Something like that.'

'How long has she known about it?'

'Not long.'

Norman filled his glass again. 'I don't understand why you didn't flee the day after I showed you his picture.'

'I love her.'

'Either that or you were gambling for her passport against my discovering what you had done.'

It's not going well, Ernst thought. He's afraid.

'Her passport had nothing to do with it.'

'What right have you got to ask me to believe anything you tell me?' Norman asked.

'None.'

'O.K. Tell me your version of what happened.'

Ernst laughed a little. 'Was it necessary?' he asked, 'to first establish that I am a liar?'

'Tell me how it happened.'

Ernst told Norman what he had told Sally. He explained that he had not wanted to kill Nicky. The murder had been an accident.

'Had you killed before?' Norman asked.

'Yes. Haven't you?'

'In the war, I have.'

'But this was your brother.'

Norman nodded.

'They all have brothers.' Ernst refused another drink. 'Do you believe my story?' he asked.

217

'Nicky meant more to me than anyone in the world.'

'I told you exactly how it happened.'

'I'm going to turn you over to the police.'

'You are?'

'That's letting you off easy.'

'You too. That's letting you off easy too.'

'I've made up my mind. I won't change it.'

'There are many ugly things I could say.'

'About her? I'm not doing it because of her,' Norman said.

'But you love her?'

'I did.'

'I pity you,' Ernst said.

'Don't.'

'You want her – you love her – but not only will you not have her, she will hate you for the rest of her life.'

'Look,' Norman said, 'he was my brother.'

'I could have run away.'

'She would never have gone with you. And another thing,' Norman said, raising his voice for the first time, 'you could have told me the story of your own accord. You needn't have made a fool of me for so long.'

'We were going to tell you.'

'Do you expect me to believe that?'

'What makes you angrier, Norman, the fact that I killed your brother, or your injured vanity?'

Norman poured himself another drink.

'I'll leave her,' Ernst said quietly. 'I won't see her again.'

'No. I told you. It's not because of her.'

'Listen – don't be a fool – what good will it do you to turn me in?'

'None.'

'What if it had been the other way round?'

'Please, Ernst, I've been over it a hundred times myself.'

'If it was the other way around you would hide Nicky. You would protect him. You would make excuses for him. Right?'

'I honestly don't know.'

'You would call that loyalty.'

'Yes,' Norman said wearily, 'I guess I would.'

'I pity you.'

'You've said that already.'

'I will say it again. I pity you.'

'Don't over-dramatise it, Ernst. You'll probably get off with five years.'

'More likely twenty.'

'I hope not.'

'If I get twenty years you would have murdered me, just like I killed your brother. But at least I was being attacked. I had no choice, but you—'

'I have no choice either.'

Ernst laughed. 'You mean you are doing this because of a principle?'

Norman nodded. 'A principle,' he said.

Ernst laughed again. His gloomy blue eyes began to shine wetly. 'During the last days of the war some people – me and my mother too – listened to an enemy broadcast describing the entry of the allied armies into Auschwitz. Everybody put the story down to propaganda. So my mother took me aside to tell me what had happened. My uncle, Heinrich Walther, had used to be a communist deputy. He disappeared in the camps. "If the Americans get here first," she said, "don't say a word about it. But if the Russians come remember that you are the nephew of Heinrich Walther." That,' Ernst said, 'you would call *un*principled, I suppose.'

'I suppose.'

'Opportunist?'

'All right,' Norman said. 'Opportunist. Get on with it, damn you.'

'Me,' Ernst said, 'I had principles. Then one day an American soldier gave me a Babe Ruth chocolate bar and told me that Hitler was dead. Kaput! Finished principles. Two weeks later I earned two packs of Lucky Strikes for spending the night with an American army colonel. O.K. Bravo. Beginning of a new principle. Truth equals Lucky

Strikes.' He eyed Norman coldly. 'Don't speak to me about principles.'

'There are such things, you know, as dignity, honour, and love.'

'Yeah. I have heard them mentioned on the radio on Sunday mornings.'

'Would you like another drink?'

'Your kind, your generation, you killed for ideals, principles, and a better world.'

Norman poured himself another drink.

'Hitler burned the Jews,' Ernst shouted, 'and Stalin murdered the kulaks, all so that there should be a better world for me.'

'You don't know what you're talking about.'

Ernst rose shakily. 'I would like to speak to Sally. I would like to see her before—'

'I'll wait for you here,' Norman said.

Ernst paused at the door. 'What is my unintentional crime,' he asked, 'compared to all those crimes your kind committed with the best of intentions?'

Ernst returned to his room just as Sally had finished sweeping up. Karp sat on the bed.

'What did he say?' Karp asked.

'He's turning me over to the police. It's a matter of principle.'

'Principle.' Sally laughed noiselessly. 'Are you pleased now? Are you satisfied now that you'll go to prison? You should have come away with me while—'

Ernst turned to go.

'Where are you going?' Sally asked.

'To the toilet,' he said. 'I'll be right back.'

Ernst walked down the stairs, out of the house, and up Belsize Avenue. He turned right on Haverstock Hill and crossed the street. In the tube station he bought a ticket to Liverpool Street Station.

*

XIV

A half hour later Norman went upstairs. 'Where is he?' he asked.

'He's gone,' Sally said.

There was a pile of money on the bed. 'It's mine,' Karp said. 'He wouldn't take it. I'm not a German, like him.'

Norman rushed to the window. 'He asked if he could speak to you first,' he said. 'I said O.K.'

'He's gone,' Sally said.

'Where's he gone to?'

'How would I know?'

'Karp?'

'Beats me,' Karp said. 'I'm a conniving Jew. Remember?'

Norman approached Karp menacingly.

'Leave him alone,' Sally said. 'We don't know where he's gone.' She looked up at Norman and laughed. 'A man of principle,' she said, 'that's what you are.'

'He left his guitar,' Karp said.

Norman banged the guitar against the floor and rammed his foot through it. 'I'll find him,' he said. 'I don't care where he goes.'

'Now Norman has something to live for,' Sally said. 'Hate, now he has somebody to hate again.'

Norman shook Sally gently. 'Did you know that he was going to run out in the end?' he asked. 'Did you plan it between you?'

'She didn't know,' Karp said.

'Take your hands off me,' Sally yelled.

'King David,' Karp said, 'sent Uriah to die in battle, so that he could make Bathsheba his wife.'

'Look,' Norman said, 'he killed my brother.'

'You see,' Sally said. 'He has principles.'

'Jesus.'

'Can't you see she wants you to go,' Karp said.

Sally seemed to notice the smashed guitar for the first time. 'Why did you have to go and do that?' she asked.

'I'm sorry.'

221

Sally began to sob. 'I always knew that it could never be,' she said. 'I always knew you'd come for him in the end. But now that it's happened— He's worth ten of you,' she shrieked.

'I ought to slap you so hard,' Norman said, 'that—'

'You're right. That's it,' she said. 'Don't you see? *You're always right*. He never was. He never had a chance.'

'You,' Norman said, grabbing her, shaking her. 'You and I,' he said, 'we could have been so happy together. I loved you Sally. Oh, how I loved you. But – How could you prefer scum like Ernst over me? And he ran out on you in the end, didn't he? You thought he wouldn't. You thought he'd stay with it. Oh, Sally, Sally. Think what you've done to both of us.'

'You lonely, foolish man,' she said. 'All that's left for you is hatred.'

'I'll find him,' Norman said, letting her go, 'no matter where he goes.'

'Find him,' Sally said. 'I don't care any more.'

After Norman had gone Karp stared morosely at the guitar. 'It's broken,' he said.

'Yes,' Sally said. 'It's broken.'

Part Four

I

Hale was shocked.

Seated opposite Norman in a frayed easy chair the next spring, Thomas Hale squeezed his big black beard and shook his head mournfully. He had been warned in Toronto, of course. Charles Lawson had described Norman's condition as psychotic. But Hale, well aware of the knack creative men have for embellishment, had not taken Lawson's story very seriously. Norman had always drunk more than was good for him – another vice of the creative, Hale reflected – but you would not have described him as an alcoholic.

'. . . and ever since,' Norman continued thickly, 'I've been looking for him. You ought to see the size of my correspondence. Once or twice I even had private investigators work on it. It seems to me that he must have gone back to East Germany. I'm thinking of going to Berlin this coming fall, if I can afford it.' Norman smiled loosely. 'Another drink?'

'No thanks.' Hale winced as Norman poured himself another stiff one. 'It's rather early in the day, don't you think?'

Norman's flat looked seedier, more disordered, than ever.

Norman was greyer. He looked plump, puffy and, if you took the lack-lustre eyes into account, a little unbalanced. Hale wished for Norman's sake that he had not told his story to many people. What an incredible fantasy, he thought.

Hale knew the truth.

Norman had fallen in love with a young Canadian school teacher who had turned him down in favour of a German boy, someone closer to her own age group. The boy, a political refugee from the East, had proven an anathema to Norman's friends. Norman had tried to ingratiate himself with the girl by standing up for her boy friend. At the same time, desperate for money, he had made an underhand deal

225

with an *emigré* producer which, had it worked, would have robbed Lawson of credit for *All About Mary*. When it was discovered, Norman, unable to cope, had taken refuge in temporary amnesia. Then – and this was the most reprehensible part of the whole sordid business – Norman had driven the German boy away somehow, hoping to rehabilitate himself in the eyes of the *emigrés*. Hale was deeply moved. The human predicament, he thought.

Norman drank his whisky neat. 'I've never told anyone the truth about Ernst before,' he said. 'I couldn't stand the idea of people gloating over what a fool I had been . . .'

Hale stroked his beard. This latest fantasy that the German boy had murdered his brother, was a clear case of mental compensation. Hale decided that he would never repeat this hallucination to anyone. For Norman, he was sure, would be himself again one day.

'What,' Hale asked, 'do you think of the Kruschev revelations?'

Norman lazily reverted to an earlier habit of mind. 'As far as I know,' he said, 'the speech you read was released by the American State Department.'

Better not argue, Hale thought. 'Well,' he said, 'I guess I'd better get moving . . .'

Norman smiled a drunken magnanimous smile. Hale came to Europe annually in the spirit of a boy visiting Coney Island. Maybe, Norman thought, his is the right attitude after all.

Hale noticed that the newspaper scattered over the floor was the Montreal *Star*. He poked a section of it with his foot. 'Homesick?' he asked.

'It's the Saturday edition. A friend at home has been sending it to me for years.'

'You ought to come home. I still think it's a waste. You ought to come home and teach.'

'Even if I wanted to,' Norman said, 'I haven't got the fare.'

'I'll gladly lend you the money.'

'Thanks.' At the door Norman pressed Hale's arm, delaying his departure. 'I mean that. Your offer is very kind.'

'I meant it.'

'I know you did. What about Charlie? How is he?'

'He's doing extremely well.' Hale clutched the door-knob tight and risked an indiscretion. 'This may be none of my affair,' he said, 'but I'd like you to know that Charlie bears you no grudge. If that's what stopping you from going home, I mean.'

'It's none of your affair,' Norman said. 'That's true.'

After Hale had gone Norman poured himself another drink. It was already 4.15. He would be late for tea with Kate and Vivian. Just this drink, he thought, and then I'll take a taxi. Once outside, however, Norman decided to take the tube. He couldn't really afford a taxi and besides he preferred tubes and buses these days. There was always the off-chance that he might run into Ernst, Sally, Winkleman, somebody, anybody, absolutely anybody, who had once been his friend. Norman saw nobody these days outside of Vivian and Kate. He had even given up travelling. He slept in until twelve most mornings, read newspapers, magazines, a book occasionally, and then he had his first drink. His money was running out.

Walking down the King's Road Norman suddenly felt a hand pressing on his elbow.

'Norman! Norman Price! You're just the man I want to see,' Colin Horton said. 'I was going to ring you tomorrow morning.'

Horton didn't look well. His bony face had filled with intricate little lines, the black hair had lost its shine. They went to the Eight Bells together. 'You saw the light before any of us,' Horton said meekly, 'so if you want to say I told you so, you're entitled to it.'

'What are you talking about?'

'Stalin,' he said.

'Oh, the speech, you mean?'

'I wrote articles against POUM in Spain, you know and in New York in '41 I helped to get a couple of Trotskyites dismissed from their jobs.'

'Not because of their political opinions,' Norman said.

'I told you,' Horton said, 'if you want to say "I told you so" then—'

'I'm sorry.'

'Norman, listen Norman. I've got a boy of seventeen in the States. I've branded him for the rest of his life. I used to consider that part of the price you paid, but now . . . What am I to write him?' Horton asked. 'He's my son.'

'Let's have another drink, eh?'

'When I think of the murders, when I remember the whitewashing articles I wrote, I'm sick to my stomach.'

'Take heart, old boy. They would have gone ahead without your permission.'

'I'm forty-five,' he said. 'I used to be so damned sure of myself. I—'

'Here, drink up,' Norman said. 'This sounds cruel – I know – but I don't want to hear about it. I've had mine, Colin.'

'The worst is,' Horton said, 'that I suspected the truth all along but kept quiet for the sake of the greater truth.' He paused to wipe his eyes. 'I had thought that the whole nature of man had been changed in thirty years.'

'Did you really believe that?'

'I was in Spain, you know.'

'The next guy who says that to me is going to get a punch in the nose. What, exactly, were you doing in Spain?'

'I was a journalist.'

Norman turned to go.

'Wait,' Horton said, 'talk to me a little. I – Excuse me.' He blew his nose. 'I – Oh, who do you apologise to?'

'Take it easy.'

'I'd like to start by apologising for picking on your friend that night. I was being unfair. I see that now.'

'Skip it,' Norman said stiffly.

'What's become of him?'

'I don't know.'

'Anyway,' Horton said, 'I was wrong that night and you were right. You're a much better judge of character than I am.'

Norman smiled lamely. 'I'm late for an appointment,' he said.

'Well,' Horton said, 'I'll see you at the party tonight. We can talk some more there.'

'What party?'

'Aren't you invited to Bob Landis's place tonight?'

Norman realised that Horton had probably been away for some time and didn't know that nobody invited him around any more.

'Sure,' Norman said. 'I'll see you later.'

Norman hurried over to the flat on Oakley Street. Kate, and Roger and Polly Nash sat around the coffee table. Kate was wearing a cashmere sweater and toreador pants. She looked lovely. Vivian saw immediately that Norman was drunk, but she made no comment.

'Sorry I'm late,' Norman said. 'I ran into an old friend. We had a few drinks together.'

Vivian, who was wearing a smart cocktail dress, poured tea. She served Norman first.

'Have you noticed Vivian's new outfit?' Kate asked.

'I think it's very nice,' Norman said weakly.

'You men,' Polly said.

'Aren't they all alike,' Kate said vehemently. 'Thoughtless, selfish, and blind to a woman's *more serious* virtues.'

Norman realised that Kate was annoyed with him. He wondered why.

Vivian passed Roger his tea. 'Norman is working frightfully hard on a new film script,' she said.

'Oh, how interesting.'

Norman winced. He imagined that Vivian had suffered more than a fistful of insults to have come to baiting Roger so blatantly, but, however just her cause, he wished she wouldn't do it. Besides she knew he wasn't working on a script.

'Roger is ever so anxious to get into film work,' Polly said. 'He has some wonderful ideas.'

Norman smiled understandingly at Roger, but before he could say anything friendly Vivian called out to him from

229

the kitchen. 'Norman, she said, 'can you give me a hand for a moment?'

Norman excused himself. Once in the kitchen he kissed Vivian mildly on the forehead.

'I hadn't counted on the others,' Vivian said. 'I thought we'd have the flat to ourselves. I know you can't bear them.'

'But I like Roger.'

Vivian shut the kitchen door softly. 'Kate's got a new boy friend. She's out most nights. Why don't you come around later this evening?'

'I'll try.'

'The Hungarian State Opera Company will be at the Palace next Wednesday. Shall I get two tickets?'

'That would be nice,' he said. 'But don't you think we ought to get back and join the others?'

II

The flat Bob had rented for Sally when she had returned from Paris in April was on a little street of shrinking grey buildings off Baker Street. She abhorred being left alone there. The combination record player and television set, a recent gift from him, was more of an encumbrance than a solace. The other gifts – the plants, perfumes, and lingerie – were not all from him. This made her feel guilty. For Bob gave so very much and, as she could not give him anything like love in return, it seemed to her that the very least she could do was remain faithful to him. He was soft. His vanity at times was insufferable. But in spite of the daily handball, the morning exercises and the occasional swim, he was beginning to spread around the middle. He was kind. He never mentioned Ernst's name unless she brought it up first. He was merely a boy. Flattering remarks were jam to him, and compliments he ravished like cookies. He was kind, merely a boy, but he was also flabby with middle-age.

Once or twice maybe she asked him about Norman. He didn't see Norman. Nobody saw him.

As Sally sat by the window watching the black tree opposite, as she glanced three, four times at the puffy grey sky, the tears swelled and broke. These days the tears came easily and by surprise. Against the tears Sally took phenobarbitol, gin, and double features.

One of those incongruously young, pink-cheeked bobbies passed below. Next came a black boy on a bicycle. Trixie, the sly terrier, led Miss Langlie down the spotted black pavement. They were late. The Volunteer must have been open for twenty minutes or more. Sally poured herself another gin and tonic. No doubt, she thought, I should have married Norman. But between them like a sore there would always have been Ernst. And Norman would have acted so correctly, with so much dignity and compassion, that he would surely have driven her out of her mind. Yet, she thought, I could have been happy with him.

'Ernst,' she called suddenly.

I mustn't. Sally thought. He'll be angry if I'm drunk when he comes. Remembering Sally got up and tottered into the bathroom and returned with a glass of water and the bottle of sleeping tablets. It was a low, desperate trick, that much she was ready to confess, but she was not going to submit to an abortion. This child she would not lose. The pill Sally swallowed went down with difficulty. She coughed and turned back to her gin. He was soft, a boy merely, and when he came to pick her up at eight – he was a most punctual man – and found her with the half-empty bottle of gin and the empty bottle of sleeping tablets beside her he would rush her to the hospital – it was nearby – and he would be so moved by her plight that he would promise her she could have the child.

A cunning, filthy stunt; that's what it was. But even as she swallowed the third pill Sally knew that this melodramatic deceit, this 'attempted suicide', was in his idiom, would do better than tears and arguments, and would win her the life of her unborn child. So Sally took another pill.

III

It was their habit to relax with a martini together before a party, so a little later Bob Landis sat down to drink with his wife.

Dark, spare Zelda Landis looked more than her thirty-nine years. Her simple black dress, the jewelled earrings which clung like bites to her ears and even the black court pumps, all added to the severity of her manner. She sat down to rest. The canapés and hors d'oeuvres and the chipolatas, were all ready and covered with napkins on the kitchen table. She had prepared a cold dinner plate for the two of them to eat before the others arrived. Zelda was a splendid hostess, but she always gave the impression that she had been specially put together just to last out one particular evening. You felt that after the last guest had gone Zelda fell apart on the floor. Bob always knitted her together again, of course. But each time there was a spare part like chip of china left over, and so when you next saw Zelda she seemed older and more prone than last time to disintegrate before the evening was done.

The living room was furnished in the best of taste. Two pictures hung on the wall. One was a Chinese print of a horse and the other a drawing of a Mexican peasant hanging from a tree by his thumbs. They were both obligatory, like pictures of the Queen or crucifixes were in homes with other loyalties.

Then, just as Bob set out to refill the glasses, the door bell rang. It was only six-thirty: nobody was expected until nine. 'Oh, I know,' Zelda said, 'It must be Mrs Deacon. The old dear offered to come round to help with the serving tonight.'

'There's a Mr Price here to see you,' the maid said.

Bob had wanted to ask Norman to their party for old time's sake, but Zelda had said no, positively no. 'Shall I ask him to stay?' Bob asked, rising.

'Certainly not.'

The number of men at Zelda's parties always equalled the number of women. Norman was extra.

'What'll we say?'

'I don't care what you say. As long as you get rid of him.'

Norman entered the room, smiling shyly. 'I was just passing by,' he said, 'and I thought I'd see if you were in . . .'

Zelda recognised the lie at once.

'Sit down.' Bob smiled his most affable smile. 'What'll you have to drink?'

But Bob, too, felt that Norman had not merely been passing by, and that embarrassed him for Norman's sake.

'Whisky,' Norman said. Then, sensing Zelda's hostility, he added, 'Look, if you're expecting people for dinner or . . . I can come by another time.'

What a cheap way to wangle an invitation, Zelda thought. But Bob was touched, he was fond of Norman, and he showed it by pouring him a very stiff drink. Then, turning to Zelda, he said, 'I'm glad you came by tonight. I've been meaning to call you for weeks and weeks.'

Zelda's cheeks flushed. 'How have you been keeping, Norman?'

'Oh, fine. Just fine.'

She noticed that Bob had poured a very stiff drink for himself too. Get drunk, she thought. You just go ahead.

Bob observed with sadness that Norman was wearing the same clothes as when he had seen him last. The cuffs of his jacket were worn, 'I hear you've been fraternising with the natives these days,' he said with forced gaiety.

'I'm going out with a British girl. But it's not serious.'

Norman asked about the Winklemans.

'*All About Mary* was a smash,' Bob said. 'It's doing great in the provinces. Sonny and Budd have formed an independent unit and they're going to make two films a year now.' Bob refilled the glasses. 'What are you working on these days?' he asked.

'I've put in for a job at one of the provincial universities,' he said. 'If I don't get it I think I'll take a grammar school job.'

Norman exuded so distinct an odour of failure that Zelda

233

was momentarily alarmed. I know now why he came here, she thought.

'Do you people ever hear anything from Sally?' Norman asked. 'Is she in London, I mean?'

Bob glanced quickly at his wrist watch. 'Last we heard she was working in Paris,' he said. 'With UNESCO, I think.' But Bob was amazed. He had thought that Zelda was the only one who didn't know that he was keeping Sally in a flat off Baker Street.

'Oh, I must tell you,' Zelda said with a smile, 'Bob bought his parents a house in Connecticut last week. It's lovely, you know, but it's left us absolutely flat broke.'

'I didn't come here to borrow money, Zelda.'

Embarrassed, anxious to create a diversion, Bob swiftly took a letter from Charlie out of his inside pocket and pulled out a snapshot and handed it to Norman. The snapshot showed Charlie holding a baby in the air. Joey sat in the background on a garden chair. Norman returned the snapshot to Bob. 'A very nice kid,' he said. 'Whose is it?'

'I keep forgetting you've been out of circulation for so long,' Bob said. 'They adopted him last year. That's why they went back to Toronto.'

Zelda rose.

'I'd better be going,' Norman said, getting up, 'I mean, if you're expecting guests, I think . . .'

'As a matter of fact,' Zelda said, 'we are just going out for dinner. Please call us soon. We must get together some time.'

'Well,' Norman said. 'God bless.'

'Wait. Have one for the road.'

'I don't think we have time,' Zelda said.

'She's right. Another time maybe.'

Bob eyed Norman drunkenly. Norman, he thought, had used to be so proper. Glancing apprehensively at Zelda, he wondered how long Norman must have wandered up and down the street – hoping to run into him accidentally perhaps – before he had dared to come without an invitation. Bob glanced at his watch. She isn't expecting me for three-quarters of an hour, he thought. So I'll be a little late. Just this once. 'I'll tell you what,' he said gaily, 'why don't you come out and eat with us. We're just going to the Chinese restaurant at Swiss Cottage, aren't we, dear?'

Zelda turned very pale.

'Well, I'm expected somewhere a little later this evening, but—'

Bob clapped Norman on the back. 'Come on.' He turned triumphantly to Zelda. 'Would you like me to get your coat, dear?'

'No thanks.'

They got into the car and drove to the restaurant on Finchley Road. Bob told a lot of jokes on the way over. As Norman got out of the car first Zelda pressed Bob's arm angrily. 'If I live to be a hundred,' she said, 'I'll never forgive you for this stupid prank.'

Bob laughed; he slapped his knees. 'You should have asked him to stay,' he said.

'Oh, you rotten bastard.'

'Come on,' he said, 'let's eat.'

Inside, Bob ordered two double whiskies. 'Excuse me a minute,' he said. 'I've got to make a phone call.'

Norman smiled uneasily at Zelda. 'Shall we pretend we like each other,' he asked, 'and talk?'

But Bob was back before she could reply. 'Line's busy,' he said. They ordered an assortment of dishes to be shared. 'The trouble with Norman,' Bob said, 'is that he was a premature anti-Stalinist.'

Zelda didn't laugh.

'How is everyone taking it?' Norman asked.

'You may not believe this,' Bob said, 'I wouldn't have myself, but when Winkleman heard what had happened to the Yiddish writers he broke down and wept. It was anti-semitism, you know, that first drew him to the Party. It was supposed to have been, quote, outlawed, unquote, in Russia, or hadn't you heard?'

'And what about you,' Norman asked, 'what do you think?'

'If it's true,' Bob said, 'then that crime and any other must certainly be exposed. But look here, Norman, I joined the Party twenty years ago because I thought that human life was sacred and that the capitalist system was brutal. I still think so. If Stalin made errors, if he was a tyrant, then I think it's a bloody shame, but I also think that it may have been a necessary stage for socialism to go through.' Bob got up. 'Excuse me. I'll be right back.'

Norman watched as Bob weaved his way unsurely between the maze of tables to the phone. 'You're not eating,' he said to Zelda.

'I'm not hungry.'

They sat in silence until Bob returned. 'Goddamned line's still busy.' Actually nobody had answered the phone. He wondered where Sally was. 'The hell with it,' he said. Bob ordered more whisky. 'Where was I?' he asked.

'Stalin,' Norman said, 'that's where.'

Bob studied Norman with glazed eyes. He's a bachelor, he thought. He might know of a safe abortionist. I must ask him. 'Look at it this way,' Bob said, 'if one generation was sacrificed then at least *this time* they died for a purpose. They died so their children could look forward to a better life.'

'You look at it *this way*,' Norman said. 'It seems to me, that aside from our political virtues, people like us never had anything else. That's a very hard fact to face at forty.'

'I didn't think you cared about these things any more,' Zelda said.

'Shettup!' Bob said.

'He showed his true political colours long ago, Bob. He—'

'Quiet! You don't know what you're talking about. Look,' Bob said thickly, 'I'm a humanist, Norman. I believe that human life is sacred. That was and still is my position.' Bob staggered to his feet. 'Excuse me, I'll be right back.'

Zelda squashed her cigarette in a plate of fried rice.

236

'We're having a party tonight,' she said. 'Would you like to come?'

'I'd love to,' Norman said, 'but I'm busy.'

'Will you please tell Bob that I asked you to come tonight and that you're busy?'

'No. I won't.'

Bob returned. 'Where was I?' he asked.

'Human life is sacred,' Norman said.

'I'm going,' Zelda said.

'See you in church,' Bob said.

'I said I was going.'

'And I said I'll see you in church.'

Zelda poked Norman. 'Tell him,' she said.

'Uuh?'

'Tell me a story,' Bob half-rose, pretending to conduct an orchestra. 'Tell me a story, tell me a story.'

'*Tell him.*'

'You tell him.'

'Is she still here?' Bob asked.

Norman nodded.

'I asked Norman to come to the party. He's busy.'

'Party,' Bob said. 'Where's the party?'

'It's true. She asked me to come.'

'Be a smarty. Join the party.'

'He said he was busy,' Zelda said. 'Now, will you please come with me?'

'I'm too busy too,' Bob said. 'These are busy times.'

'*Your* guests will soon be arriving.'

Bob glanced at his watch, 7.40. 'I have to make a phone call,' he said. 'Look, Zelda, I'll be there in an hour. I have to see somebody first.'

Zelda hesitated.

'I'll get him back to your place by eight-thirty,' Norman said. 'That's a promise.'

As Zelda left Bob rose shakily again. 'Be right back,' he said. But he was gone five minutes. 'Can't understand it,' he said when he got back. 'No answer . . .' He grinned broadly. 'Where was I?'

237

Norman told him where.

'Yeah,' Bob said, 'have you any idea what the infant mortality rate was in Russia *before* the revolution? Has there been a pogrom in Poland,' he asked with feeling, 'since the communists came to power?'

They talked and drank for another half hour and then Norman helped Bob out of the restaurant. 'Here,' Bob said, handing him his car keys. 'Will you be a good chap and drive?' They stumbled into the car together. 'Take me to—' he gave him Sally's address '—first, wilyu?'

'I promised Zelda to deliver you at eight-thirty,' Norman said. 'It's now a quarter to nine.'

'Oh,' Bob said, 'is it?'

Norman assured him it was.

'A quarter to nine, huh?' Bob tried hard to think. Why doesn't she answer the phone? She's angry, he thought. She's gone out. I'll call her in the morning. 'All right,' he said. 'Home, Trotsky.'

Norman drove Bob home. The party didn't break up until four and Bob slept in the next morning. So Sally died.

IV

'What time are they expected?'

'Not for another hour,' Miss Greenberg said.

Except for the rasping of the old man in the room opposite his and the occasional tap of a nurse's heels as she hastened down the corridor, this ward of the Montreal Jewish General Hospital was quiet. His leg, which had been broken in three places, was suspended by an elaborate system of pulleys. 'There will be no photographers,' he said. 'You promised.'

'No,' she said. 'There will be no photographers. Would you like me to turn on the T.V.?'

'O.K.'

But Mr Gordon got there first. Fat, shaggy-haired Hyman Gordon came every afternoon to sit with him. Miss Greenberg wished that he would go. His inscrutable smile vexed her.

'A moment,' he said. 'Would you brush my hair a little?'

'Certainly.'

She went to it gently, with pleasure. 'You need a haircut. Don't you, Joseph?'

'Yes,' Ernst said. 'I suppose so.'

'Are you excited?'

'No.'

'This is a great honour, you know. We're all proud of you here.'

'Thank you, Miss Greenberg.'

'Trudy,' she said.

'Trudy.'

The television set went briefly wavy, then it cleared. A short squat bearded man with a worm-like bit of moustache filled the screen and smiled at Ernst, Trudy, and Hyman Gordon.

'Good evening ladies and gentlemen. My name is Thomas Hale. Every Friday we have the pleasure of bringing you *Controversy*, a three-way discussion of a topical subject. Tonight's guests are—' the camera drew back '—to my left, Miss Lucy Morgan, critic, poet, and travel writer.' Hale paused; he smiled. 'I understand, Miss Morgan, that you have a new collection of poems coming out later this autumn in Boyd & McEwen's Folio Series. Is that right?'

Miss Morgan smiled, a thin alarmed smile. A frail, bony creature with fierce black eyes, a remarkably wide mouth, and a huge quantity of black fuzzy hair, she gave the impression that she was propped up on pillows or a couple of telephone directories. Her deep gravel voice came as a shock.

'Yes. *The Traffic of the Fire* will be out on November the *nineteenth*. It costs a dollar ninety-*eight* a copy.'

In reply to Mr Hale's next question Miss Morgan said that she counted Dylan Thomas, Mallarmé and Fraser's *The Golden Bough* as her primary influences.

239

'And to my right,' Mr Hale said, 'we have Charles Lawson, television playwright and film writer. I understand, Mr Lawson, that your latest film, *All About Mary*, will have its première at the Shea's tomorrow night. Is that right?'

'It must be. Otherwise how could I afford this suit?'

In reply to Mr Hale's next question Mr Lawson said that his most significant influences were his analyst, his wife, and money, in that order.

Thomas Hale's glad face filled the screen again. 'Tonight's controversial question,' he said, 'is do you think Canadian artists must leave the country in order to develop?' Hale paused; he smiled. 'We ought to be in for some truly partisan discussion tonight as Miss Morgan is sailing for England next week. I believe she hopes to settle there. While Charles Lawson, an expatriate for years, has recently returned to settle *here*.'

'Would you like me to try another channel?' Trudy asked.

'No,' Ernst said. 'I want to see this.'

'Charles Lawson is a good man,' Hyman Gordon said.

'I saw one of his plays last week,' Trudy said. 'What corn!'

'Charles Lawson,' Hyman Gordon said reverently, 'could have been a big man in Hollywood but he stood up for freedom of speech. That counts for something.'

'Is Lawson a commie?' Trudy asked.

'Quiet,' Ernst said.

'To stand for freedom these days,' Hyman Gordon said, 'that counts for something.'

'Quiet,' Trudy said. 'Joseph is trying to listen.'

'. . . that Canada is starved for culture,' Miss Morgan concluded.

'I'm not trying to say that Toronto rivals London as a theatrical or literary city yet,' Mr Lawson said. 'But – and this is a big but, mind you – Canadian artists cease to have value to their own country once they become expatriates. I've lived in London. I've seen too many highly promising talents end up at the bottom of a bottle of Johnny Walker.'

240

'Are you suggesting that I'm liable to become a dipsomaniac once I've moved to London?'

'Mr Lawson, I'm sure was only speaking metaphorically.'

'I'm a Canadian,' Mr Lawson said, 'and proud to be one. Miss Morgan has a point. This is no cultural paradise yet, but,' he said angrily, 'if our gifted poets continue to run off to safer – and I use that word advisedly – to *safer* climates, then we will never develop culturally.' He leaned forward. 'England is dead, Miss Morgan. Finished.'

'Maybe so,' Miss Morgan said, 'but at least there are people who read poetry there.'

Thomas Hale leaned back in his chair. 'That's a very disputatious remark, Miss Morgan. I'm a Canadian. I read poetry.'

'An old maid,' Hyman Gordon said. 'Phooey.'

Trudy Greenberg stiffened.

'Gogol,' Hyman Gordon said. 'There was a poet for you.'

'Please,' Trudy said, 'Joseph is trying to listen.'

'Byron,' Hyman Gordon said, 'that's what I call a poet.'

'. . . just because of class distinctions?'

'I'm sorry,' Mr Lawson said, 'but we didn't want to bring up our child in a mesh of prejudice, privilege, and pomposity. We certainly weren't going to send David to a public school.'

'I fail to see what that has to do with the subject at hand,' Miss Morgan said.

'A point well taken,' Thomas Hale said. 'The problem of how you choose to educate your children is not germane—'

'Sure, sure,' Mr Lawson said, 'but I'd like to discuss this problem of expatriates with Miss Morgan again after she's lived in London for a bit.'

'I repeat,' Miss Morgan said, 'Canada is a provincial country. My going to London is not going to change that.'

'A provincial country,' Mr Lawson said, 'but a very exciting one. Sensational things are beginning to happen right here in Toronto. Take the Stratford Festival, for instance—'

'You're not going to claim Shakespeare as a Canadian writer. Are you?'

'Ho, ho, ho,' Mr Hale said.

'You interrrupted—'

'You called the London theatre decadent. Am I right in saying that you failed to get any of your plays presented in—'

'Look here, when you observe that Canadians don't read poetry what you really mean to say is that they don't read *your*—'

Poing, poing, poing, went the bell before Thomas Hale. Music crept in. 'Ladies and gentlemen,' he said, 'you have been watching . . .'

'Turn it off,' Ernst said.

Hyman Gordon switched off the set.

'Are you all right?' Trudy asked.

Ernst's forehead was sweaty.

'Come on, hero. Give us a smile.'

'I would like to sleep for a while,' Ernst said.

'Certainly,' Trudy turned expectantly to Hyman Gordon.

'After you, Miss Greenberg.'

Trudy joined Hyman Gordon at the door.

'A moment,' Ernst said. 'How soon are they expected?'

'In about a half hour,' Trudy said. 'I'll come to wake you first.'

Outside the studio in Toronto, Joey waited in the Buick. Charlie kissed her warmly. And then Joey showed him the clippings that had come with Karp's letter from Israel.

'Why, the poor girl,' Charlie stared at a rather bad newspaper photograph of Sally. 'The poor, silly girl.' They drove in silence for a while before he asked, 'How's David?'

'Sleeping like a lamb.'

'That poor girl,' Charlie lit two cigarettes and passed one to Joey. 'What does Karp write?'

'He's not liked over there. He's having trouble. People suspect him because he survived.'

'Poor Karp.'

And suddenly all Charlie could think of were the friends he had lost and the friends who had died and the friends who had turned into enemies and how everyone, himself included, tried and tried and tried and only ended up hurting each other worse. He could only think that here he was at last with a wife and child and something like celebrity and yet inside him, deep inside, was sourness and a sense of having been cheated. There was fear of discovery not of an act, but of an attitude. He thought of Norman and wondered whether he had it any better. I doubt it, he thought.

'Any mail?' he asked.

'An invitation to Eckberg's for dinner Saturday night. You've been invited to speak at Carleton College on the twenty-fifth.'

'The twenty-fifth, eh?'

'And the Y.H.M.A. would like you to act as judge in a playwriting contest.'

'The poor silly girl.'

'Seymour wants us to come round for drinks tomorrow night. I – what did you say?'

'Nothing.'

'Are you O.K.?'

'Maybe,' Charlie said, 'David will grow up to be somebody big. An artist, maybe.'

Ernst's journey from Munich, Paris, London, to the Jewish General Hospital in Montreal had been a long and circuitous one. Stowing away at Liverpool had been easy, and once in Montreal Ernst ate where Sally had used to eat and walked where she had walked before. He went to the bars she had described as fun and, in the telephone directory, he looked up the names of people she had mentioned and went to stand in front of their houses until they appeared. At least once a day he walked by her house in N.D.G. The second time, Ernst recognised her father from a photograph she had shown him. A thin, greying man with calm blue eyes, Mr MacPherson, his pipe turned upside down against the

243

rain, seemed the epitome of the Scots schoolmaster. Ernst watched him pass with longing and much regret and then followed him like a supplicant for a few blocks.

Everywhere Ernst went he pretended to be waiting for Sally. There was a soda shop near Montreal High School that she had often gone to in her teens. Ernst went there and feeling foolish and conspicuous he nevertheless sat on each stool and at every table, until he was sure to have sat where she had sat before. In one of his many dreams he came home to Sally in N.D.G. and she hold him that her parents were coming home for dinner. Mr MacPherson was very fond of Ernst. They smoked a pipe together and the good old man told him stories of Sally as a child. Ernst rose and said, 'You don't have to work any more. I have been given a big promotion. We are going to buy you a house.'

Mrs MacPherson kissed Ernst. 'You are like a son to us,' she said.

On Sunday mornings they went to church together and in the afternoons they went driving. There were three children. A boy and two girls. When Ernst got his next promotion they bought a little cottage in the Laurentians.

'What a happy couple,' people said.

Ernst did not eat very much. He lost weight. Nights he spent alone in his room. As the weeks passed, as he began to fall behind with the rent again and the first snows came, he realised that something would have to be done. But Ernst had lost his drive.

Ernst worked one week as a dishwasher and the next he shovelled snow, he waited at table, drove a taxi, sold magazine subscriptions, shined shoes, delivered coal, and at last went to work in a furniture shop on Saint Lawrence Boulevard. Between jobs he sometimes slept for two days at a time or went from one movie to another. From not eating enough he turned to gorging himself. Four meals a day became his average fare. He grew fat. But one thing he did accomplish. When he read in the *Star* that a German 'new Canadian' had been killed in a traffic accident he went to the funeral and arranged to buy the dead man's papers from the

244

widow. On these papers he forged the name of a dead comrade. Joseph Rader.

The furniture shop on Saint Lawrence Boulevard was owned by a man called Steinberg, who had once owned a furniture store on the Theatinerstrasse in Munich. There he had sold hideous modern furniture on the instalment plan to a hard-pressed but Aryan clientele. When the hard-pressed Aryans had smashed his shop and burned his account books in '36 Steinberg had fled to London. He had been interned there in a camp as an enemy alien and then he had been sent to Canada, where after a short period in another camp he had been released. Now Steinberg once more sold hideous modern furniture on the instalment plan to hard-pressed Aryans. He even had a few of his old customers back. But this time he kept his account books locked in a fireproof safe.

Steinberg bullied Ernst. He paid him poorly. He mocked the boy: he didn't like him.

Nobody in the neighbourhood, in fact, liked Ernst. He claimed to be an Austrian, but they knew better. Nobody could understand why Ernst wanted to live and work in a Jewish quarter. When Ernst ate every day at Hyman Gordon's lunch counter in the basement of the Klassy Klothing Building next door nobody sat at his table. Hyman Gordon always served him last.

Spring came. The snows shrank greyly, grass sprung up on the mountainside, and St Catherine Street thickened with pretty girls in cotton dresses. Next door to Steinberg's furniture shop an old factory building was being demolished. Often, during the noon hour break, Ernst stopped to watch the men at work. Hyman Gordon and others also stopped to watch, but they never acknowledged Ernst's presence.

The only person Ernst visited in all that time – and he saw her as seldom as possible – was the widow Kramer, the 'new Canadian' from whom he had bought his papers. Inge Kramer, who was in her late thirties, worked as a housekeeper for a family in Westmount. She was a tall, bony, severe woman, very thrifty, and frankly dishonest. Frau

Kramer longed to marry again, a man with some money, someone who would start up a small business with her. She lived frugally, hoarding her salary with fanatical care. She was vehemently proud of the fact that her late father had served in the S.S. and Ernst was a little frightened of her sometimes.

After his accident, when he revived in a private room of the Montreal Jewish General Hospital, the first thing Ernst did was to call for the newspaper reports of the incident. He examined all the photographs that had been taken of him under the rubble and was satisfied that nobody could recognise him.

He's been working for me for three months,' Steinberg told one of the reporters. 'A boy to be proud of.'

The crowd collected on the hospital sunporch, waiting to get in to see Ernst, included many reporters, some officials, a few doctors, and three press photographers.

'Why can't we get in to take his picture?' one of the photographers asked Trudy Greenberg.

'He's shy,' Trudy said. 'I told you that.'

'Give us a break, eh?'

'What I want,' another photographer said, 'is one of *you* and Joey *together*.'

'Be a sport Miss Greenberg.'

'I told you,' Trudy said. 'I'll try my best.'

'Now we hear you talking.'

'There's a honey for you.'

A reporter stood off to one side with Frau Kramer. They spoke in hushed voices. Two other reporters were interviewing Hyman Gordon.

'It all happened so fast,' Hyman Gordon said. 'One minute I was standing there, watching the demolition men at work, and the next people were yelling, "Watch out", "Run", "Look out, Hymie" . . . I'm telling you when I looked up and saw that wall swaying I just froze on the spot. I couldn't move to save my life . . . And the next thing I knew a push from behind – whew! and I was knocked flat,

246

but clear of the wall. The dust, the dust from that wall . . . People came running. Shouts, screams, sirens. A business.' Hyman Gordon wiped back his shaggy grey hair and shook his head reverently. 'And there buried underneath the rubble was the boy we wouldn't talk to or eat with or even stop to say hello. There was Joseph, who had pushed me and saved my life. I'm telling you I still ask myself why he did it. The others could have . . . They didn't and I don't blame them for a minute. You could be killed. You had to be crazy . . .

'There was Joseph with his mouth full of dust and his forehead split by a brick; there he was buried under all that crap and not a complaint from him. Three hours it took to dig the boy out . . . Tell me I'm crazy, tell me anything you like, but when we all stood around him with encouraging words and cigarettes and a little for him to drink I could swear that he smiled and that he was happy. I never saw him look happy before . . . I,' Hyman Gordon lifted his hands and let them drop to his lap, 'I never really talked with him before . . .'

The officials waiting to see Ernst were from the Bnai Brith, Kiwanis, and the Rotary Club. Ernst had won a thousand dollar reward for bravery. A league for Jewish-Gentile friendship was going to give him a citation. Yet another organisation had promised to give him fifty dollars a week until he was able to work again.

'All right,' Trudy said to the photographers, 'wait here. And remember,' she added, 'I'm not promising anything.'

Ernst woke from a dream of Sally to find Trudy Greenberg smiling at him lavishly. 'They're coming,' she said.

Ernst glared at the system of weights and pulleys that tied him to the bed. Then he heard them approaching. There were the public officials, the reporters, the doctors, and three photographers.

'There he is,' a reporter said.

'God bless him.'

'Smile,' a photographer said.

'Hey, Hey, Joey. Look this way. Atta boy!'

Then Ernst saw her. Frau Kramer approached him with a

thin smile. Ernst pulled despairingly at his leg, but it was no use. As she bent over and kissed him again and again the flashbulbs popped. Frau Kramer, her cheeks stained with tears, turned to face the others. 'I'm his fiancée,' she said. 'We are going to get married.'

The following day, Saturday there was a photograph of Ernst in the *Star*. It was three columns wide. The image was clear.

V

Two weeks later Vivian took Norman to visit her mother. Mrs Bell's council flat in Fulham was damp and reeked of bacon fat. Everywhere you turned there were little tables adorned with crocheted mats and bowls of artificial flowers. The National Health Service had issued Mrs Bell with a hearing aid and glasses and an upper plate that clacked when she spoke. She was a round, plump woman with grey hair and big blue eyes. Her rosy cheeks gave her an aura of constant blushing girlish surprise. Mrs Bell, who was probably sixty-five spoke in a poignant whisper of a voice.

Norman and Vivian ate supper with her in the parlour off blue plates which – once you have cleared them of roast beef and mashed brussel sprouts – revealed greasy and crackled likenesses of King George V and Queen Mary. Mrs Bell spoke endlessly of Diana.

Vivian's older sister Diana had been killed in the blitz, a week before she was to have played her first featured role in a film and two weeks before a famous artist was to have completed his portrait of her. After supper Mrs Bell led them into Diana's room. 'Diana would have been thirty-five a week on Wednesday,' she said. 'Isn't that so, Vivian?'

Vivian nodded.

'Vivian's the practical one,' Mrs Bell said. 'Oh, had my Diana lived she would have had the world at her feet today. When I think of all the hearts she broke . . . We were ever so close, you know. She used to tell her mummy everything. Why when she broke with Lord Dinsdale the poor boy took to drink, and do you remember Tommy Boswell, Vivian? There was a proper gentleman.' Mrs Bell giggled softly. 'He took Diana to a ball at Oxford, where they ate swan steak . . . Isn't that so, Vivian?'

The unfinished portrait of Diana hung on a wall in the room. The room, in fact, was full of mementoes – yellowed theatre programmes and pressed orchids, a warped scrap-book and frocks slightly moth-eaten – the room, in fact, was exactly as Diana had left it fifteen years ago, the night of her death, when she had gone off to the hunt ball with flying-officer Denis Graves. As Mrs Bell led them out of the room again she said, 'Vivian's a bit ashamed of her mum, you know. I'm not one for reading and that's the truth of it. But Diana and I were ever so close. Like sisters . . .'

Vivian leaned close to Norman. 'The family bought her off,' she said. 'That's why she broke with the Dinsdale boy.'

After Norman had walked Vivian back to the basement flat on Oakley Street she invited him inside for a nightcap. Kate was out. So this, he thought, is as good a time as any to tell her that I'm leaving the country.

'I think we'd better stop seeing each other,' Vivian said suddenly.

'Why?'

'You feel obligated to me because I took care of you while you were ill.'

Imitating a posture of Kate's she stood beside the fireplace with one elbow balanced on the mantelpiece. Her loose, fluffy sweater was calculated to underplay her small bosom, and her tight skirt succeeded in forcing attention to her attractively broad hips. But the clothes, just like the boy-ishly smart haircut, were sadly out of character. Kate never should have tried to make her over, Norman thought.

'So,' she continued in an edgy voice, 'I think it would be best if we didn't see each other again.'

Norman fiddled anxiously with his glasses. 'Would you like to marry me?' he asked.

Turning away from him, Vivian knelt and busied herself with the fire. When she turned to him again her eyes were moist. 'Please go,' she said.

Norman started towards her.

'No,' she said. 'I want you to go.'

But she followed him out into the hall. 'Why do you want to marry me?' she asked.

'I love you,' he said.

'Really?'

'Yes,' he said.

'All right then. I'll marry you.'

Norman kissed her on the mouth. She did not respond very warmly.

'Good night.'

'Good night,' she said.

He was wakened by the phone shortly after eight the next morning.

'You don't have to go through with it,' Vivian said.

'With what?' Norman asked thickly.

'You asked me to marry you last night.'

'I thought that was settled,' he said. 'I thought you said yes.'

'I did. But I haven't told anyone yet. There's still time for you to change your mind.'

'Jesus,' he said.

'I beg your pardon?'

'Let's get married.'

A thoughtful pause. 'I don't even know your religion,' she said at last.

'I'm a Seventh Day Adventist.'

'Good Lord,' she said. 'Are you?'

They were married in the Chelsea Register Office on a rainy Saturday afternoon. Mrs Bell, Kate, and Roger and Polly Nash, came to the ceremony. Bob and Zelda Landis sent a telegram. The Winkleman's sent a bouquet of roses and a cheque for fifty pounds. Norman had no idea of how they found out about the wedding. But it was nice of them anyway, he thought.

Norman had not counted on the party afterwards. Roger and Polly Nash aside, he did not care for the people who came to the basement flat on Oakley Street. Vivian, of course, had few friends and so most of the guests were friends of Kate. The party, a sort of surprise, had been arranged to take place in Norman's flat. Downstairs Norman noticed that in the excitment of the last three days he had forgotten about his mail. He emptied the box of a few letters and bills and a rolled copy of the Saturday edition of the Montreal *Star*. Norman drank too much at the party.

All the gay, sophisticated men gathered in his flat could be divided into two groups. Those who wore extravagant waistcoats and those who went in for extravagant moustaches. The first group, it seemed, was made up of journalists, advertising writers, assistant film and television directors, and non-figurative painters. Most of them had been to minor public schools. They were, on the whole, amusing, clever, and with a tendency to get drunk as a matter of pride. The extravagant moustaches talked about their sports cars, past and present, with a mixture of energy, nostalgia, and passion that one usually associates with talk about one's mistresses. They wouldn't speak of their jobs. 'You've got to earn a crust of bread somehow,' was about as concrete as one of them got with Norman. But, it appeared, they were mostly businessmen of one sort or another and they were far more political. They thought the country was going to pot. There was a dream of a Northern Rhodesian farm, an Australian sheep ranch, or an oil job in Saudi Arabia in their futures. They were shorter, redder, and more inclined to corpulence than the others. Through their contact with the extravagant waistcoats they had acquired a taste for French salads, but nothing would make them give up tomato sauce. Most of the girls – actresses, models, dancers – were extremely attractive and, contrary to legend, far more decorative than their American or continental counterparts.

Roger Nash came down with a thud on the arm of Norman's chair. 'You're being anti-social,' he said. 'I thought Americans liked to be liked.'

251

'Do you really want to write film scripts?'

'I don't really want to do anything very much.'

Vivian came to collect Norman. 'There are some people I want you to meet,' she said.

They were, as he expected, extravagant waistcoats. But there were also three authentic friends of Vivian. Her friends were marked by beards and corduroy trousers. 'I say,' one of them said, 'are you and Vivian going to settle here or in Canada?'

'Here,' Norman said.

Kate passed with a tray of drinks and Norman poured two into one glass and took it. He kissed Kate on the cheek.

'Norman is going to write films here,' Vivian said to a bearded man. The bearded man managed a smile. 'Cyril is a film editor for the coal board,' Vivian said coolly.

Norman was concerned because he realised for the first time that there was a streak of malice in Vivian. She had invited all these people here with cruel intent. She appeared to have told all of them that Norman was a King's College man, a former RCAF pilot, and a successful film and thriller writer. Norman was dismayed because he did not care for these people and he was not interested in helping Vivian to get her own back. She didn't seem to know that he wanted to settle down and return to teaching.

As Norman helped himself to another drink somebody tapped him on the shoulder.

The small, spare man with the black fuzzy hair wore horn-rimmed glasses and a cheesed-off smile and had no chin to speak of. Haig was a social scientist. He tapped Norman once, twice, three times on the shoulder. Norman whirled around drunkenly.

'I suppose you were in Spain?'

Haig had a high, scraping voice.

'What?' Norman asked.

'Vivian told me you were in Spain.'

'Yeah,' Norman said, 'I was,' anticipating, not without pleasure a little praise.

'Was that where you were wounded?'

'No. I was a pilot.'

'A *pilot*?'

'In the RCAF. I was shot down over the Channel.'

Pretty girls predominated in the group around them so Norman was anxious to come off well.

'I don't mean to be offensive,' Haig said, 'but physical courage is a form of ignorance, actually.'

'Jesus,' Norman said. 'I wasn't a hero.'

Haig snapped his hand open like a knife and pointed a white blade-like finger at Vivian. 'He was decorated,' he said, 'wasn't he?'

'It was only a formality,' Norman said. 'After you've taken part in so many missions you automatically—'

'The fact remains that you were decorated.'

'Honestly, I can't imagine anyone more remote from the heroic than myself.'

'You *were* involved in the Spanish fiasco?'

'Yes, but—'

'There,' Haig said.

'You're right,' Norman said. 'I'm a hero.'

Haig retired with a triumphant, waspish smile. And Norman grasped for the first time that he was a character, an ageing pinko, ineffectual and a bore, and, as far as Haig's crowd could see, the fossil of a sillier age like the player-piano. Norman retreated to a comparatively unoccupied corner of the room.

Slumped glumly in the corner Norman recalled something he had once read in an atlas somewhere. Off Vancouver Island there was a vast area of sea known as the zone of silence. No sound penetrated this sea. A stillness prevailed. And since no siren or bell warned ships of dangerous reefs the floor of the zone of silence was strewn with wrecks. This, he thought, was surely an age of silence. A time of collisions. A place strewn with wrecks. This time of opinions, battle-stations, and no absolutes, was also a time to consolidate. This time of no heroes but hyperbole, where treason was only loyalty looked at closely, and faith, honour, and courage had become the small change of crafty politicians, was also a time to persevere. To persevere was a most serious virtue.

If there was a time to man the barricades, Norman thought, then there is also a time to weed one's private garden. The currency of revolution is invalid as long as both tyrannies bank big bombs. Each age creates its own idiom. This was a time to drop a nickel in the blind man's box and to recommend worth-while movies to strangers, it was a time to play *their* game but to make your *own* errors, a time to wait and a time to hope. The enemy was no longer the boor in power on the right or the bore out of power on the left. All alliances had been discredited. The enemy was the hit-and-run driver of both sides. The enemy, no longer clear, could still be recognised. His cause was just. He knew what was good for you and he was above small virtues. Charlie who hadn't talked and Jeremy who had, Karp inside and Ernst out, Joey, the Winklemans, all moved unknowingly through the same ogre-like zone of silence, which made a necessary sacrifice of the Nickys and Sallys, leaving the less beautiful behind to pick at the bones of their discontent. So in this time of wrecks, Norman, at the age of thirty-nine, chose at last to lead a private life. Ernst was, as he had once told Joey, the creation of their own idealism. So wherever he is let him go in peace. Let him be.

Without actually taking part Norman shook hands and waved goodbyes to his guests. See you Henry, so long Jori, thanks for coming Tony, goodbye Derek, don't mention it John.

Vivian kicked off her shoes and went methodically through the living room, emptying ashtrays. 'The Jarrolds,' she said, 'have asked us to dinner next Sunday.'

'You got out of it, I hope.'

'No,' she said. 'I thought you'd like to go. They're going to have some of the others around later. It should be fun.'

'Well,' he said, 'maybe.'

'I was hoping you might be able to do something for Cyril, actually. He's the one with the coal board. He used to write the cleverest film reviews for *Isis* and he'd so much like to get on.'

'You seem to have forgotten that my old friends are no longer interested in me, darling.'

'Didn't Mr Winkleman send you a gift?'

'Yes . . .'

'And your friend Bob sent a wire, didn't he?'

'Yes. That was a surprise. But all the same—'

'Aren't you pleased?'

'Certainly I am, but—'

'I knew you would be,' she said happily. 'I phoned them.'

'You *what*?'

'I phoned to say you were getting married. Mr Winkleman said he'd like to have a talk with you any time you're free. He's holding some money for you, or something, he said.'

'I'm to appear before them, am I?' He laughed. 'I wonder if there are any names I can give them.'

'Oh, don't pretend to be angry. I knew you were too proud to call them, so I did it myself.'

'Vivian.'

'You're glad,' she said. 'Admit it.'

Norman fiddled anxiously with his glasses. 'I'm going back to teaching,' he said. 'I've put films and all that behind me.'

'Nonsense,' she said. 'You'd never be happy in some ghastly provincial university. I know you so well, Norman.'

'Look here, Vivian, there's a book. Something I've been promising myself to finish for years, and I—'

'A novel,' Vivian said, excited. 'You're writing a novel.'

'No, not quite. It's meant to be a scholarly – About Dryden and his period. You see – '

'Oh, Norman.'

'I know it doesn't sound like much,' he said, 'but it's rather important to me.'

'I promised Cyril you'd introduce him to Winkleman.'

Norman looked at his wife and wondered if a year or two of these people would be enough for her. She's an intelligent

255

enough girl, he thought. 'O.K.,' he said. 'I'll see what I can do.'

Vivian brought him a whisky and soda, his mail, the Saturday edition of the Montreal *Star*, and his slippers.

Norman immediately came across Ernst's picture and the story. He read how one Joseph Rader had saved Hyman Gordon's life, won awards, cheques, and was going to marry a German widow. Then, for the first time in months, Norman recalled Hornstein vividly. Once again the ferocious little man climbed back into his machine and dived it into the Thames. 'Vivian,' Norman called thickly.

'Yes?'

'I'd like for us to have a child. Almost right away, I mean.'

'A child? Good Lord!'

'Yes,' he said. 'As soon as possible.'

She tried to hide her displeasure. Norman was eleven years older than her, and that was plenty, but she hadn't realised until now that he was middle-aged.

'Maybe next year,' she said.

He made no attempt to conceal his disappointement.

'I thought we might do some travelling first. A child, you know, is a full time job for a woman.'

'It doesn't have to be, Vivian. I mean—'

'You're being a bit selfish, I think.'

Norman got up, went into the kitchen, and threw the *Star* into the waste basket. When he came back he said, 'We'll wait one year for a child, but that's all.'

Vivian abandoned her broom and fled into the bedroom. Sitting on the edge of the bed, she lit a cigarette. Vivian was scared. Gradually, however, she began to calm down. Flipping through an old copy of *Life* she came across a picture of Grace Kelly. I wonder, she thought, if I can persuade him to take me to the Cannes Film Festival next year.

Norman poured himself a stiffer drink. He wondered whether Vivian would object to asking Kate round to dinner tomorrow night.